ON LINE

FICTION
Russe
Russell, Sheldon

The Yard Dog

# THE
# YARD
# DOG

## ALSO BY SHELDON RUSSELL

*Dreams to Dust*
*Empire*
*Requiem at Dawn*
*The Savage Trail*

# THE YARD DOG

## SHELDON RUSSELL

MINOTAUR BOOKS ☆ NEW YORK

This is a work of fiction. All of the characters, organizations, and events por-
trayed in this novel are either products of the author's imagination or are used
fictitiously.

THE YARD DOG. Copyright © 2009 by Sheldon Russell. All rights reserved. Printed
in the United States of America. For information, address St. Martin's Press, 175
Fifth Avenue, New York, N.Y. 10010.

www.minotaurbooks.com

Book design by Phil Mazzone
Maps by Paul J. Pugliese

Library of Congress Cataloging-in-Publication Data

Russell, Sheldon.
    The yard dog / Sheldon Russell.—1st ed.
        p.   cm.
    ISBN 978-0-312-56670-8
    1. Prisoner-of-war camps—Fiction.   2. Conspiracies—Fiction.   3. World
War, 1939–1945—Prisoners and prisons—Fiction.   4. Oklahoma—History—
20th century—Fiction.   I. Title.
    PS3568.U777Y37 2009
    813'.54—dc22                                                    2009012727

First Edition: September 2009

10   9   8   7   6   5   4   3   2   1

Dedicated to my agent team,
Michael and Susan Morgan Farris

# ACKNOWLEDGMENTS

My father worked as a machinist on the Santa Fe Railway during the time of the great steam engines. In fact, most of my relatives were railroaders of one ilk or another, as were my friends' parents. I grew up listening to their stories, which were clever, witty, and sometimes even true. I'm indebted to that oral history and to the men who passed it along to the younger generation.

I'm also indebted to the factual accounts of that era in such fine books as *The Rape of Europa*, by Lynn H. Nicholas, a fascinating tale of the Third Reich, and *The Barbed Wire College*, by Ron Robin, which chronicles America's attempt to reeducate German prisoners of war.

To be successful, a writer must be surrounded by smart, supportive people. In that respect, I am fully prepared. The help and support I've received has been exemplary.

I owe thanks to my editor, Daniela Rapp of St. Martin's Minotaur, for her insight and for her excellent editorial skills; to my agents, Michael and Susan Morgan Farris, who supported me when times were lean; and of course to my wife, Nancy, who has never lost faith in me.

# THE
# YARD
# DOG

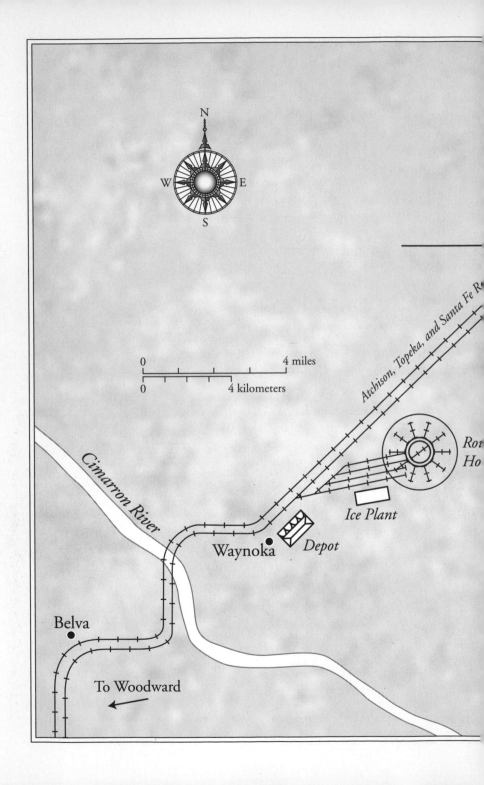

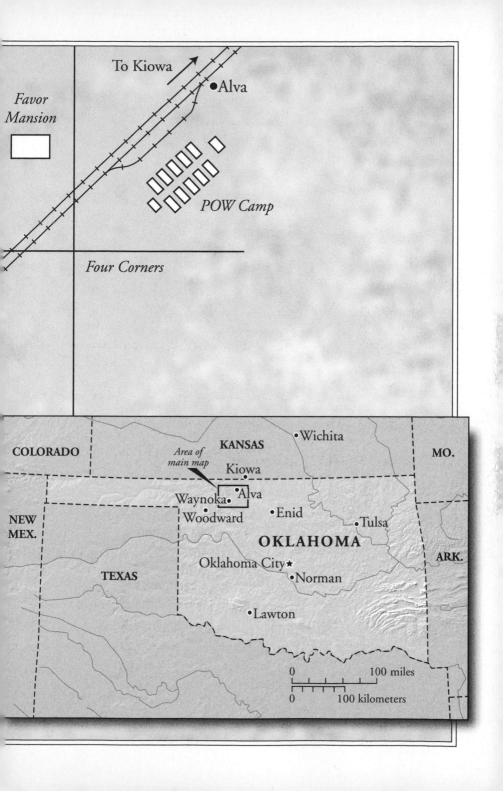

Favor
Mansion

To Kiowa

●Alva

POW Camp

Four Corners

COLORADO

KANSAS

●Wichita

MO.

_Area of_
_main map_

Kiowa

●Alva

Waynoka●

NEW
MEX.

●Woodward

●Enid

●Tulsa

OKLAHOMA

ARK.

Oklahoma City★

TEXAS

●Norman

●Lawton

0          100 miles

0          100 kilometers

# PROLOGUE

No ONE KNEW the Waynoka rail yards better than Spark Dugan. No one knew better where doors were unlocked, where a man could sleep on a bitter night, or where the squabs were nested for gathering and eating during sparse times. No one knew better the scheduled runs, the refuse piles, or the machine shop with its gears and belts and wheels. The yards had been Spark's for as long as he could remember, since after the Depression, since after the land had fallen silent beneath the Oklahoma dust.

When Spark's family left for California, he stayed behind. Too slow in the head to find work on his own, he lived in the shack under the bridge. After several weeks, he received a card in the mail with a picture of a cactus on it, big as a man with arms outstretched. He couldn't read the words, but he knew they were from them. After that, he never heard again.

The first time the river flooded his shack, he went to the yards looking for shelter. Lights winked behind clouds of steam, and cars rumbled out of the darkness. Tracks struck off to worlds far away. Steam engines thundered and hissed through the yards, and the earth trembled beneath him. The smells of oil and creosote were thick as syrup in the night, and he knew that this was where he belonged.

He learned to gauge train speeds with accuracy, to leap from car to car, to roll under moving stock and come out on the other side. Once, he caught his overall's strap over the door lock of a cattle car and was dragged to the end of the yards. Holes were worn in both his boots, and his big toe turned black as an eggplant.

Soon he discovered bits of coal scattered along the tracks and a ready market for them as well. Picking coal wasn't much of a living for most, but for Spark, a man whose thinking lurched and hitched like the freight cars about him, it was enough. A good day brought cash for shine, Bull Durham for smoking, bologna for frying. Sometimes the coal cars would slow enough that he could tail up, fill his bucket, and drop off before the speeds wound up again. On a lucky day, the cars would stop long enough for him to pitch coal over the side for gathering up later. On those days, the chunks of coal were big as melons, the kind Hook Runyon, the railroad bull, liked best for his stove.

He'd known Hook Runyon a long time, maybe forever. He couldn't be clear on that. The coal he gave Hook was not for bribing purposes, though some might think it. He brought coal to Hook's caboose because Hook was his friend, because Hook would slap him on the back and laugh, a laugh all full of power like a steam engine pulling grade.

Hook never cussed him, or cuffed him to a car ladder, or cracked his head with a stick. But even if he had, Spark would have brought him coal anyway. He didn't have many friends like Hook, in fact *none* that he could remember. Hook could drink Runt Wallace's shine straight up, didn't talk 'til it mattered, didn't whine or ask for more than he was worth.

THE YARD DOG | 3

As Spark saw it, he and Hook had much in common. Like him, Hook was a collector, even though Hook collected books, which seemed a useless thing. Spark himself liked rail spikes, high-carbon ones with "HC" stamped on the heads. Last count, he'd collected nearly three sacks full and had them stashed down by the river. Come time, he'd sell them at the salvage yard and have himself a shine-on weekend.

Since the war, the yards had picked up business, making night picking more dangerous with so many men about. The trains ran with hardly a breather in between. There was more opportunity for trading here and there, though so many strangers made him uneasy.

Tonight the yards hummed, and his bucket brimmed with coal. He squatted in the darkness to take measure of the yard and the movement of the cars. A switch engine eased a line of reefers in for icing. He could smell the heat and steam of the engine, feel its throb and pulse in his bones. When the brake was set, the cars rumbled away like rolling thunder. The engine bell pealed again and again. He loved the sound. It filled him and spilled over into his soul.

He turned down the tracks to Hook's caboose as he had a thousand times before. But for Spark on this night, the bell fell silent and would be heard by him no more.

# 1

HOOK RUNYON ROLLED over in his bunk as engine 3768 pulled out of the yards, a mile-long trail of reefer cars at her back. The cadence of her 4-8-4s and eighty-inch drivers was distinct as she labored against the enormity of her load. Dawn's light cast through the gray window of his caboose, which sat on the siding. Pulling the covers over his head, he squeezed his eyes shut against the throb. It was Sunday, thank God, and there were twenty-four hours left to nurse the ravages of Runt Wallace's popskull whiskey.

When he awoke the second time, the sun bore through his lids, and he groaned. Prying open an eye, he took in his graceless surroundings: the coal stove; the stacks of books, like the ruins of a bombed-out city; the boxes of photographs with their edges curled with moisture. In the far corner, an empty quart bottle lay on its side as dead and useless as a corpse.

Sitting on the edge of the bunk, he waited for the whirl in his head to subside before slipping on the prosthesis. They'd taken his right arm below the elbow, leaving him movement, but even after all this time, the stump seemed foreign, as if it belonged to someone else. The hook lay cold against his leg as he worked on his britches. Afterward, he tied his shoes, a task that had taken him weeks to master, and then he lit a cigarette against the dreariness of the morning.

When he checked the coal box under the entrance step, he found it empty. Spark Dugan filled his box without fail. Hook wondered if something might be wrong. Even in the coldest mornings, it was topped with coal and slid under the steps to keep it dry. Spark Dugan gathered his bounty along the tracks, where it fell from the cars as they rattled their way to the power plant in the southern part of the state. His best pickings were at the switches or where the engines stopped and started.

The divisional supervisor had accused Spark Dugan of stealing and asked Hook, as the local Santa Fe bull, to arrest him for trespassing, but he hadn't the heart. Spark Dugan was just slow in the head, that's all, a lonely man who lived in a tar-paper shack under the trestle. He was without friend or kin and talked to no one, not a hello or good morning as he shuffled along the tracks, his cuffs frayed from the bedding rock. What coal he didn't use himself, he sold around town, most often to the blacksmith shop on Main or to the widow women who traded baked bread and custards for a share.

Little was said between him and Spark, but over time they had become friends. Spark reached out with what he valued, with what he could, and that was coal. Even though slow-witted, Spark had his ways and did not depart from them without cause. Maybe he would swing by and check on him today, make sure he wasn't laid up sick somewhere.

Dumping what coal was left into the stove, Hook dribbled in kerosene from the lantern and lit it, waiting for the flames to struggle to life. The mornings were still cold, and the water bucket was glazed with ice. Breaking it with the dipper, he filled the pot and set it on the stove. Lighting another cigarette, he sat on the edge of the bunk, pulling the blanket over his shoulders. Living in a caboose was like living in a rowboat. When a train went by, which was every fifteen minutes, she pitched and rolled and threatened to swamp.

But from here he had a good view of the roundhouse and the yards, and the price was right. The caboose had been part of the deal when he was transferred out of Flagstaff. He was neither trained for nor inclined to law enforcement, but like most things in his life, fate had dealt her hand. He had discovered a propensity for the work, an ability to step outside himself and to see through others' eyes, to think through others' thoughts. He'd been around enough to know that the skill was instinctive, an intuition tucked away in some primitive lobe of his brain.

The aroma of coffee perking brought him about, and he snuffed out the cigarette. Drawing cold water, he filled the basin and whipped up a lather in the shaving mug. He examined his beard in the cloudy mirror. The gray was showing more each day. At forty, he was still lean and strong, not from exercise, but from a constitution that defied the harsh realities of his life. He was tall, six foot two, as his father had been, but his black eyes and straight black hair had been inherited from his mother's side of the family. Indian blood, though not uncommon in Oklahoma, was not a point often touted when he was a child.

He poured himself a cup and sipped at the coffee as he stood at the window, wiping the steam away with his sleeve, looking down at the yards. Engine 4801 rolled onto the turntable to await maintenance at one of the stalls, and a cloud boiled from the steam jenny down at the machine shop. Morning shift was changing, and men, black with grease, lunch boxes in tow, struck out for their frost-covered pickups. Since the war had started, they'd worked twelve-hour shifts, seven days a week, and the wear was taking its toll. Twice now he'd broken up fistfights down at the ice plant.

If not for the arm, he might have been a soldier himself by now, fighting the Germans, or an archaeologist like he'd always planned, or a teacher at the university. Janet had been driving, the streets black with ice, and even now he remembered the sounds of breaking glass, the cries for help, the smell of his own flesh rendering in the fire. The amputation of his arm had been as certain and swift as Janet's departure. Soon after, she'd married the lieutenant in charge of food service down at the army air-force base.

Hook wasn't one for crying about what couldn't be changed, but a big chunk of his spirit went the way of the arm. And then when Janet left, he'd spun downward in despair, a man lost in a dark sea with no shore in sight. At some point, despair turned to bitterness. He buried his feelings deep, so deep that even he could not find them. But with time, he'd struggled back to make a life. Even still, in the silent hours of night, the old memories sometimes rose up out of the darkness.

Hopping a freighter, he spent a year on the rails. During that year, he'd learned how to survive, how to fight for a scrap of food, how to roll a man off the rods in the dark of night. During that time, he'd developed a taste for whiskey, changed his name from Walter to Hook, and nursed the smoldering rage within him.

Pulling up a chair, he read over yesterday's paper in search of an auction. Books were his passion and his salvation. Without them he would have perished from boredom long ago in this godforsaken place. But the auctions offered little in the way of interesting material, mostly farm estates, tools and kitchen utensils, the occasional collection of *Reader's Digest* or *National Geographic,* the rare book, the odd reader. It was the uncommon farmer who left a library behind when he went to his Maker.

Searching through his stack of books, he landed on Conrad's *Heart of Darkness*, a library copy he'd scavenged at a school fundraiser. This was a day for such diversions, a day for placating guilt and easing the thump in his head.

The whistle from the six o'clock northbound wailed in the distance. It would be filled with green troops from the Texas training camps, boys on their way to the front. The caboose rocked under the rush of wind when the train roared by, the guards in the doorways in their brown uniforms, their rifles slung from their shoulders.

The knock at the door was loud and urgent, and Hook jumped, the hair crawling on the back of his neck. When he opened it, Jake Campbell stood on the porch, his hands over his ears against the morning cold.

"What is it?" Hook asked.

"I think you better come," he said.

"I'm not on duty. You boys got any fighting to do on Sunday, just have at it."

Looking down the tracks, Jake blew into his hands.

"You better come, Hook," he said. "There's a body under a reefer car over to the ice deck. They think it's Spark Dugan."

# 2

AFTER SENDING JAKE for the sheriff, Hook donned his coat and slipped the camera over his shoulder. As he made his way to the ice plant, his empty stomach protested under the assault of black coffee and nicotine. Kicking a rock down the track, he cursed under his breath. Dragging bodies from under trains was not how he'd figured on spending his Sunday.

A death was bound to stir up trouble, and Eddie Preston, the divisional supervisor out of Chicago, was less than enamored with him as it was. Being a Baldwin-Felts detective, Preston considered Hook unqualified for the job and had done everything he could to prevent his being hired in the first place.

A line of reefers stretched from the ice deck to the supply sheds. Reefers were the railroad's pride and joy, a fleet of freight cars laden with perishable fruits and vegetables. The Green Fruit Express, GFX, as it was called, coursed from California to New York in frantic runs through the desert, the difference between riches and ruin a matter of the three-hundred-pound blocks of ice that cooled their cargoes. As a major divisional point, the Waynoka, Oklahoma, yards touted the largest ice plant in the United States and labored twenty-four hours a day to keep the cars iced.

Men gathered around the reefer, their breath rising in the morning chill. The switch engine puffed and sighed, and steam shot from her sides. Ten or so German POWs watched from atop the ice deck. A prisoner-of-war facility had been built in Alva, twenty miles north. Prisoners were assigned to the ice plant as part of their labor program. They worked no more than eight-hour shifts, as dictated by the Geneva Convention, dragging the blocks of ice into the bunkers situated atop the reefer cars. A camp guard watched on, his weapon at the ready.

Ross Ague, the night foreman at the ice plant, pushed back his hat and wallowed a cigar stump into the corner of his mouth as Hook approached.

"It's a goddamn mess, Runyon," he said, "and there's cars waiting to ice. That produce goes to mush, someone's ass is going on the line, and it ain't going to be mine."

Leaning down, Hook looked under the car, his stomach lurching. An arm was severed and tossed against the rail, its fingers curled. Caught by the undercarriage, the torso had dragged backward down line, the skin and muscle scoured away by bedrock. There was no mistaking the frayed cuffs or the wear of Spark Dugan's heels, and there was flesh on the two right forward wheels. In spite of the gruesome condition of the corpse, there was no spray of blood on the undercarriage.

When Hook bent under for a closer look, he could see Spark Dugan's face, like he'd dropped off to sleep. The smell of carnage rose in the cold, and Hook leaned against the reefer to catch his breath.

"What happened?" he asked.

"Goddamn if I know," Ague said, spitting between his feet. "We was finishing up the shift when Jake spotted him. Figure he was sleeping under the car." Taking out a match, he snapped it against the button on his fly and lit his cigar. "Had you boys run ole Spark Dugan off like you was supposed to, we wouldn't be sweeping him up this morning."

Stepping back, Hook clicked off a picture and rolled up the next frame.

"Spark didn't have anyone that I know of," he said.

"No," Ague said. "He's lived in that shack under the trestle for as long as I can remember, if you call it living."

"It was damn cold last night for sleeping under a reefer car."

"Maybe he was drunk," Ague said. "Everyone knows Spark Dugan liked his hooch. Maybe he was jerking off for all I know. He wasn't none too bright, you know."

Dropping down on one knee, Hook focused in on the twisted form and took another shot.

"What's in the reefer?"

"Reefers are sealed at the point of origin," Ague said. "You know that. Keeps yard dogs from poking around and spoiling the goods."

"I could check with the divisional office," Hook said, lighting a cigarette. "'Course it might take awhile. You know how efficient *those* bastards are."

Ague rolled his eyes and pulled a wad of papers from his pocket. "Cabbage, out of Oceanside, California," he said. "Why? Is being run over by cabbages better than being run over by oranges?"

"Who was working graveyard?" Hook asked, ignoring him.

"Me, and them union busters up there on the deck, and that guard, if you call sitting on your ass working. There was the switch engineer and Jake. That's about it. We had a grapefruit run out of Texas and didn't look up until sunrise."

"Would those POWs have seen something?"

"Can't see squat from the deck, Runyon, not at night. Jake was checking angle cocks when he spotted ole Spark Dugan, or what's left of him. No one even knew he was there until then."

"You don't mind if I ask them a few questions?"

Tossing away the cold cigar, Ague said, "You can take them to Sunday school for all I care, but it ain't up to me. You want to talk to them Germans, you'll have to clear it with the commander at Camp Alva. I ain't got no say one way or the other. Besides," he said, "they don't talk nothing but Kraut."

Hook framed the prisoners in his camera and snapped off a shot. He walked around to the tracks that ran parallel to the reefers. Spark's coal bucket lay spilled down the center of the tracks.

"You boys didn't move Spark's bucket, did you?"

"We ain't touched nothing," Ague said. "Given how sensitive you yard dogs are."

"Where's this car headed?" he asked, slipping the camera strap over his shoulder.

Shrugging, Ague checked his schedule again.

"Destination for RD 32 is the Camp Alva spur. Kraut for them fuckin' Nazis, I reckon."

From across the way, the sheriff's car pulled into the parking lot, its red light spinning. Sheriff Donley and Jake picked their way over the switches toward them. Donley was renowned in the county for his ability to break a man's jaw with a single punch. But he was equally renowned for his inability to fill out traffic-violation reports without the help of the court clerk. When he abandoned giving tickets altogether, driving in town soon degenerated into a contest of wills.

Squatting, Sheriff Donley shined his flashlight under the reefer and silently studied the ball of gore that was once Spark Dugan. Retrieving a handkerchief from his back pocket, he dabbed at the perspiration on his forehead.

"Jesus," he said.

"Look, Sheriff," Ague said. "We got a line of reefers waiting to be iced by the morning shift. Can't we move this along?"

Clicking off his flashlight, Sheriff Donley worked it into his back pocket and looked down the line of cars.

"Knew ole Spark Dugan was going to get it someday," he said. Steam shot from the switch engine, drifting off in the chill.

"You figure it to be an accident then?" Hook asked.

"I been called out a dozen times on Spark Dugan, getting drunk, sleeping it off here and there, wherever he took a notion. Once he drank a quart of shine and passed out on Bell Watson's porch. She shit a brick when she went out for the mail."

"There wasn't much blood, Sheriff, not for the mess he's in, and he's lying on his back. He had to be facing that car when it ran over him, and what's his bucket doing over there on those other tracks?"

"He was probably froze up, Hook. Maybe he tripped over the rail. It was cold last night, and I don't think Spark Dugan heard none too good. I never could get him to answer up one way or the other."

"This took place on railroad property, Sheriff. It will have to be cleared with the divisional office."

"There's forty cars waiting for ice," Ague said. "Maybe we could talk over old times some other day."

Taking a pack of Beech-Nut chewing tobacco out of his pocket, Sheriff Donley loaded his jaw and turned up the collar of his coat.

"I got a prisoner pickup at eight o'clock for Judge Mason, Hook. Maybe you could finish up here for me?"

"What about the body?"

Taking another look under the reefer, Donley spit a brown glob onto the track.

"The county fund ought bury him, if you'll get hold of Bud Hanson, the digger."

"I guess I could do that."

Tossing his flashlight onto the seat of the car, the sheriff got in and rolled down the window.

"Some things are worth stirring up trouble for," he said, starting up the car. "Spark Dugan ain't one of them." Backing around, he stopped, looking out from under his hat. "You know how the goddang government is about reports, Hook."

"Consider it done, Sheriff."

"Thanks," he said, hanging his enormous arm out the window as he pulled off down the road.

Ague tore off the wrapper of a fresh cigar, wetting one end of it and then the other, rolling it into the corner of his mouth.

"There's a extra arm under that reefer, Runyon," he said, "if you're in need of one."

Reaching over, Hook snapped Ague's cigar between the tongs of the prosthesis, bending it up at a right angle.

"No. Thanks," he said. "This one works just fine."

As he turned away he could hear Ague cussing above the din of the switch engine.

The sun fell warm across Hook's shoulders as he walked the line of reefers to the operator's office. Water dribbled from the bunker drains, and the smell of creosote and coal hung in the air. The earth trembled beneath his feet as engines and cars rumbled through the maze of switches. It was going to be a fine spring day, for everyone except Spark Dugan.

At the depot, the operator handed Hook the phone and turned back to his telegraph. When Eddie Preston came online, Hook cleared his throat.

"Hello."

"Eddie, this is Hook Runyon."

"Runyon, you know what day it is?"

"Sorry I disturbed your Sabbath, Eddie, but we had a reefer car turn a local citizen into roadkill last night."

"Oh, Christ. Was the signal out?"

"It happened in the switchyards down at the ice plant. They found him this morning."

"What happened?"

"Backed over. Dragged a hundred feet or so by the looks of it."

"This could be a lawsuit, Runyon. I'll send an agent down."

"I *am* an agent, Eddie. Remember?"

"This sort of thing has to be handled by professionals. No offense."

"Look, his name was Spark Dugan, a coal picker, an indigent hereabouts."

"Oh," he said.

"The sheriff figures it was an accident, least that's what he says."

"Wrap it up then, Runyon."

"I'm not so sure it was an accident, Eddie. There wasn't much blood and . . . well, there was no fear on Spark Dugan's face, none at all, like he'd gone to sleep."

"What the hell you talking about?"

"It's just this feeling."

"You wouldn't know a feeling if it squatted on your face, Runyon. Just wrap it up."

"You're a real sensitive guy, Eddie."

"Yeah, well, that's why I'm divisional supervisor, and you live in a caboose," he said, and hung up.

Hook sat down in the chair that overlooked the yards and rubbed at the throb in his head. Gathering up pieces of a man's friend did not make for a good day.

Turning to the operator, he said, "Joe, you worked graveyard, didn't you?"

"Low man on seniority always works the shit shift."

"Was there anyone about, besides the regular crews, I mean?"

"I hear poor ole Spark Dugan was strung out clean to the turntable."

"You can't believe what you hear around a place like this, Joe."

"That's certain," he said.

"You see anybody about?"

Leaning back in his chair, Joe hooked his hands behind his head. There was a stub pencil in the pocket of his overalls, and a smear of mustard on the cuff of his shirt. Joe always ate a mustard and bologna sandwich for his midnight lunch, dill pickle and black coffee on the side.

"Most folks sleep nights, Hook, though I do recall a Favor Oil truck about daybreak."

"Anything unusual?"

"Picking up a load of drill bits down at the siding. Signed in, signed out, just like always."

"Listen, if anyone needs me, I'm going over to the funeral home."

"By the looks of it, they might put *you* in a casket, Runyon."

"Thanks, Joe. Given your caring nature, maybe you would call Supply and see if they'll deliver some coal to the caboose?"

"Sure, Hook," he said. "What else I got to do besides take care of your needs?"


Bud Hanson stood at the doorway in his robe, a cup of coffee in his hand. The veins in his nose were purple and spidery, and the fuzz in his ears was transparent in the sunlight.

"It's Spark Dugan, you say?"

"Out at the ice deck," Hook said.

"The county paying?"

"That's what Sheriff Donley says."

"The doctor will have to sign off before I can move him," he said. "I'll give him a call and be on out."

"Thanks," Hook said. As he started to leave, he turned. "What kind of a funeral does the county provide?"

"I keep cardboard boxes in the back for delivering indigents to the university medical school. It pays enough to make it worth the drive."

"I want him buried proper," Hook said, "and with a marker."

"Gravediggers are hard to come by since the war, Hook, and markers don't come cheap, neither."

"Send me the bill, and could you get someone for a graveside service?"

"The preacher over at the Holy Roller church will send him off for twenty bucks. It's got to be cash, though."

Reaching into his billfold, Hook peeled off the bills and handed them to him.

"Tell him I want a song, too."


With one last stop, Hook headed for the sheriff's office. The deputy checked Hook's badge and handed him a form, directing him to a small room adjacent to the jail in the basement. The smell of urine and tobacco hung in the dankness, and cockroaches dashed from shadow to shadow.

There was much he was unable to complete about the life of Spark Dugan: date of birth, next of kin, social security number. When he reached the bottom of the form, he took out a cigarette, lit it, and studied the last question: probable cause of death?

After several minutes, he squashed his cigarette, leaned over, and scribbled in "Homicide."

# 3

A COVEY OF quail exploded from out of the brush, and adrenaline coursed down Hook's spine. Waiting for his heart to level out, he lit a cigarette and propped his foot on an old tire that was half-buried in the mud. Below him, the Salt Fork twisted into the prairie, its banks the color of blood. The train trestle, a contraption of steel beams, rivets, and rust, arched over the water. Hundreds of blackbirds gathered on the trestle, twittering and clamoring for position. Not a hundred feet from the water's edge, in a stand of willows, Spark Dugan's shanty leaned on a foundation of sandstone.

Working his way down, Hook flipped his cigarette into the water and watched it drift downstream. There were footprints in the mud, but old ones filled with water, their edges worn away by the elements. The smell of oil and sewage hung in the air, and clouds of mosquitoes whined above trapped pools of water.

Tar paper covered the walls and roof of Spark Dugan's shanty, and the rim of a tractor tire served as its front step. Halfway up the door was a high-water mark, and on the south end, a single window with a diagonal crack across its surface. Stepping up on the foundation, he peeked through the window. He could see an old boot encased in a spiderweb on the window sill and on the kitchen table, a jar lid filled with cigarette butts.

The door gave way with a shove from his shoulder, and Hook waited for his eyes to adjust to the darkness. A coal stove squatted in the center of the room, its rusted pipe striking through a hole in the roof. There were scores of empty milk bottles scattered about the room. Spark Dugan was obviously a white-rabbit hunter, stealing milk off the front porches of homes.

A patchwork quilt lay on the floor, its innards strewn about by rats, and an old card table was shoved in the corner. On it sat a half-burned candle sticking from a Hill and Hill whiskey bottle. Under the table was a cardboard box, limp with river damp and stuffed with shredded paper that smelled of rat droppings and urine. Pulling some out, Hook held it to the light that bled through the door. Foreign print of some kind covered the paper. Spark Dugan probably used it for kindling in his stove. The one thing Hook had learned was that a man could never have too much kindling.

Sunlight shot through the holes in the roof, and mud daubers buzzed from the darkness of the corners. Standing on his toes, he retrieved a rucksack hanging on a nail that had been driven into the ceiling joist. Dumping its contents on the card table, he sorted through the items: two pair of cotton trousers, a pair of leather gloves, black brogans, socks, white boxer drawers, undershirts, and a raincoat. They were all new. They were all unmarked, and they were all army issue. Holding up the raincoat, Hook shook his head. The one thing a man didn't need in this country was a raincoat.

Walking to the doorway, he lit a cigarette and looked down on the murky waters of the river. Where the hell did Spark Dugan get military issue? There was no army base around except Fort Sill, and that lay two hundred miles to the south. He'd seen the

German work crews from the prisoner-of-war camp over at Alva wearing army issue, but always with a foot-high "PW" sewn on the back.

A cloud drifted through the sky, its tail looped over its back like a scorpion, and a mosquito tapped a vein on the back of his hand. He smeared it away. Who would want to kill Spark Dugan, a man so far removed from society that he posed a threat to no one beyond himself? Even if someone had a reason to kill him, why would they use a reefer car to do it? It was like killing a fly with a sledgehammer. Maybe Eddie Preston was right. Maybe he did deserve to live in a caboose.

Hook first heard the absence of the birds, and then his own heart beating in his ears. The alarm sounded somewhere deep in his brain stem, and when the two men stepped from around the shanty, he reached for his sidearm. But his coat was buttoned, and the holster was snapped.

The tall one wore boots, big, and an overcoat. He had a white beard, and a pint of whiskey stuck out of his pocket. The other man was short and stocky, a ball cap cocked on his head. He carried a walking stick, which he tapped over and over in the palm of his hand.

"Who are you?" Hook asked, dropping his arms.

The bearded one moved to one side, increasing the distance between the men.

"Might ask you the same," the short one said.

"I'm the railroad bull."

"Why ain't you out picking up runned-over dogs, then?" the tall one asked.

"Look," the short one said. "He ain't got but one arm."

Circling out wider, the tall one grinned. "I ain't never heard of no one-arm yard dog before."

The short one cocked his walking stick and moved in. Hook worked at the snap. Out of the corner of his eye, he could see the tall one circling low like a coyote. Just then the short one caught Hook in the ribs with the walking stick, and his air rushed away. Staggering, he struggled to stay on his feet, his lungs afire with embers, and ash, and molten lava. From the other side, the tall one rushed him, his eyes fierce beneath his brows, his beard flowing.

Leaning over, Hook gasped for air, waiting for the moment to slam the steel hook across the tall one's nose. When he did, the man teetered, his face ruined, his eyes rolling white in his head. Hook caught him again above the ear, dropping him into the dirt. Blood dripped from his nose, clotting in his beard, and in the corners of his mouth. Only then did Hook notice the army brogans, the tread clear and distinct.

But there was little time to reflect, because from behind him a scream rose, filled with fear and rage, as the short one charged. Once again, Hook scrambled for his sidearm, but just as he managed to free it, the blunt end of the walking stick plowed an inch-long furrow into his brow and spewed stars into the blackness behind his eyes.

When he awoke, the last rays of sunset lit the river into an orange ribbon. His hair was encrusted with blood, and a lump the size of a walnut thumped over his eye. Mosquitoes fed at the tops of his ears, and blackbirds once again gathered in the trestle, chattering and preening as they prepared for the night.

Sitting up, he waited for his head to steady before checking for his sidearm. He must be losing his edge. There was a time he would have had both those bums in cuffs. It was not that he minded that so much, but his clothes were a mess, and the lump on his head would take days to heal. He looked in his wallet. Whatever they were after, it wasn't his money. But they had to be here for a reason. No one came to Spark's shack without a reason.

Steadying himself against the door of the shanty, he waited for the nausea to pass before checking inside. Nothing had changed except for the spots of blood on the card table and the missing rucksack and clothes.

In the waning light of sunset, he eased down the bank of the river, Spark Dugan's shanty looming dark and lonely behind him in the willows. Lighting a cigarette, he studied the fresh boot tracks at the edge of the river. He hadn't surprised his attackers as he had first thought. They'd probably followed *him* instead, set upon him with intent. Maybe they were afraid he would find something? Maybe he had. A petty black-marketing scheme was little enough to kill a man over, but when he'd been on the bum, he'd seen men killed for less.

As he climbed from the valley, the lights of the Waynoka yards shimmered in the evening. His friend Spark wouldn't be sleeping at home tonight or ever again. He didn't understand why a man like him should die. But then he'd stopped expecting justice a long time ago. He just took his hits as they came and hoped to fight again another day. Maybe he never would know why Spark had to die, but he was damn sure going to try to find out. The first thing he had to do was to get his first real look at a prisoner-of-war camp.

# 4

HOOK'S EYE THROBBED as he made his way back to the rail yards. How he'd wound up a railroad detective, he couldn't know. His talents were cerebral, his inclinations reclusive. Nothing pleased him more than a free day to read, or walk, or think. He could have been a monk, come to think of it. But here he was getting his head busted by a couple of thugs down on the river bottom. All and all, none of it ranked high on his wish list.

His life had taken odd turns, driven by fate and bad luck, and at some point he'd lost hope in its control. Too much had happened, too much pain and disappointment.

If only he had not lost that arm, had not met Janet, had moved with purpose in his life instead of drifting this way and that. But then most folks could say the same, he supposed, if they were honest. Life caught a man up, swept him along like a fast-flowing river, and dumped him on shore wherever it took the notion, if he was lucky enough not to drown along the way.

As he walked down the tracks to the depot, birds banked in formation across the sky, coming about for a second run over the yards.

He found Joe half-asleep in his chair, his head bobbing.

"Fire!" Hook said.

Joe dropped his feet and swung around in his chair.

"Goddang it, Hook. What the hell you do that for?"

"Trying to save your mortgage, Joe. A man sleeping on the job can get his ass canned."

"What the hell you do to your eye?" he asked.

"What eye?"

"You only have two, Hook. It's the one with the black under it."

"You don't like my eye?"

"I like it fine," he said. "In fact, I think it improves your looks to a large degree."

"Want one just like it?"

"Don't you have something to do besides threaten the employees, Hook?"

"Listen, Joe, you ever know Spark Dugan to do any black marketing?"

"Spark wasn't bright enough to market anything besides coal. Maybe if someone else put him up to it. Spark could be talked into anything other than work."

"You haven't seen any issue coming out of that POW camp in Alva, have you, Joe?"

"Nope. But then again I haven't been looking. They have a small camp outside of Waynoka that they use during the week. From what I hear, they run a pretty tight operation, and it's all controlled by those Kraut officers."

Hook lit a cigarette and studied Joe for a minute. "What do you know about Ross Ague?"

"A lot of goddang questions, ain't it? I didn't know you went to law school," he said.

"Maybe you could just answer a question without a lecture."

Joe checked his telegraph before turning back to Hook.

"You remember the kid who bullied everyone at school? Well, that's Ross Ague, except he ain't a kid. I hear tell he shoved his fireman out the engine cab over in Winslow and cracked his head open. Ague denies it. Said the fireman tripped over his lunch bucket. Division was going to give him a Brownie, but they couldn't prove anything. It was his word against the bakehead's. Guess who won that one?

"Why do you ask?"

"I was thinking to send him a Christmas card."

"Why don't you just adopt him if you love him so much?"

"Then what would you do for a daddy?"

"Got to go," Hook said, before Joe could answer. "Try to keep awake, will you, Joe? We've got real trains on those tracks out there."

"Don't you worry so much about me," he said. "And you better not mess with that Ague. A man could wind up with *two* black eyes."

Hook walked down the tracks toward his caboose. He always had it sided at the top of the grade, where he could see the entire works. Any number of times while having his morning coffee, he'd caught hobos moving across the yards.

Pausing, he checked over his shoulder. No place was more dangerous than the yards, cars being switched here and there, sometimes moving down line without so much as a whisper. Many a switchman had lost life or limb by failing to take a look back once in awhile, and anytime flesh came up against tons of moving steel, flesh lost.

Locusts hummed, a perfectly rendered sonata from the prairie. Being a railroad yard dog had its difficulties, but moments like these made it all worthwhile. So often he'd ridden an ole boxcar into the evening, leaving behind the miseries of life itself. He promised himself to remember such occasions next time he had to look upon the remains of a man crushed to death under the wheels of a train.

When he topped the grade, he stopped, looking first left and then right.

"Where the hell is my caboose?" he said.

Turning toward the roundhouse, Hook kicked gravel down the track. No one messed with his caboose without checking with him first. It was his home, and it was to be treated as such. He worked his way down to the machine shop where Buzz Hendricks worked at firing up the Babbitt furnace. Tools big enough for giants were scattered about, open-end wrenches four feet long, nuts and bolts too heavy to carry. Buzz took out a cigarette and stuck it into the furnace flame as he listened.

"You lost your caboose?" he said, grinning through his beard. "Jesus Christ, Hook, maybe it's time you gave up drinking shine altogether."

Fred Brummer, the machinist apprentice, stuck his head out of the service pit, his face covered with grease.

"Maybe you got the wrong railroad, Hook," he said, glancing up at Buzz. "This here's the Santa Fe."

"Thanks a lot, you bastards," Hook said.

"Well, now, if you're going cry," Buzz said, "I did see a bobcat moving a caboose down line about two hours ago."

"Who the hell was it?" Hook asked.

"I believe it was Ross Ague," he said.

"What the hell was he doing with my caboose?"

"Well, he didn't say, did he? Maybe he was taking it to salvage where ought go."

"Where is he now?" Hook asked.

"Well, sir, time and again I've asked Ross Ague to report to me,

but seeing as how I'm low man on the seniority, and I ain't as important, say, as a yard dog, he just goes on about his way."

"Next time your lunch box is stolen, you can just call someone
else," Hook said, stomping off.

He searched the supply office and then went down to the boiler-
makers' shop. There he spotted his caboose sided right next to the
steam-jenny room that supplied the power to the machine shop.
She spewed steam and smoke and thumped day and night like the
heartbeat of a dragon.

When he opened the door to the caboose, he found his books
spilled everywhere. The coffeepot had turned over and leaked black
coffee all over his only copy of H. G. Wells's *The Time Machine.*

"Damn it," he said, wiping off the dust jacket.

He'd not get a bit of sleep this close to the jenny nor could he
see what was going on in the yards. In any case, no one moved his
caboose without orders, not Ague, not anyone.

Stepping into the jenny building, he found Bet Summers working at a brass fitting. "You see Ague?" Hook asked.

"Yeah," he said. "He's as ugly as ever."

"Where did he go?"

Bet laid down his wrench, pulled out his pocket watch to check
the time.

"I guess the foreman failed to tell me it was my turn to keep
track of Ague."

"Do you have to be a smart-ass to work for this place?" Hook
said.

"Well, now, they hired you, didn't they?" Bet said, dropping his
watch back into his overalls' bib.

Hook turned to leave when Bet said, "Ague gets off at three. His
truck is usually parked over there by the drainage ditch behind the
roundhouse."

"Thanks," Hook said.

"Maybe you ought try living in a house like regular folks, Hook.

They ain't got wheels, so the chances of finding one where you left it is considerable."

"Yeah? Maybe I'll move into your house," Hook said, "while you're working graveyard shift."

He found Ague's pickup parked on the hill overlooking the drainage ditch just like Bet had said. The employees liked to park there because it was out of view of the yard office in the event they needed to confiscate a few supplies.

Ague had left the windows rolled down against the heat. Hook pulled the seat forward to check behind it. Nothing he'd like better than to nail that son of a bitch for pilfering Santa Fe supplies. Unfortunately, he found only a roll of cable, probably railroad property, but there was no way to identify it as such.

"What the hell you doing?"

Hook turned to find Ague standing behind him. He had a cigar stuck in his cheek, and his hands pinned on his waist.

"I've been looking for you," Hook said.

"Yeah? Well, you found me."

"Someone moved my caboose," Hook said. "I hear it might have been you."

"And what if it was?"

"Did you have an order?"

"I don't need an order to move anything interferes with the smooth operation in these yards, that includes that ole crummy you live in."

The heat rose in Hook's face. "Any son of a bitch moves my caboose without orders has me to deal with."

Ague took his cigar out of his mouth and leaned in. Hook could smell the tobacco on his breath.

"I figure that wouldn't be much of a job without you hiding behind that badge."

Hook unpinned his badge, dropping it into his pocket.

"There's nothing I do with this badge that I can't do without it, Ague."

Ague looked over his shoulder as if someone might come along and stop them.

"How am I to know you wouldn't change your mind after a good beating, you one-arm prick?"

Hook reached back through the window of Ague's truck and popped the shift into neutral. At first the truck didn't move, and then it eased forward, gaining speed until it roared down the hill toward the drainage ditch.

Hook waited until Ague's truck plunged nose first into the ditch, the back tires spinning in a cloud of dust, before he turned. Ague's mouth hung open.

"You'll just have to trust me, I guess," Hook said.

"You son of a bitch," he yelled, spittle flying out of his mouth. "You've ruined my truck."

"And now I intend to ruin your face," Hook said.

Ague's jaw tightened, and he dropped his cigar. Hook squared off, determined to make the first blow count. If Ague ever got him pinned, he'd be in big trouble.

Ague charged toward him, his eyes ablaze. Hook sidestepped, bringing his prosthesis across the bridge of Ague's nose, which cracked like gunfire. Ague bellowed, spinning about, his eyes filling with water. Hook circled, waiting his chance. When Ague dropped his arms, Hook moved in and delivered a blow to his jaw with the full weight of his body.

Ague's legs wobbled, and he pitched forward, rolling down the hill and up against the back bumper of his truck. Hook blew on his hand, which ached from the impact with Ague's jaw, and began working his way down the hill toward the truck. As he approached, Ague shook the cobs from his head and started to get up.

Hook reached over, unlatched the tailgate, and let it drop with a thud on top of Ague's head. Ague's eyes rolled white, and he slumped to the side.

Hook climbed back up the embankment, put his badge back on, took out a cigarette, and lit it.

"I was figuring on moving that caboose to the Alva spur anyway," he said. "But next time you might want to ask first, or I might take offense."

# 5

Dr. Reina Kaplan pushed back from her typewriter and read over the review. It was crap. Saroyan's *The Human Comedy* was a bore, and the prospect of selling it as entertainment to a bunch of Nazi degenerates was as ludicrous as her own messed-up life. But it had been the selection committee's choice for the month and fell to her to make Holtzclaw's review palatable for *Der Ruf,* a newsletter that went out to every prisoner-of-war camp in America.

For six months now she'd worked at The Factory, a secret propaganda machine put together by the Special Projects Division out of Fort Kearney, Rhode Island.

The idea was to direct the paper to the POW intellects, to the cultured and curious who would be drawn in by logic and philosophical debate, and then to analyze their editorial responses as a way of infiltrating the camps themselves. It was propaganda in its subtlest form.

But as it turned out, the staff was the real human comedy, an amalgamation of liberal arts professors, denazified prisoners, and gung ho military men set on making everyone's lives miserable. But nothing was more preposterous than their mission: to mold democracy-loving citizens out of the 150,000 boot-stomping Krauts that now occupied every shit-hole camp in America.

Sliding back in her chair, she stared out at the gloom. Her own doctorate was in English literature, with an art history minor, the sort of thing that a young Jewish girl could depend on in the city. Language was her thing, and she was bright, scary bright sometimes, and within a short time, she'd risen through the ranks of the university, claiming her tenure and then her professorship within the minimum limits. No one had ever jumped the hoops faster, higher, or with fewer enemies in the wake.

It was her own Jewishness, she supposed, or some patriotic sensibility maybe, or some madness that drove her to abandon a perfectly fine career for the absurdity in which she now found herself.

Lighting a cigarette, she read over Holtzclaw's review once again. The man was a moron and wrote with an academic tedium that bordered on the criminal. *Mein Kampf* was more engaging. Instead of rewriting the review, she could have crafted it herself and saved everyone a lot of grief, but the truth be known, she'd been little more than a glorified secretary since her arrival. Most of her time had been spent patching up Holtzclaw's drivel or kissing Major Dunfield's ass for a chance to write.

Striking out the first sentence, she started over, rearranging the lead idea. Laying her cigarette in the ashtray, she studied the words, reading them aloud. Holtzclaw wouldn't know a well-crafted sentence if it were stuck up his blowhole. Still, not all her problems could be blamed on Holtzclaw. Truth be told, she'd been hot to leave the university because of personal problems.

Robert had called twice since she'd left, once when he'd made tenure in the English department and again when he'd gotten published. Neither time had either of them spoken of his affair. It was the *way* she'd found out about the affair that hurt the most: from her own students. So, when the offer had come from the Special Projects Division, she'd jumped at the chance to leave.

Through the window, she could see Major Dunfield's orderly coming across the compound. When he opened the door, she squashed out her cigarette.

"Dr. Kaplan," he said.

"Come in, Austin."

"Major Dunfield asked if you could come over to headquarters."

"Now?"

"At ten, if that would work for you."

"Are we having another literary crisis, Austin?"

Stuffing his hands into his pockets, he shrugged. "I don't know, Dr. Kaplan."

"No, of course you don't. I'm sorry, Corporal. Ten will be fine."

"Yes, ma'am," he said, and ducked out the door.

At five 'til ten she tossed Holtzclaw's review into the out basket and covered the Underwood typewriter. It wasn't the best work she'd ever done, but it was a hell of a lot better than what it had been.

As she entered the compound, eyes followed her from the doorways. Tucking her coat about her, she cut between the barracks and behind the hedgerow that led to Major Dunfield's office. Even though the POWs were hand selected for their intelligence and anti-Nazi politics, they were still men who had been incarcerated a long time. Being one of only two women in the camp brought with it an uneasy notoriety.

Corporal Austin pointed to Dunfield's door before turning back to his log. Rising, Dunfield locked his hands behind his back, nodding for her to take a chair. In spite of his balding pate, he was not a bad-looking man, especially for someone whose face would shatter like a dirt clod if it ever broke a smile.

"Dr. Kaplan," he said.

"If this is about Holtzclaw's review, I finished it this morning."

"No, no, it isn't that," he said, commencing a pace behind his desk. "Have a chair."

"Look, I'll get right on that Hemingway thing. It will have to be rewritten from scratch, and I can only take Holtzclaw's prose in measured doses."

"This is not about the Hemingway piece. If you'll take a chair, I'll try to explain."

Sometimes Dr. Kaplan's directness shortcut his strategy. He preferred to carry out his plan his own way and at his own pace. She was always ahead of him putting up roadblocks. Even though she was the best writer he had, not to mention being easy to look at, he would not be sorry to see her go.

Sitting down, she pulled her dress over her knees.

"Now, as you know," he said, "the Geneva Convention restricts the use of propaganda on prisoners of war. It's very clear on that point."

"Yes. I'm aware of that."

"And The Factory has not done that. Even though we've been a secret operation, we've been very careful to follow the dictates of the convention." Walking to the window, he spoke with his back to her. "We've not had anything to hide because we're in the business of education, not propaganda. Still, the enemy is always looking for a reason to mistreat our soldiers, so you have to be damn careful, that's all. It's prudent."

"I understand how the program works, Major."

"Anyway, the point here is that we're in the business of enlightenment, of education, and in no way a propaganda machine. That's all we've ever been, ever intended to be. The Factory has never violated the intent of the convention."

Reina watched him as he resumed his pacing.

"The difference between propaganda and education is not always clear," she said, "particularly to the uninformed. We're just introducing the Teutonic mind to a bit of real culture. Right?"

"My sentiments exactly," he said, taking up his chair. There was a photograph on the desk, a young woman with a hairdo from a different age, and she was holding a small girl on her lap. "You care for a drink?"

"It's a little early for me."

"Oh, yes, so it is. Well, as you know, the war has taken a turn of late and on every front."

Reina's stomach knotted. "If you're unhappy with my work—"

"No, no, it isn't your work. We believe that for a woman . . . I mean for someone like yourself, a woman in a man's world like this, that you've done just an admirable job."

"I've done what any good secretary could do at half my salary. Suppose we get down to it, Major."

"Fact is," he said, folding his hands on the desk in front of him, "that we've got German prisoners coming into the United States from the London Cage  faster than we can process them. It's clear to everyone, except maybe the hun himself, that we're winning this war."

"That's a good thing, isn't it?" she asked.

"Of course, but it presents a different set of problems for The Factory. Look, it's dawning on the public, and even the politicians, that we're going to be sending these prisoners back to Germany sooner than later."

"That's a good thing, too, isn't it?"

"Not if they go back as rabid Nazis. We'll be fighting this war for the third time. It's a lesson we've learned the hard way." Leaning forward, he pushed aside the ashtray. "The point is that the Office of the Provost Marshal General has made the decision to take the reeducation program public, to push it for all its worth. It's the last chance to civilize these bastards, isn't it?"

"Public?"

"We're placing assistant executive officers into every district in the country to work with camp commanders, you know, to establish on-site reeducation programs. No more hiding behind *Der Ruf*. We're going to move in and kick ass, if you'll pardon the expression. We're going to set up course work, especially English, libraries, and music. Hell, we're even going to show them American movies. What better way to turn their minds to shit than Hollywood, that's what I want to know?"

Reina stood, moving to the window. Below, POWs gathered at the canteen for their morning break. They would be discussing the latest articles they'd written for *Der Ruf*. The newsletter had proved to be an effective propaganda instrument, especially among the German officers. It was the prisoners themselves who knew best how to weave the propaganda into the writing. But it had failed to reach the rank and file, of that there was little doubt.

"So now they're looking for someone?" she said.

"That's right."

"And that would be me?"

"We want you on board, Dr. Kaplan."

"I see."

"The committee has decided that you would be best utilized at Camp Alva. We think that you could have a strong impact on the population, and Mjr. Stan Foreman is one of our best commanders."

"Camp Alva is the Nazi dump, as I recall—a little getaway for war criminals."

"We believe you're just the person," he said, dabbing at his mouth with his sleeve. "You've keen insight into human behavior and can be quite persuasive—it's a clean camp, too," he said. "We have fewer discipline problems at Camp Alva than anywhere in the system."

"Discipline has never been a problem for the Nazis."

"You're well prepared for this," he said. "We're talking about a discerning population, very suspicious of American propaganda.

It will take someone with, well, a woman's touch, someone less threatening."

"I'm an English professor, Major. Interrogation 101 was not part of my academic course work."

"The job is to educate, Dr. Kaplan, not interrogate."

"And where is this Camp Alva?"

"Oklahoma. All the camps are remote by design, making escape impractical."

Standing, she buttoned her coat. Sweat had gathered on Major Dunfield's bald spot, sparkling under the hanging light.

"The decision has been made, hasn't it?" she asked.

"I wouldn't put it that way."

"I'm assuming you know that I'm Jewish?"

"Well, yes, I suppose I do," he said, looking up through his brows, "but we can change your name. Who's to know?"

Walking to the door, she held on to the knob and steadied herself.

"Me, for one," she said, closing the door behind her.

# 6

RUNT WALLACE STOKED the stove with wood, cranked open the damper, and waited for the flames to crawl to life. Starting the fire fell to him every morning, but he didn't mind. The kids had a long hike to school and getting up to a warm house eased that burden. Ma would fix breakfast while he milked the cows and did the separating. The cream brought in a little cash, about the only cash to be had, except what he managed from the still now and again.

Times had always been hard on their scrub farm, but since his pa had died, they'd gotten even harder. Then Cinch and Rollins, his older brothers, were drafted and sent off to fight the Germans. On top of that a drought had set in, months without rain, or promise of rain. Had it not been for the milk cows, slopping hogs, and the still, they'd starved clean through.

Slipping on his shirt, he went in to wake Billy Joe, which often took some doing on a cold morning. Billy Joe was buried beneath the covers. Runt poked his shoulder.

"Time to get up, Billy Joe."

Billy Joe rolled over. "Is the stove warmed up yet?"

"Yes it is, and it's your turn to take out the chamber pot."

Billy Joe kicked his feet and pulled the covers down tight. "Oh, all right. In a minute."

Runt pushed a few more sticks of wood into the stove. Sometimes it was hard being left behind to take care of family. The army had classified him 4-F because of his size. At first it had hurt, being rejected by his own country like that, but it was just as well in the end. Without him home to help out, things would have fallen apart long ago. He'd not grown as he ought, like a runt pig without a tit, they said. Still, he was strong in his arms, strong as a gorilla, and could lift Rosston Hendricks over his head to a count of ten.

"Billy Joe," he called. "Get up now. I got milking to do."

"I'm coming," he said.

Sometimes Runt wondered if he belonged to this family at all. Unlike Cinch and Rollins, his hair was red, orange actually, orange as a Popsicle, and his arms and face were covered with freckles. His ma always said his eyes were the exact color of the bluing she put in the wash to whiten up the sheets. In the summer, his freckles joined together into patches until he was more freckle than not. One of them was the exact outline of the United States of America.

But all that aside, he could hold his own when it came down to it. Milking cows morning and night had turned his hands to vises and his forearms to steel. There wasn't a man in a hundred miles who could break his grip if he took a notion to hold him.

Since graduating from the eighth grade, he'd worked the fields, mostly at home, for a neighbor now and again. But it was seasonal work, shocking feed, putting up prairie hay, some broomcorn down on the river bottom. Even though his size got in the way on occasion, he made a hand when it came to field work.

From the back bedroom, his ma stirred, long sighs from under the covers. It was the way she awakened every morning, as if some sadness had to find its way free before the day could begin. While Billy Joe and Essie washed up for school, she'd make her baking-powder biscuits and white gravy, then proof the sourdough for the day's bread. Her ritual varied little, except on Sundays, when biscuits and gravy gave way to corn bread and milk, so she could fix chicken and noodles for dinner. It was the sorry hen who failed to produce her quota of eggs for the week.

Without complaint Ma had turned the running of the farm over to Runt when his pa died. But an emptiness had come that hadn't been there before, a distance, as if she'd stepped back just out of reach of the world. Still, his place in the family had more importance than ever before, even to the younger ones who turned to him for advice and for the settling of arguments.

The separator house smelled of sour milk, as it always did, and cats dashed from all corners, their tails frayed with cold as he poured the milk through the strainer and into the steel bowl. When he leaned into the crank, it growled in protest, gaining speed like a train leaving the station. As it leveled out, he slacked off to let her ride, a feel that came with experience. Turn too fast and the cream would thicken to mud. Turn too slow and it would escape back into the milk.

Afterward, he mixed the separated milk, blue as water now, with mash from the still. Its pungent smell was unmistakable and carried with it a certain risk. But such a risk had to be taken. Without the nourishment from the mash, the hogs would squeal and run the fence until they were skinny as jackrabbits.

Smoking a cigarette, he watched the hogs wolf their feed, bubbling and snorting and scooping mash up on the ends of their snouts. Slopping hogs gave him comfort, a contentment to be found in the gluttony.

Runt had learned shine from his pa, who in turn had learned from his own pa, who always said that Prohibition was his salvation, and the Women's Christian Temperance Union his own best friend. Back in early forty, his pa had even campaigned for the drys. With a grin big as sunrise, he'd carried a sign down Main, damning all liquor and those hungry to tax her evils.

The still, well hidden, had been in the same location down at the gypsum cave for as long as he could remember, accessible only by wading Dead Man Creek a full quarter mile, and then up a ravine clogged with bramble sharp as barbed wire. So dense was the undergrowth that a man could stand within feet of the entrance and never see it. Yet that same man could stand at the opening of the cave and view the entire length of the creek.

According to his pa, Runt's granddaddy had buried twenty quarts of shine to age out in the bramble. When the cows ate the redbud marker, the whiskey could never be found again. That was forty years ago, and not a day had passed that Runt hadn't looked for that shine when he made his way to the still. Forty-year popskull would make a splash for a man with the price.

Because of its location, the still had been built permanent, with copper boilers and a worm for burning off smoke. The temperature in the cave was perfect for storing, and working, and taking summer naps. Walnut and pecan for the fire grew nearby, and even juniper berries for snapping up the Blue John. Shelves, carved by the stream into the gypsum walls, held sacks of sugar, yeast, and cornmeal, and the spring never went dry, even in the worst of times.

In the good crop years, they'd kept it going as much for tradition as for profit, but since the drought, it had been the difference between eating and not eating. The drought had taken its toll. Cash-starved customers had lots to trade but precious little to pay, and because of the war, sugar and meal were getting harder to find.

Oh, there were a few about with good-paying jobs, railroaders, government men out of Camp Alva, truck drivers over at Favor Oil, but country folk, the ones he depended on the most, were as dried up and broke as the land they worked. Then he had to pay up the annual donation to Sheriff Donley's charity, and the cost of fruit jars down at the general. All and all, things had turned sour, and that's why he'd decided to make his move.

As he walked to the house, smoke from the chimney curled into the blue sky, and the smell of biscuits rode in from the kitchen. The kids would be up, warming their clothes on the stove and fighting over whose turn it was to carry out the thunder pot.

Setting the cream on the icebox, he took off his coat and hung it on the nail behind the door.

"What's for breakfast, Ma?" he asked.

"What you think?"

"Ole Shorty's got a cut tit. She 'bout kicked my head off this morning."

Breaking up his biscuits, she poured gravy over the top and set the plate on the table.

"How you like somebody squeezing your sore tit, and with cold hands to boot?" she said, pouring him a cup of coffee and then another for herself.

Sprinkling black pepper onto his gravy, he said, "I been thinking, Ma."

Hooking her elbows on the table, she looked out the window and watched the chickens scratching under the lilacs.

"Them kids been fighting all morning over emptying that chamber pot," she said. "It's high time someone took a switch to them. They ain't figured out what taking turns means."

"I been giving some thought to getting a job, you know, what with the drought and all. I don't mean putting up hay or such but a real job what pays real money."

"That ole leghorn ain't laid but two eggs this week," she said, leaning toward the window, "and one of them was bloody."

Runt studied his biscuits. "I hear they're looking to hire over at Camp Alva," he said.

Turning her cup, she studied the crack under the handle.

"Why couldn't a man get on the railroad, or Favor Oil?" she said. "It's good work, and it's safe."

Scooping up a fork of biscuits, Runt chewed and listened to the rooster down at the creek. Every morning he wandered a little farther. Soon enough a coyote would have him for breakfast.

"They don't hire but able-bodied men, Ma," he said, loading his fork. "The camp hires what it can get, they say, and the money's not bad."

"And you know why, Runt. Them's Nazis out there, five thousand of them. Them's devils out there."

Voices rose from the bedroom, and Runt slid back his chair.

"Billy Joe," he yelled, "it's your turn, and I don't want to hear another word from either of you."

"It's a fair piece to drive, too, in that ole pickup," she said.

Mopping up the last of his gravy, Runt slid his plate to the side and lit a cigarette, hooking it in the corner of his mouth as he searched his pocket for a match.

"You kill that leghorn," he said, "and you ain't going to have eggs for Essie's cake."

"That ole hen ain't but eating grain and squatting for the rooster anyway," she said.

"I figure to hop the Green Fruit Express, least most days," he said. "She slows for the grade over at Four Corners."

"A man could get caught by the bull, Runt, or dragged under even."

There wasn't anyone in the county who hadn't heard about Spark Dugan's accident, but his death, like his life, had been but a ripple. Runt had sold Spark Dugan a thousand quarts of shine over the years, he supposed, and never got much past a nod between them. Most folks liked Spark Dugan well enough, much as they could at least, but he was like a feral dog, fetching his food in quick bites before slipping away into the darkness.

Fact being, Spark Dugan's getting drunk didn't surprise much of anyone. He was laid up drunk in the yards a good bit, but no one who knew him figured on him dying under the wheels of a reefer car. He was too savvy about the rails for such as that.

"I got an order from Simmons for a quart," Runt said. "Maybe I can trade out for a couple of them Rhode Islands what roosts in his barn."

Walking to the window, he flipped the ashes from his cigarette into the palm of his hand and watched as Billy Joe waddled over the hill with the thunder pot in tow. Runt had done that job himself as a child, and he knew its burden.

"It's a worry, Runt, thinking about you hopping them freighters, working with them Nazis."

"I don't see no other way, Ma."

She rose from the table, took up the plates, and dropped them into the sink.

"I suppose a man's got to do what's got to be done," she said, turning to her dishes, her back bent under the weight of the years.

# 7

HOLDING HIS EYE open, Hook bent down to check out the damage in the mirror. Being tall had its downside, especially when living in a caboose. Blood had seeped into the white, and it glowed red as a fire engine. His looks bordered on the rugged side at best anyway, with a strong jawline and a Roman nose, but they'd served him well enough in the past. Women liked him far as he could tell, found him comfortable and easy to talk to. Anyway, it was the rare woman who wanted a man prettier than herself. In any case, in a couple days he'd have a real shiner, an event that would provide far too much entertainment for the crews.

After his coffee, he went through the local paper in search of an auction, finding one scheduled for Saturday three miles north of town: land, house, tools, things too numerous to mention. Taking his notebook out of his pocket, he entered the date and location, more *Reader's Digest* magazines, probably, or another collection of Louis L'Amour, folks having an insatiable appetite for him in this part of the country.

One couldn't rule out the possibility of a first edition of Steinbeck's *The Grapes of Wrath*, a volume both read and despised by the locals. He might stumble on a treasure even in the most humble of homes. Not two months ago he'd found a mint copy of Kipling's 1902 *Just So Stories* tucked away in a box of McCormick Deering operating manuals.

Somewhere along the line his reading interest had evolved into a collecting interest, and then into an addiction as consuming as Runt Wallace's whiskey. At first he'd sought out quantity, to possess as many titles as he could drag home. When the caboose began to creak under the weight of books, he'd turned to first editions only, and then rare editions, and then to signed rare editions, of which he'd found only two, Browne's *Adventures in the Apache Country,* and George Wharton James's *Indian Blankets and Their Makers.* Collecting had become an obsession, an absurd obsession for a railroad bull.

When he heard the whistle of the work train, he downed his coffee, checked the film in his camera, and headed for the yards. The last car was just being made up as he arrived.

"Hey, Frenchy," he said, holding his hand against the morning sun. "You headed north today?"

The engineer leaned out the cab, pushing his hat back.

"Nice-looking eye," he said, grinning.

"Yeah, thanks for the sympathy. Now how about a lift to the Camp Alva spur?"

"It ain't but a twenty-mile drive as the crow flies, Hook."

"I'm not a crow, and I can't fly."

"Don't you have better things to do?"

"Than to spend the morning with charmers like you?" Hook said.

Taking out a cigar, Frenchy rolled it under his nose before biting off the end.

"I won't have to listen about no goddang books, will I?"

"Long as I don't have to listen about no goddang fishing trips."

"Climb aboard then, and try to stay out of the fireman's way."

Moving to the back of the cab, Hook found a place to sit among the lunch boxes. Bulls rode free and without notice. It came with the job. The morning warmed, and the smell of spring filled the air. Thank goodness for nice weather. Come summer, the cab of a steamer turned into the hottest place on earth.

Neither the fireman nor Frenchy spoke as the engine chugged out of the yards, gaining speed on the flat run north. At the Avard crossing, Frenchy lay in on the whistle and then lit his cigar, hanging his elbow out the window.

"Hear they had to gather up Spark Dugan down at the ice deck?"

"Sunday morning," Hook said.

"Heard that reefer strung him clean to the sand house."

"Things get exaggerated, Frenchy."

"You figure to talk to them Krauts up to Camp Alva?"

"Just routine," Hook said.

"Hell, you been reading too goddang many books. Them Krauts are under guard every second. Everyone knows that." The fireman checked a pressure gauge, glancing up in agreement. "Damn shame, though," Frenchy added. "Ole Spark Dugan could be a nuisance, but he never hurt no one."

Hook lit his cigarette and flipped the match out the door.

"Don't let me keep you from your morning snooze, boys," he said.

"Engineers work for a living, Hook. Don't have the luxury of laying around reading books, like some I know."

"Ought to try it sometime. Probably wouldn't make you any smarter, but it would damn sure make you a rarity."

Grinning, Frenchy lit his cigar again and turned back to his work.

At Four Corners the steamer drew down to walking speed as she labored against the grade, black smoke rolling across the countryside. The terrain leveled out, and the engine gathered momentum for the final leg to Camp Alva. On a good day with no siding stops, the trip could be made in forty minutes.

Featureless, the flat plain stretched to the horizon. Tumbleweeds gathered in the fencerows, and dust drifted and swirled ahead of the wind. A great many trees had succumbed to the drought and now stood with arms outstretched, like skeletons rising from their graves.

"Spur's just ahead," Frenchy said. "I'll be back through about four. You ain't here, it's a goddang long walk back to the yards."

"I'll be here and don't forget to stop. I carry a sidearm, you know."

"Ain't seen a bull yet could hit a goddang freight train," he said, laughing, his cigar clamped between his teeth.

Holding the camera under his bum arm, Hook swung out on the steps and waited for the engine to slow. He dropped down and waved them off, picking his way through the Johnsongrass that grew in a tangle along the right-of-way. The work train waddled off down the track, its clatter fading into the horizon.

Camp Alva cropped from the spur's end, its gun towers rising like the pilasters of some forgotten civilization. A ten-foot fence encircled five compounds covering six hundred and forty acres, and behind it were row upon row of barracks, each mounted on blocks, each covered with tar paper nailed down with strips of lath. Identical wooden steps led from identical doorways and onto identical dirt roads, a place void of artistry, a mindless refrain, a graveyard of uniformity.

As he approached, the cadence of jackboots thumped like a heartbeat, and the smell of cooking cabbage wafted in on the breeze. The spur ran parallel with the mess-loading dock, and a reefer car had been pulled alongside. Even from the road, Hook could see the RD 32 number, the same reefer car that had ended Spark Dugan's life.

A military policeman stepped from the guard shack, his rifle across his chest. Shaving soap had dried on his collar, and the imprint of missing chevrons could still be seen on his sleeve.

"Halt," he said, "and state your business."

"I'm a railroad agent, a detective, and I'd like to see the commander," Hook said, showing him his badge.

"You have an appointment, sir?"

"No."

"The commander don't see locals without an appointment. It's the rule."

Lighting a cigarette, Hook looked up at the guard tower where the barrel of a tommy gun had been leveled at him.

"A man died under a reefer over at the ice plant. One of your crews worked on the ice deck that night. It's possible someone may have seen something."

"No exceptions," he said, "'less you're a general."

"I'm an arm short for a general, as you can see."

"Then you need an appointment. That's the rule."

"What I do have, Soldier, is the authority to shut down that railroad spur while I conduct an investigation. You boys could be eating field rations by the time it all gets straightened out."

"Step behind that line, sir," he said. "I'll be right back."

Through the door of the guard shack, Hook could see him talking on the phone. When he came out, the guard motioned him forward.

"The commander will see you, but you'll have to be searched before you can enter the camp. No cameras. That's the rule. Do you have weapons to declare?"

"I carry a sidearm," he said, showing his holster, "and a pocketknife for paring my nails."

Taking the weapon, the guard examined it. "This is a German P.38, an officer's sidearm."

"So it is," Hook said.

Hook's father had been an importer in El Paso, tequila from old

Mexico, food deals, trinkets, sometimes just things he didn't talk that much about. He'd traded the P.38 for a case of tequila. Sometimes his father disappeared into Mexico for days, for weeks, returning with a round of deals and ideas, of which he then boasted about to anyone who would listen.

Though a natural beauty, his mother had been quiet, introverted, with a mind that required feeding through books, dozens of them carried home in paper bags from the library each week.

She shaped him with her intellect, molding his curiosity about the world. She read the books at day's end, cherished the words, presented theories to him like jewels in the sun. When he'd gone to college to major in archaeology, she'd cheered. When he'd met Janet, the love of his life, she'd accepted her as a friend, as someone to care for as much as her own son, and when his father failed to come back from Mexico one day, she went down into the basement and blew her brains out with the P.38.

"All German weapons are subject to confiscation by the U.S. Army," he said.

"That so?" Hook said.

"That's the rule. Now, the corporal over there at the gate will escort you to the commander's office and back again. You see that chalk line just inside the fence?"

"I see it."

"That's the zone of the interior. Any man steps over that line is shot. *Any* man, you understand?"

Following the corporal through the gate, Hook turned back to the guard.

"I won't be stepping on your chalk line, son, but that P.38 has a bad history, if you know what I mean. First came the German officer whose body they took it from, and then the woman who ended her life with that barrel in her mouth—oh, and then that soldier down at Pete's bar last Saturday night. 'Course, he didn't die."

"He didn't?"

"No, no he didn't," he said, holding the hook up for the guard to see. "Dying would have been a blessing, though, given the condition of his nose."

Mjr. Stan Foreman, Camp Commander, reached out to shake Hook's prosthesis before realizing his mistake.

"Oh," he said.

"It's a cold greeting," Hook said, reaching over with his good hand. "My name's Hook Runyon."

"Won't you have a seat, Mr. Runyon?"

Pulling up a chair, Hook took in the room: army-issue desk, green filing cabinet, wire wastebasket, typewriter with folders stacked on top. There were no curtains, no pictures, not even a rug against the cold of the plank floors.

An overweight man in his late forties, Mjr. Stan Foreman eased himself into his chair. His eyes were the color of ash, and a twitch worked at the corner of his nose, as if he were about to sneeze.

"Mind if I smoke, Major?" Hook asked.

"I'd rather you didn't, Mr. Runyon."

"Oh, sure," he said, slipping the pack of cigarettes back into his pocket.

"Now, my guard tells me that you are the railroad bull and that you've threatened to close down our spur."

"Well, not exactly, but I do need to talk to some of your prisoners."

"And why's that?"

"We had a death at the ice plant, an indigent killed by a reefer car."

Picking up a pencil, the major clicked it against his teeth and rocked in his chair.

"Yes, I've heard. It's a tragedy, but I suspect that indigents die fairly often on your railroad."

"A prisoner crew from your labor program worked the ice deck that night. I thought perhaps they saw or heard something."

"Nothing has been reported to me."

"It's just that he lay flat on his back."

"On his back?"

Leaning in, Hook said, "The cars were being backed in to the ice deck. The victim would have been facing them. Why didn't he see them coming?"

The major's nose twitched again, and he rubbed the sneeze away.

"I'm sure I don't know. But I have been in combat and have some idea what happens to the human body when it comes up against something as big as a reefer car. He could have rolled over a dozen times, for all that. The fact he ended up on his back is pretty weak evidence of foul play."

"You're absolutely right, but I've got to clear the record before I close out the case. I'm sure you understand. So, if I could speak to the work crew?"

"Mr. Runyon, do you have any idea what this community went through to get this camp located here? Favor Oil donated land. The city piped water in and piped sewage out. The railroad, your railroad, built a spur and guaranteed delivery of food. Politicians sold their souls and the souls of their children. And then there's the branch camps, half a dozen scattered all over this county, working roads, farms, railroad.

"There's over six hundred locals employed right here in one way or another, people who would be on the public dole, feeding their kids on lard and biscuits or making shine down on the river, without this camp. Do you know that this very day, there's not a vacant room to be had in all of Alva?"

"What's your point, Major?"

"Word gets out that our prisoners are being investigated about some death or other, and everybody gets Kraut fever. Everybody gets to thinking there's Nazis on the loose, climbing into their bedrooms at night and raping their women. Pretty soon everybody's got a hell of a lot of trouble, including you, Mr. Runyon."

"I don't see any reason to make this public."

"Then there's the Geneva Convention, and the Red Cross, and worst of all, the Swiss Legation, who come in here and talk to the ranking German officer any time they want and with no one else around. These Nazis got more power than I do, and if Germany finds out their men are being interrogated, bad things could happen to our own prisoners there. It's a damn touchy situation."

"All I'm asking is if they saw anything."

Taking out his handkerchief, the major waited for the sneeze, which failed to materialize. He folded the handkerchief up and put it back into his pocket.

"Top it off," he said, "the army in all its wisdom has decided to start a reeducation program. They're going to teach civics and English to the Germans, show 'em movies and give 'em diplomas and tuck 'em in at night so they won't have murdering ideas when they get back to the homeland."

Sneezing into his hand, he shook his head. "They're sending an assistant executive officer out here to start the whole thing up. Know who? A woman with a Ph.D., by God. Oh, not just any woman with a Ph.D., but a Jewess with a Ph.D. Now, doesn't that make a lot of sense?"

Hook took a cigarette out of the pack and pushed it back in.

"Look, Major, I'm not interested in busting up your party here, but I have a report to make, and I've got to have the facts. Spark Dugan lived in a shanty down on the river, and I had the opportunity to go down there. I discovered some interesting things."

"Oh? And what would that be?"

"Well, a rucksack for instance, filled with military clothing, unmarked issue. Now, for the life of me, I can't figure how poor ole Spark Dugan wound up with an entire issue of military clothing.

Looked like the same issue your prisoners wear, too, except without the 'PW' stamped on the back."

Rising, the major walked to the file cabinet and leaned on it with his elbow hooked over the top.

"What is it you want?"

"The truth might be a good place to start. Couple boys showed up at Spark Dugan's house and worked me over pretty good, as you can see. I'd guess they were unhappy with me poking around, digging up military clothes and the like. Now, I'm not one quick to anger, but when a man starts pounding on my head, I can't help but get a bit riled."

"I know what you must be thinking," he said, "but I keep very careful control of supplies around here. I'm not saying that there couldn't be a little black marketing going on, because there usually is around a military installation. Given the number of people employed, there's bound to be some of that, I suppose, but I run a tight operation. I want you to know that. I keep that sort thing to a minimum."

"I'm sure you do."

A twitch set up under the major's nose again, and he dabbed at it with his handkerchief.

"I'm not saying it's impossible, but it's not something I condone."

"So, why don't you just call in your man, ask him if he's heard anything about Saturday night, and we'll let it go at that for now?"

Walking to the window, the major watched a tumbleweed race over the horizon.

"Okay," he said, "though it's against my better judgment. The son of a bitch is not some German national, you know. He's not some Austrian yodeler signed up for the duration. Served under Göring himself, and he could still have someone shot back in Germany. Of that I have no doubt. So just be damn careful what you say. He speaks English, too."

"I'll be careful."

Opening the door, he called to the corporal, "Go get Colonel Hoffmann. Tell him I need to talk to him about the soccer-game schedule."

Colonel Hoffmann snapped his heels together when he entered, his arms locked at his sides.

"Major," he said.

He wore an officer's field jacket, long since stripped of its medals, and his eyes, the color of glacial ice, bore through thick glasses. A braid decorated the bill of his hat, an eagle with its wings out-stretched on the crown, yet another above his right pocket. A two-inch leather belt, now absent its Luger, cinched his middle.

"Colonel Hoffmann, this is Mr. Hook Runyon, a railroad detective from out of the Waynoka yards."

Turning, Hoffmann took in the scuff of Hook's shoes, the artificial limb, the two-day beard. Hook dropped his jacket over his arm.

"Ah," Hoffmann said, "so, we talk of the death of the American vagrant."

"Mr. Runyon needs to clear up his report. You know how railroads are."

"I know the German railroads," he said. "There is little trouble."

"How is it you knew about the accident, Colonel?" Hook asked.

Pointing his chin to the compound, he said, "My men report to me. We are soldiers. We rise each day at four to prepare for the Füh-rer. The German officer knows his command."

"Did your men see or hear anything out of the usual that night on the ice deck?"

"No," he said, folding his hands behind his back. "My men saw or heard nothing. This is a minor loss, no?"

"Not for me. I don't suppose your boys would know why there were military clothes in Spark Dugan's shack?"

"Army supplies are prohibited to prisoners," he said.

"Then you would have no objections to me asking the work crew a few questions?"

"You speak German?"

"No."

"I would interpret," he said.

Hook looked over at Major Foreman. "You don't have your own interpreters?"

"Interpreters are in much demand on the front, as you might guess. Prisoner-of-war camps are not high priority. We do the best we can with POWs."

"Thanks, anyway, Colonel. It won't be necessary," Hook said.

"Well, then," Hoffmann said.

"Thank you, Colonel Hoffmann," Foreman said.

After the colonel had left, Foreman took his place behind the desk.

"As you can see, no one maintains better discipline in the camp than the Germans themselves. It's a trade-off we make. The less we interfere, the better things go. It's as simple as that."

"Thanks, Major. I think I've found out what I needed to know. Perhaps someday you could give me a tour of the camp. I find it intriguing, having never been a soldier myself."

"Because of the arm?"

"Yes," he said, "because of the arm."

"Well perhaps we can, someday. Good-bye, Mr. Runyon."

"Next time make an appointment," the guard said, sliding first the camera, then the knife, then the P.38 through the window slot. "It's the rule."

"Right," Hook said, dropping the sidearm into its holster.

Making his way down the spur, Hook glanced at his watch. If he hurried, he could get to the spur by four. Work trains were not that reliable, being subject to any number of delays, so he was delighted to see the black smoke churning over the horizon as he approached.

Swinging onto the engine ladder, he tossed his camera into the cab and climbed in after it.

"Glad you made it on time for once, Frenchy," he said, settling in among the lunch boxes once again.

"Didn't want my goddang engine shot up, did I?" he said, opening the throttle, listening for the telltale rumble as they took up slack.

Hook rolled up his jacket for a pillow and lay down, propping his feet against the cab as they gathered up steam. The heat from the boiler warmed the cut over his eye, and the pulse of the engine relaxed him.

"Frenchy," he said, "I'd like to have my caboose moved up here for a while. You got a siding available?"

"Park you down by the grain elevator. It ain't used but harvest time. Given the rain in this country, that ain't all that often. We will need an order from the operator."

"Thanks. Wake me when we get back, will you?"

Frenchy struck a match, watching it dip and flare as he brought his cigar back to life.

"Boys got a game going down at the signal shed tonight. Starts about seven."

"Thanks anyway, Frenchy," he said, dropping his hat down over his eyes. "I've got a funeral to attend tomorrow. I best get my rest."

# 8

WHEN THE GFX roared by the caboose, Hook sat straight up in bed as he struggled to orient himself. Funeral day. He hadn't known Spark Dugan that well, but he hated funerals on principle, any funeral, hated its despair and its inevitability.

Shivering, he searched for his robe in the twist of covers. Hopping from one foot to the other, he went out on the step to get some coal and found the box empty. From the yards came the thump of the steam jenny, which meant the machine shop was up and running, which meant that supply was up and running, which meant that the bastards didn't intend to bring him any coal.

Stumbling over a stack of books, he cursed and held his toe. The shaving water was cold, the soap melted to slime, the razor dull as his pocketknife and clogged with whiskers. His eye looked like a piece of raw meat. When he cut himself, blood oozed into the creases of his neck. "Damn," he said, staring into the mirror. Crow's-feet pulled at the corners of his eyes, and his sideburns were gray beyond repair. He'd aged ten years living in this hole, no doubt about it. Too much going on, the booze, the rough living, the need to press too hard. Might be the loneliness that sometimes nibbled away inside him like termites in a house. From the outside everything is fine. Push too hard, probe too deep, and the whole structure collapses into a pile of dust.

Afterward, he splashed on aftershave one-handed, slapping away the sting. When he put the prosthesis on, it smelled of creosote. His best shirt looked like a mophead, and when he tried to button the collar, the button sprang away, bouncing three times before disappearing into the mountain of books. It took the handle of a tablespoon to pry on his loafers, and when he got them on at last, both feet went numb.

Spark Dugan's nose stuck over the rim of the casket in the back of the room.

"You're the first and only to come," Bud Hanson said. Most folks called Hanson "the Digger" to his back, not a term that he cared for that much. "I'll go turn on the organ music."

"It's not necessary," Hook said. "You get the arrangements made?"

"The preacher's to meet me at the cemetery for the graveside," he said, rolling down his sleeves, buttoning his cuffs. "The son of a bitch kicked up his fees. Said burying indigents didn't pay, 'cause of the poor turnout and low recruiting potential."

"I'll pick up the difference," Hook said.

"Well, never mind about that," Bud said, pursing his lips. "A deal's a deal far as I'm concerned. Anyway, I'll get my coat on, and we'll get Spark Dugan planted. He's back there if you want to pay your respects."

"You mind if I ride out to the cemetery with you?" Hook asked. "I don't have a car."

He shrugged. "You'll have to wait until I get the equipment loaded before we come back."

"I can wait," he said, feeling the need for another cigarette.

Spark Dugan looked odd all dressed in a gown and scrubbed clean as a newborn. His skin, having been covered with dirt and coal dust for most of his life, now shined white as paper. The putty-filled cavity in the back of his head drooped from the sunlight that poured through the window.

Spark Dugan, in spite of his violent death, had a look of peace on his face. A wreath of plastic daisies lay on the coffin, and the stink of formaldehyde hung in the air.

"Well, Spark," Hook said, "the bastards didn't bring my coal this morning."

"I been talking to him for two days," Bud said from behind, "and he ain't so much as spoke a word."

Turning, Hook said, "He didn't have all that much to say alive, as I recall."

Bud dropped the casket lid with a bang and slid home the latches.

"We best be on the way."

"Need a hand?"

Wheeling the cart about, he said, "It's a one-man job."

As they pulled onto the lane that twisted up the hill to the cemetery, Hook lit a cigarette, letting the match burn awhile before blowing it out.

"Is it true," he asked, cracking the window, "that whatever a man's feeling when he dies is frozen on his face?"

"Here comes that Holy Roller preacher," Bud said, looking in the rearview mirror, "smelling his money."

"I heard that you can always tell," Hook said.

"It's bullshit," Bud said. "Dead's dead, and everything else is bullshit."

Hook took a drag off his cigarette and aimed the smoke at the crack in the window.

"I know how it feels to lose an arm, like someone reached in and pulled out your guts. But Spark Dugan looked like he just went to sleep."

"Dead's dead," he said, driving the hearse up to within feet of the grave.

When Hook got out, he could see where their tires had run over the top of a grave. The heart-shaped tombstone read, "Sarah Favor, Our Angel, Born: Jan. 6, 1939, Died: Feb. 10, 1939."

As they were maneuvering the casket onto the wench, the preacher arrived. He drove a Chevy coupe, with a visor that had been caught on a tree limb, or something of that order, now bent at an angle so that anyone on the passenger's side would have been hard put to see out the window. The windshield had been cracked, a spider crack that radiated in all directions. The paint had worn away from atop the fenders, and a grease rag had been stuffed into the gas-tank spout.

Lunging against the door with his shoulder, the preacher emerged with Bible in hand. Dressed in green pants and white shirt, he looked like one of the plastic daisies on Spark Dugan's coffin. Both knees of his britches shined with wear, and he'd slicked back his hair with oil.

"This is Rev. Bentwell from over at the Pentecostal church," Bud said.

Hook could smell Mennen aftershave in the mounting heat.

"Thanks for coming out," Hook said, shaking his hand.

Rev. Bentwell looked about. "Ain't many here, is there?"

"Spark ran alone," Hook said.

"Though a gentle soul, Spark Dugan lost his way in an evil world," the reverend said. "Some say he wasn't smart as he ought be and ought be forgiven for his transgressions. Maybe so. Others say it was the hunger for shine what led him astray. Maybe that's so, too. Lord knows shine has taken its share of sinners to their damnation." Clutching his Bible to his breast, he looked down on the casket.

"Judgment Day has arrived, it appears, and will be weighing that out one way or the other." He opened his Bible. "Now I'll be reading the Lord's Prayer, fittin' words for Spark Dugan as he stands before his Maker."

Just as he finished the prayer, number 5003 out of Clovis rumbled on the horizon, her whistle wailing at the crossing south of town.

"And may God in his mercy forgive this man his drinking and his stealing milk bottles off the porches of God-fearing citizens."

As the reverend turned to leave, Hook said, "I paid for a song, Reverend. Would like for Spark Dugan to get his money's worth."

Glancing over at Hanson, the reverend shrugged and struck a rendition of "Amazing Grace." When he'd finished, he walked back to the coupe, whacked the car-door handle with the heel of his hand, got in, and drove away.

Before lowering the casket, Bud Hanson took off the plastic daisies and tossed them in the back of the hearse. Just as they finished loading the equipment, the day warmed to hot.

Climbing into the hearse, Bud Hanson dabbed at his head with a handkerchief before backing, once again, over the tiny grave. Hook lit a cigarette as they turned onto the lane, taking a final look back at Spark Dugan's resting place.

Loosening his tie, Bud rolled down his window.

"I'll get that marker up soon as the dates are engraved."

"Thanks," Hook said. "Maybe you could drop me off at the drugstore. I got some film I need developed."

"He ain't much of a preacher," he said, wheeling out onto the road, "but he could sing a man right out of the bowels of hell."

As they pulled in front of the drugstore, Bud paused, both hands on the wheel.

"Just send the bill to the operator over at the depot," Hook said. "He'll see that I get it."

"Maybe it ain't bullshit," Bud said, "not all the time, I mean. Maybe I *have* seen it on their faces, the fear, the pain sometimes." He dropped the hearse into gear and gave a wave of his hand. "You tell anyone I said so, I'll burn your goddamn caboose down."

The operator handed the message over his shoulder to Hook.

"Eddie Preston, the divisional supervisor, called," he said. "Wants you to call him back. Seemed kind of hot about something."

"Eddie's always hot," Hook said, dialing the phone. "That's why he's divisional supervisor, and I live in a caboose."

When Eddie came online, he puffed.

"Yeah?" he said.

"Eddie, this is Hook Runyon."

"Hook, goddamn it, I just got word that you have that indigent case listed as a homicide. What the hell is going on?"

"We just buried him today. Aren't you in kind of a hurry?"

"Listen, my ass is on the line with this stuff, not yours. When I say close out a case, that's goddamn well what I mean. The longer these things are on the books, the more shit can go wrong."

"Eddie, Spark Dugan had been facing those cars when they ran him over."

"What the hell does that prove?"

"And then I found a set of military issue in his shack. While there, a couple of boys split open my head with a stick. One of them wore army brogans. I figure the boys over to Camp Alva got a black-marketing scheme in the works. Maybe Spark Dugan was involved."

"Hell, no one gets killed over a little black marketing. The army couldn't run without it. You know that. You just keep to the railroad, and let the army worry about the army."

"There's something about this case that stinks."

"You buried it this morning. Now, close it out, or I'll get some-one down there who will."

Frenchy switched out the grain cars and backed the caboose onto the siding. The setting sun lit the white elevator towers in a spray of color.

"I hear tell they got rats big as house cats in them grain eleva-tors," Frenchy said, leaning out the window of the cab. "Might want to set the brake on that caboose."

"Thanks for the advice. Don't suppose you'll be seeing Runt Wallace, will you?"

Frenchy struck a match and lit his cigar. "Seems likely," he said.

"Tell him I'm out of goods, will you, and that I've moved."

"A man needs his goods," he said, waving as he eased the throttle forward.

After lighting the lantern, Hook picked up the books that had been scattered the length of the caboose from the ride north. He checked the bruise under his eye and hung the prosthesis over the chair. After undressing, he blew out the lantern and slipped under the covers. The morning promised to be cold, and there was no coal for the stove.

Having grown accustomed to the noise of the yards, Hook felt the quiet now press in about him. Through the window of the ca-boose, he could see Favor Mansion looming on the horizon, a single light shining from the blackness and, beyond that, the lights of the watchtowers at Camp Alva.

Maybe he should close out the case on Spark Dugan. Nobody cared, not the sheriff, not the army, and damn sure not the rail-road. But Spark Dugan's death cried out for justice, maybe because of his backwardness, or his timidity, or the loyalty of his coal deliv-ery. Maybe it was no more than Hook Runyon getting his head cracked and his feelings hurt. It wouldn't have been the first time he'd let revenge override reason.

As weariness swept over him, he closed his eyes. What the hell, he'd give it a couple more days and close the thing out. Be done with it forever like everyone else.

# 9

BEYOND REINA'S TRAIN window, the land-
scape raced by as bleak and empty as her own spirits. For days
they'd driven into the heartland, and with each passing mile her
regret mounted. The vastness of the prairie shriveled her, and she
longed for the city, for its energy and comfort. She'd been dropped
into the sea with no shore in sight, no ship, no hope but to paddle
against the inevitable.

Pulling her legs under her, she lit a cigarette and listened to
the clack of the wheels. At least she didn't have to read Holtzclaw's
drivel anymore, or feign interest in Major Dunfield's postulations
on the theory of inner emigration.

As the train rounded a corner she caught a glimpse of the troop
cars behind and of the end car filled with German prisoners who
were also headed for Camp Alva. At the longer stops the prisoners
stretched their legs, while an armed guard stood watch from atop
the car. From her window, they seemed clean-cut boys, and she
found it hard to fathom them as killers.

Rubbing at the weariness in her feet, she ignored the baby who had screamed all the way from Kansas City and whose face had turned the color of a purple plum. There'd been no sleeper cars available, the demands of the war having made such luxuries rare. There was only the single car for civilians, a coach overcrowded to the point of hysteria. Snuffing out her cigarette, she curled into the seat and let the sun fall warm across her face.

When she awoke, the sun had moved to the other side of the car, and the baby had stopped crying, now watching her with swollen eyes. The conductor walked the aisle, his ebony skin glistening against the starched white of his shirt.

"Next stop, Alva. Alva, fifteen minutes," he called.

"Conductor, could you help with my luggage, please?" she asked.

"Why certainly, Miss," he said, pulling her luggage from the overhead rack, "but this is Alva, Miss. You sure this is where you want off?"

She could smell the richness of his cologne and the clean of his uniform.

"Does the train stop at Camp Alva itself?" she asked.

"You wouldn't want to go there, Miss," he said. "We'll switch off the prisoners' car, but it's no place for a lady."

"Then Alva it is," she said, picking up her luggage.

When she stepped from the train, the wind, warmed from the sun and smelling of sage, swept in. An old truck sat under a tree, the tree long since dead from heat and thirst. Kids played under the shade of the tailgate, dust gathering in the corners of their eyes.

The town lay in a basin, and the houses, spare as the land, squatted among the ravines like toads. At the far end of the basin, grain elevators rose into the sky, white cylinders as stark as the valley. The population couldn't be more than a few thousand strong, and the town itself had that lean look that comes from the lack of good jobs and good paychecks. But it had survived the Depression and the drought and now the war. Like a weed, it clung to life on the hillside.

Finding a telephone in the waiting room, she dialed the number Major Dunfield had given her.

"Camp Alva," a woman said, "may I help you?"

"Yes, perhaps. My name is Dr. Reina Kaplan, Special Projects Division. I'm to report to Major Foreman at Camp Alva in the morning. Might you suggest a place for me to stay the night?"

"Oh, yes. We're expecting you. One moment please." Several minutes passed before she came back online. "I'm sorry, Dr. Kaplan, but Major Foreman is tied up. He suggested that I pick you up in the staff car."

"That would be great, Miss . . ."

"Oh, I'm sorry. My name is Amanda Roswell, Major Foreman's assistant. I'll be there in about twenty minutes."

By the time Reina had freshened up and smoked a cigarette, a staff car pulled in front of the depot. A petite girl in her early twenties climbed out, her dark hair tucked behind an ear.

"Dr. Kaplan?"

"Yes."

"Hi. I'm Amanda Roswell."

"Pleased to meet you. I hope I'm not keeping you over."

"No, it's fine, really. Major Foreman gave me the staff car for the rest of the day. Perhaps you'd like to eat?"

"Well, yes, if you don't mind. The food on the train lacked inspiration, I'm afraid."

"I hope you like chicken-fried steak. It's the local fare."

"At this point anything will do."

The Corner Café sat on the corner of the main square. Flies, bewitched by the flickering neon sign, buzzed against the gray window.

A fan rattled above the side door, its exhaust smelling of onion and cigar. Somewhere inside, a jukebox moaned of wreck and ruin. Pickups lined the street in both directions, temples of despair, with their cracked windows, drooping mirrors, and threadbare tires.

Inside the café, old men sat at the counter, their hats pushed back, their skin browned from the sun, their boots hooked over their chair rungs. They looked up when the women entered, but with a deference born of the frontier, a trait long since extinct in their city brethren.

"I'm sure you're used to much better restaurants," Amanda said.

"You must not apologize," Reina said. "It's refreshing not to be undressed when I walk into a room of men."

"Oh," she said, blushing.

"I've embarrassed you. I didn't mean to be so direct. It comes from living among men, I suppose."

"Sometimes the prisoners look at me that way," Amanda said. "It's very uncomfortable."

The waitress poured them coffee and took their orders, barking them over her shoulder to the fry cook, who stood at the service window, his apron covered with the day's menu.

Reina studied Amanda's quiet beauty through the steam of her cup and understood why the prisoners might stare.

"So, what hotel would you recommend, Amanda?" she asked.

"Fact is," she said, pouring sugar into her coffee, "there hasn't been a place to stay in town since Camp Alva opened, not even boarding rooms down at the Commercial."

"Ah," Reina said, "then Major Foreman plans to put me up at the camp?"

Stirring her coffee, Amanda looked out the window. The sunset cast pink against the whiteness of her skin.

"I know it's not my place to say this, but I think you should not expect much help from Major Foreman."

"Oh?"

"I mean, he believes that a prisoner-of-war camp is no place for a reeducation program, and, well, there's resentment about the camp in any case."

"In what way?"

"Folks around here see it hard," she said, testing her coffee. "We've had the drought, and then the Depression, and then all the men going off to war. Many of the families don't even have decent food." She wiped her lipstick off the rim of the cup and added another packet of sugar. "Their kids are living off corn bread and milk. You can understand, and it doesn't matter what the Geneva Convention or anyone else says about it. They know that when the enemy eats better than they do, something is wrong."

One of the men at the bar said something to the waitress, and a laugh rippled down the counter.

"And then there's the labor program," Amanda said. "The railroaders see the German work gangs coming in, taking up their jobs, working for ten cents a day. It frightens them. They fought for those jobs, to make them what they are, and now the enemy is taking them away. Not a week ago, Spark Dugan lost his life under a reefer car in the Waynoka yards." Looking out the window, she paused. "They say it was terrible, what they could find left of him, I mean."

Stirring her coffee, Reina studied the girl. She'd forgotten such innocence existed in the world.

"And who was Spark Dugan?"

"Oh, nobody, really," she said, "just a coal picker who lived under the trestle. Spark Dugan didn't talk much, but sometimes he'd smile or wave from across the tracks. He traded out coal for whatever he needed, mostly food or whiskey, I suppose. Some said he stole milk off porches, but I never saw him do it. He drank too much and wasn't all that clean, but he didn't deserve to be run over." The bell rang, announcing an order up. "Some say he got drunk and went to sleep under the car. Some say the Nazi prisoners killed him. Others say the union put him under the car, so they could blame his murder on the Germans. The sheriff told Bet Summers that the yard dog's investigating it as a homicide."

"Yard dog?"

"The railroad agent, Hook Runyon."

"I see," Reina said, setting down her cup. "And then I show up, a Yankee, a woman no less, who's going to provide yet more advantages to the enemy."

In the back the jukebox changed tunes, the twang of guitars and mandolins over an ancient Scottish beat.

"Folks are pretty touchy about the Germans, I guess."

"So where is Major Foreman putting me up?"

"There's a barracks outside the compound for temporary personnel," Amanda said, looking up at Reina. The flicker of the neon light played in the blackness of her eyes. "The military police are rotated every three months for security reasons, to keep down fraternization, bribery, that sort of thing. They stay in the barracks while they are being processed."

"So, he thinks that would be a good place for me to stay?"

Before Amanda could answer, the waitress came with their orders, chicken-fried steaks smothered in white gravy, hash brown potatoes, white bread, and a side order of coleslaw.

"You girls be wanting pie?" the waitress asked, refilling their coffees. "Got cherry, apple, and sour cream–raisin."

"Oh, I don't think so," Reina said, looking at the chunk of meat that had been beaten, breaded, and deep-fat fried beyond recognition.

"Listen, honey," the waitress said, totaling the ticket and then sticking the pencil behind her ear, "you got to keep your strength up, you hear?"

"Thanks anyway," Reina said. "Amanda?"

"No thank you."

Taking the ticket, Reina squared off at her plate. Halfway through, she lay down her fork and leaned back in the booth.

"I may never eat again," she said.

"Would you excuse me a moment?" Amanda said, pushing aside her plate. "I need to make a phone call."

"Of course."

While waiting, Reina lit a cigarette and studied the town square through the window. The courthouse sat in the center surrounded by what had once been a park, a grassy area long since destroyed by encroaching pickup trucks. The county sheriff's car was parked outside the jail, the gold badge on the door nearly obscured with red dirt. On the north side of the square, a sign touted billiards, King Edward Cigars, and Days Work chewing tobacco. An old man in overalls sat on a bench in front of the pool hall, his hands crossed at the wrists, his hat ringed with oil. A crow picked at some obscenity in the gutter and then lifted away.

When Amanda slid back into the booth, she smiled.

"I called my father," she said.

"Oh?"

"I thought maybe you could stay with us."

"That's nice of you, Amanda, but I don't think so," Reina said, dropping her cigarettes into her purse, checking her lipstick in the mirror. "It would be an imposition, and I'll need a place to work, privacy and quiet, you understand."

"My father is Hugh Favor's chauffeur," she said, "Favor Oil Company, and we live in Mister Favor's carriage house. It would be a perfect place. Father says he'll check with Mr. Favor tomorrow but that in the meantime, you are to come as our guest."

"I don't know. What about your mother?"

"My mother left many years ago," she said, glancing away. "Look, Dr. Kaplan, there's an extra room with a kitchenette and everything. There's no place else to stay in the whole of this town, really, and you just can't move into that barracks."

Clicking her purse shut, Reina looked out the window. The sun edged below the rim of the basin, and the sky churned with the first colors of sunset. The old man had gone, and the crow had settled back to search under the bench.

"For tonight, Amanda," she said, "but you simply must stop calling me Dr. Kaplan."

As they pulled into the drive of Favor Mansion, the sun puddled on the horizon, and columns of orange shot into the sky. In the city, the day ended under a curtain of darkness, a shutting off of the lights, as it were. Out here, the day exited with theater and drama. Rolling down her window, Reina could smell the loam of the prairie.

Favor Mansion loomed in the distance, an Italian villa, with its gables, and arches, and red-tiled roof. Even from this distance, its immensity and extravagance dominated the horizon. Marble statues stood like guards at the entrance, while fountains spewed water that drifted in the wind.

"My god," she said. "It's unbelievable."

"I know," Amanda said, negotiating the curves.

"All this came from oil?"

"Yes," she said, pulling up in front of the carriage house, "oil and more oil, all belonging to Hugh Favor. He's drowning in oil. Come on, I'll show you how the servants live."

The carriage house sat not far from the main gate. It, too, had been built of limestone and with the same architectural grace as the mansion but was miniscule in comparison. Wrought iron adorned the windows. Black streaks of rust washed into the white of the limestone.

"How charming," Reina said.

"It would be a wonderful house anywhere else," Amanda said, making certain she'd retrieved the key from the staff car, "but here it's like living in the shadow of a giant. Each day is a reminder of your insignificance."

Amanda's father met them at the door, a man in his late forties, bespectacled and balding, who showed her about the cottage with the reserve of a butler. The back room looked just as Amanda had described it, small, but quaint and welcoming. A separate entrance had been put in the back and a stove and refrigerator provided. There was even a corner table and bookshelves built at the head of the bed.

"It's lovely," Reina said, "much nicer than what I had at Fort Kearney. I wonder what the rent might be?"

"It was used as a tack room at one time," Amanda's father said, pushing a strand of hair over his bald spot, "but then was converted for the stonemason who traveled here from Italy during construction." Burying his hands in his pockets, he stood in the doorway. "I'll ask Mr. Favor, if you like."

"Yes, please. The quiet here is marvelous."

"Would you care for a cup of tea?" he asked.

"Thank you, no, if you'll forgive me. I'm quite exhausted from the train ride."

"Certainly," he said, ducking through the door. "Good night."

"Good night," she said. "And good night, Amanda. I'll see you in the morning."

After they'd gone, she put on her pajamas and opened the side window to freshen the room. The smell of moisture from the fountains drifted in on the breeze. The lace curtain brushed her face like delicate fingers. A single upstairs light in Favor Mansion flickered through the sway of tree limbs.

Lying down, she pulled the covers over her feet, the clack of the train wheels still resounding in her head. So many miles she'd come, so far from family and friends. She thought of Robert, of his affair. She thought of Spark Dugan and the terror he must have known under the wheels of the reefer car, and she thought of the prisoner-of-war camp just miles from where she lay, a cage teeming with Nazis.

# 10

RUNT CAUGHT THE early run north, trotting alongside the grain car, pulling himself up and into the door just as the train slowed at Four Corners. The clack of the wheels rumbled in his chest, and he hung on tight as the train picked up speed. Yesterday, he'd delivered a quart of shine to the digger and endured a blow-by-blow account of Spark Dugan's missing body parts. Runt figured anyone who hopped trains had some inkling as to the grisly consequences of a misstep, but the digger had left little doubt as to the reality of such an event.

In any case, he was glad to be on his way to work. Soon enough he'd have his first real payday in a good long while. The hiring officer down at the courthouse had walked around Runt twice, looking him up and down.

"You're kind of puny, ain't you, son?" he asked.

"Yes, sir, but I can lift Rosston Hendricks over my head to a count of ten."

"The hell you say?"

"Yes, sir. Maybe longer."

"Hell, that's good enough for me," he said, laughing. "Go on in there and fill out your paperwork."

The secretary had questioned him about his military standing, whether or not he was mentally impaired, and whether or not he had ever been convicted of a felony. He'd answered no, and they'd hired him as the assistant manager of the Camp Alva bakery. No one asked if he could bake, and it didn't seem mannerly that he should bring it up on his own. Anyway, as he saw it, a man who could make shine to the discriminating taste of lifelong clients ought damn well be able to bake a loaf of bread.

The morning chill bit through him as the train sped along, but dawn broke with the promise of a warm day. Clouds raced across the horizon, their bottoms fuming with the pinks and golds of sunrise. Blackbirds lifted in alarm, banking into the dawn as steam boiled from the stack, and the throb of the engine rendered the morning quiet. Eddies of wheat dust, with their smell of earth and sun, stirred in the corners of the car, and an empty pint of store-bought gin sparkled in the sunlight.

Holding his hat against the breeze, Runt lit a cigarette, leaning back. It wasn't smart to smoke at an open door. Many a bum had been snagged with the drift of tobacco smoke. But then, he did know Hook Runyon, the local yard dog, having delivered a quart of shine to his caboose every week since his arrival from Arizona. Frenchy had told him just yesterday that Hook had moved and had asked for delivery of more goods, so he figured he was safe enough, even if he did get caught.

He and Hook had hit it off from the start, though one could never be certain about the law. 'Course, it wasn't all that clear that a yard dog *was* the law, not in any real way, not like the county sheriff, or the highway patrol who rode up and down Highway 14 in a black-and-white.

When a field mouse dashed from the darkness, Runt grabbed

the cuffs of his overalls and held them about his ankles. A mouse had climbed his leg out in the cornfield once, all in all an unsettling experience.

Disoriented, the mouse darted to the door, his black eyes snapping with fear, his ears lying back in the wind as he debated the perils of jumping. Deciding to take his chances with Runt, he dashed back into the shadows and buried his head in the corner.

"Know the feeling," Runt said.

When Runt spotted the guard towers of Camp Alva, he dropped his legs over the side and waited for the train to slow. Instead, it picked up speed, passing the spur without so much as a blow of the horn.

"Shit," he said, as the spur disappeared behind him.

When the train reached the city limits of Alva, it slowed enough for him to jump. "So long, mouse," he said, dropping off the side.

Catching his toe on a loose spike, he tumbled into the bar ditch, taking a fair amount of skin off the heel of his hand in the process. Sucking away the sting, he looked back at the distant guard towers.

He checked the position of the sun and struck off down the track. He'd be damn lucky to make it back on time. Moments like this he wished his legs were longer.

At the switch point, the Favor Oil land came into view: the spiraling drive; the limestone wall, dry stacked like a crisp, clean ribbon; the lush trees like an oasis rising from the barren land. Beyond those trees somewhere sat a citadel of wealth and privilege, a place that men like him could not even imagine. Favor Mansion, a fortress, held at bay the Depression, the drought, and the unclean who roamed the byways of this country like lost children. For as long as Runt could remember, it had been so.

Rumors abounded of Hugh Favor himself, of how he'd swindled the landowners, sucking oil from under their feet, of his great wealth and taste for art. But sightings of Hugh Favor were rare—an occasional glimpse of his Cadillac, or of his private plane as it banked its way out of the basin.

When Runt reached Camp Alva, the sun rose hot in the eastern sky, and sweat rings grew from under his arms. Heat came early in this country. The smell of cabbage and pork hung in the morning. Brushing the dirt from his knees, he approached the guard shack.

"State your business," the guard said, holding his rifle at the ready.

"I'm the new assistant baker. Come reporting for my job," he said.

"Assistant baker," the guard said, laughing. "You a local, shorty?"

"Yes, sir."

"Thought so. Let me see your paperwork."

"Yes, sir," he said, digging the chit from his pocket. "Says I'm to report here at seven."

"It ain't seven no more, shorty."

"Name's Runt Wallace," he said.

"Hell, that's worse than shorty, ain't it?"

"Maybe you could tell me where to report?"

"First you got to be searched," he said. "Any weapons to declare?"

"No, sir."

"Lean against that rail," he said and patted him down. When finished, the guard picked his rifle back up. "That military policeman inside the gate will take you to security, where you'll be issued a badge."

"Yes, sir."

"Show your badge here in the mornings, and you'll be passed on. No badge, no work."

"I understand," Runt said, taking back the chit.

"See that chalk line on the other side that fence?"

"Yes, sir."

"Well, that's the zone of the interior, and ole Marino up there has a tommy gun."

Runt glanced up at the tower, at the blue of the gun barrel in the morning sun.

"I see him."

"Well, Marino hates locals as much as he hates Nazis. Step over that chalk line, and he'll blow your goddamn head off. You can pass on in long as that's clear."

As Runt entered through the gate, he could see the guard laughing and giving good ole Marino the finger through the window of the guard shack.

After having issued Runt his security badge, the guard escorted him to the bakery. German prisoners stood in rank, or marched through the dusty streets, or gathered in groups to await work trucks. Others sat on the barracks steps, smoking and talking.

A flagpole sat in the center of the compound, Old Glory flapping over the enemy below. Signs, boards with white backgrounds and black letters, distinguished the otherwise identical buildings, the post exchange, canteen, and mess hall. At the far end of the compound, some prisoners played soccer.

These were the enemies, the men who would kill him under different circumstances. These were the same men his brothers, Cinch and Rollins, were fighting, maybe even dying by their hand. The hair crawled on his neck.

"Don't worry about them prisoners," the guard said. "There's tommys in every one of them towers. Besides, these bastards ain't got nowhere to go without dying of old age before they get there. This is a high-security Nazi camp, run by Nazis for all that, and nobody does spit without an order. These bastards got their ways. All we do is keep 'em inside this fence. Sometimes," he said, turning, "I ain't so sure about that."

The bakery sat next to the mess hall, a wooden structure identical to the others. The smell of baking bread wafted through the door when the prisoner opened it for them to come in. He looked to be in his thirties, close to Runt's own age, with blond bangs that fell across his eyes. Perspiration glistened on his upper lip, and his skin had turned red from the heat of the ovens.

"This is Corporal Kurt Schubert, Afrikaner, POW, and the best goddamn baker in the German army. Schubert, this here is Runt Wallace, your new assistant."

"Did you say baker?" Runt asked.

"Ain't none better. Major Foreman just hires an assistant so these boys don't pilfer goods for their raisin wine. Ain't that right, Schubert?" Smiling, Kurt shrugged his shoulders. "Schubert here cooks for the work crews from time to time, when he can't stand the food here no more. Ain't that right, Schubert? And he speaks English better than the locals, but then, who don't?" the guard said, laughing. "So be careful what you say. Anyway, having someone to talk to is going to make the days a lot shorter in this hellhole, even if it is a Kraut. Sometimes we even use Schubert here for an interpreter, and he tells us just what we want to hear. Ain't that right, Schubert?"

"No, sir," he said, reaching for Runt's hand.

"Glad to make your acquaintance," Runt said. "I guess it's only fair to tell you that I don't know much about baking."

"Why, that's good," the guard said. "Then you won't be fuckin' up ole Kurt's baking."

"I'll teach you," Schubert said. "The baking is over by ten, then cleanup. Come on. I'll show you around."

Runt glanced over at the guard.

"Come quitting time you just make your way over to the gate," he said. "Be sure and bring your badge in the morning. There ain't no getting in here without it. Oh, and paydays are on Fridays for locals. You can trade for coupons and use them at the exchange or canteen if you want. Prices are a hell of a lot better than in town."

"Thanks," Runt said.

"Keep your eye on these boys," he said, as he went out the door. "They ain't above stealing the gold right out of your mouth."

Heat from the ovens filled every cranny of the building, and steam gathered on the windows. Sweat raced from Runt's brow and off the end of his nose.

"You'll have to work in light clothing," Kurt said. "It's permitted in the bakery."

Slipping off his outer shirt, Runt hung it on the pegs behind the door.

"How many men do you bake for?" he asked.

"All of them, about five thousand, depending on how many are shipped in or out on any given day. Now," he said, pointing the way, "this half of the building is where we keep supplies, both for baking and for the mess hall itself. Fresh vegetables and fruit are shipped in by rail. The flour and eggs are purchased locally and brought in by truck. We do the unloading. The mess cook takes care of the rest. This room is where the food for the camp is kept."

The room overflowed with food and fifty-pound sacks of flour. There were bags of sugar, cakes of yeast, and baskets of brown eggs. Tins of coffee, tea, and spices were stacked under the windowsill. There were boxes of raisins and of salted cod and herring, sacks of almonds, and jars of pickled pigs' feet. Sides of bacon and smoked hams hung from hooks attached to the ceiling joists, along with smoked pork hocks, jowls, and cured sausages of every kind. Inside the walk-in cooler were cans of milk, cream, sides of beef, barrels of lard, blocks of butter, crates of cabbages, carrots, and yellow onions. There were containers of apples and oranges from California, and grapefruits from Texas. Carrels had been built in the center of the room to hold tow sacks of potatoes, turnips, and sweet potatoes. Never had Runt seen so much food in one place.

"This is all for the prisoners?" he asked.

"Your job is to keep the inventory of bakery goods," Kurt said, "what comes in, what's used in the course of a day."

"I've never seen such food," Runt said, his stomach growling at the banquet before him.

"When we first came here, they fed American food," Kurt said, "but Colonel Hoffmann complained to the Swiss Legation. Now we eat the German food. Your government puts much store in the Geneva Convention. Anyway, there is less waste now."

"Did you eat like this in Germany?"

"On the front line we ate sauerkraut and pork knuckles every day, cooked in pots that smelled of the barnyard. Sometimes not even bread. Sometimes we could not eat anyway because of the stink of death on the desert."

"And what's that room there?" Runt asked, pointing to the locked door.

"Clothing and tool supply. Opened only by the duty guard."

As they moved into the bakery area, the aroma of sourdough and yeast hung in the sodden air, a smell not unlike the separator house, Runt thought. Prisoners worked at loaves of bread, putting them onto trays, which they slid into the stacked ovens. There were mixers big as wagon beds, proofers, cooling shelves, and tubs of dough that rose and sighed in the warmth. Sinks stretched the length of the back wall, spilling over with pots and pans from the morning's activities.

Kurt introduced Runt around, the prisoners nodding from behind their aprons, turning back to their work without comment. Afterward, Kurt showed him how to keep the tally sheet and then took him through the steps of the morning bake.

"Once a week the supply truck comes," Kurt said. "You are to tally the inventory. You'll eat with the guards and the other locals. The food is free."

"That's all I have to do," he asked, "take the tally and keep watch over these supplies?"

Dabbing the perspiration from his forehead with his apron, Kurt shrugged.

"There's no shortage of men in a prisoner-of-war camp."

Taking out a cigarette, Runt offered him one. Kurt took it and put it in his pocket.

"No smoking in the bakery," he said.

"I wasn't raised to stand around while other men worked," Runt said. "Maybe there's something I could do to help out, pass the time?"

Leaning against the doorway, Kurt glanced down at Runt, the stunted frame, bent legs, and twisted pelvis.

"I don't know," he said. "The others did not ask."

"I'm stronger than I look," Runt said.

"There's always those," he said, pointing to the pots and pans. "They await the end of the day like the executioner's pole."

"Maybe I can whittle them down a tad," Runt said, rolling up his sleeves.


At eleven thirty, Kurt came for him. Taking off his apron, Runt dried his hands.

"Your boys steal any raisins while I was busy?" he asked.

"We have our raisins this month," Kurt said. "You go eat now. Then come back here."

The lines were only beginning at the mess when Runt arrived. His tray heaped with food, he took a table. Kurt was right. The food looked delicious, and he had taken a shameful amount. He lay aside his spoon for a moment to gather up control of his hunger.

Soon, a line formed out the door, guards for the most part, with their military-police armbands and their silver whistles; a few truck drivers from the motor pool; some construction workers building a drainage ditch along the road. A half dozen women gathered at a table near the door, their laughter like bells among the voices of the men.

Runt spotted her as she searched for a place at the table, her tray balanced on her hand, her black hair tucked behind an ear. He recognized her as Amanda Roswell from school. She'd grown into quite a beauty. Sitting down, she smiled at the other women.

Runt watched her. When she looked up, he turned to his tray. How often he'd seen them lower their eyes or move away at the sight of his body. He learned not to look back, not to invite it, if he could keep from it. After finishing his meal, he sipped his tea and waited until she'd left before making his way back to the bakery.

By day's end, he'd washed all the pots, lining them up on the shelf for the morning run. Kurt nodded his head in approval.

"Good, for an American," he said. "Sometimes it's late before the cleanup is finished. Take your tally now and go home."

When Runt had finished, he donned his shirt and headed across the compound. Prisoners watched him from the steps of the barracks as he waited for security to open the gate. Kurt, who stood in the doorway, did not look up.

Runt waited in the stand of sumac as the five o'clock train switched out empty reefer cars from the Alva spur. With a full head of steam and a light load, they were soon at Four Corners and by the time the sun eased below the horizon, he'd finished the milking and brought in wood for the night.

Ma stood at the stove, stirring the gravy she'd seasoned with black pepper and bacon grease. Essie and Billy Joe were shooting marbles at the cat's feet and laughing each time he vaulted into the air.

"You get them hens?" she asked without looking up.

"I didn't have time, Ma. I'll do it Saturday. I got to take some goods to Hook Runyon anyway."

"Come on, kids," she said. "Supper's on."

Essie and Billy Joe climbed up on their stools and waited while Ma drizzled gravy over their bread. The stools were painted nail kegs, and hardly a meal passed but what one of the kids didn't spill over backward.

"Is there any milk?" Billy Joe asked.

"There's not milk for you and them hogs both, Billy Joe," Ma said, "and we can't eat you for breakfast meat, can we? Here, have a little of my coffee."

"I don't want no coffee," he said. "It taste like ole tobacco juice."

"You just watch your mouth, buster," she said, scraping the last of the gravy out of the skillet, "or you'll be going to bed with nothing but squeaks in your belly."

After supper, Ma heated bricks on top of the stove, wrapping them in brown paper bags for the kids to warm their feet on in bed. And when they were quieted down at last, she sat in her chair by the stove and took up the rag rug that she braided on in the evenings. Runt smoked a cigarette and read an article in *Capper's Weekly* on the eating behavior of tomato worms.

Putting out his cigarette, he laid the magazine aside.

"Did you know that a tomato worm can eat a full-grown plant in twenty-four hours?"

"I been thinking about Cinch and Rollins all day," she said, "and about all them Germans over there in Camp Alva. I ain't had a moment's peace, I tell you."

"Oh, Ma, it ain't like you think. They don't have weapons or nothing, and the feller I work with seems right decent. There's ten-foot-high fences and guards with tommy guns everywhere you look. Even if them Germans could get out, there ain't no place to go. It's a million miles back to Germany."

"Bess Hendricks says they're Nazis and that there ain't no one safe long as they're right here in our backyard. She says they killed Spark Dugan, stuffing the German flag in his mouth so's he couldn't scream out while they cut off his arms and legs."

"Oh, Ma, that's downright foolishness."

"Well, that's what she told May Bohn down at the creamery."

Laying her rug down, she looked up at him. "Suppose they make a break, Runt? Suppose they get loose? What would they do to you? What would they do to all of us?"

"Bess Hendricks is just an ole sittin' hen," he said, stretching his arms above his head, "squawking at every peep in the henhouse."

"There's some truth in the biggest tales, Runt, even Bess Hendricks's."

"I get paid on Fridays, Ma, and we get post-exchange privileges. You make out a list of what you need, and I'll carry it home."

When she didn't answer, he rolled up the magazine and slipped it into the stove.

"I better get my rest, Ma. I got chores before daylight, and them pots and pans near whipped me today."


Crawling under the covers, Runt shivered against the cold spring night, wishing he, too, had warmed a brick for his feet. The wind whipped across the plain, rattling the screen on the window and thumping at the door like some lost spirit. As he lay in the dark he could hear the creak of Ma's rocking chair as she worked at her rug. It was her way, and the way of other folks in these parts, to stir up fear of strangers. And when the strangers were Nazi and gestapo, the fear might likely be considerable.

But Ma had a point, something that lay unsettled in his own mind. Many times he'd seen Spark Dugan hop a freighter. Dead drunk, he could do it better than most sober men. No one in the yards knew trains better than Spark Dugan, and that was just a fact. Trains were his home, his company. For him to lie down under a reefer, sided for icing, was for him to commit suicide, and Spark Dugan liked his shine far too much for that.

# 11

THE KNOCK ON Hook's door sat him straight up in the bunk.

"Yeah?" he said, his voice hoarse.

"Hook Runyon?"

"Who is it?" he asked, reaching for his sidearm.

"Corporal Hensley, dispatch from Camp Alva."

Hook slipped on his robe in the dark, opening the door. The corporal's chevrons were clear in the moonlight, and he held a piece of paper in his hand.

"Camp Alva?" Hook asked.

"Yes, sir," he said. "I have a message from Major Foreman."

"What is it, Corporal?" The corporal handed him the dispatch, which Hook couldn't make out. "Maybe you could just tell me."

"Yes, sir," he said. "We had an escape from Camp Alva tonight, a commander out of the panzer division."

"Panzer?"

"Yes, sir, tank commander from the Africa Corps. We think he managed to go out with the garbage truck sometime after dark. At least he wasn't there for roll call."

Hook rubbed the sleep from his eyes. "What does this have to do with me, Corporal? I'm a railroad bull."

"Major Foreman thinks there's a good chance he'll hop a freighter."

"What makes him think so?"

"How else could you get out of this country, begging your pardon, sir? It's a thousand miles to nowhere."

Hook stepped out on the porch. The moon cast his shadow across the tracks.

"Ask Major Foreman to call the Waynoka operator. Tell him I'll be hopping the next freighter through here. You got that?"

"Yes, sir."

"What's this prisoner's name?"

"Mjr. Erik Fleischer."

"Is he armed?"

"We can't be certain, sir. You never know what these prisoners got stashed away somewhere."

"Okay, Corporal. Make sure that call is put through."

"Yes, sir," he said. "And, sir?"

"What is it?"

"Major Fleischer is a highly decorated soldier. He's smart, and he's a mean son of a bitch."

"Thanks," Hook said.

Hook got dressed in the dark. He checked the clip and snapped his sidearm into his shoulder holster. Having only one arm made a quick draw pretty much impossible, so over the years he'd concentrated on accuracy.

The freighter should be slowing through the spur. He'd wait for the bouncer, catch the ladder, and then work his way toward the engine. If the prisoner had hopped the freighter, he'd not go for the caboose. There would be too much chance of encountering people.

He'd most likely go for something near the middle of the train, probably on the west side, away from the POW camp. In the end, he'd have nowhere to move but forward.

Out of Alva they would gain speed, not slowing again until Wellington, and bailing from a speeding freighter would be a daunting prospect even for a man like Fleischer. Of course, if for some reason Fleischer hadn't hopped the freighter, then Hook would have a long trip back.

He donned his jacket against the morning cool, locked the door, and walked down the track to where he could get a clear run at the caboose. The spacing of the ties was not conducive to running alongside, one tie being too short for a step, and two being too long, like running with your pants around your ankles. Better to reach out, grab the railing, and hope the damn thing didn't pull off your arm, a particularly distressing thought if you had only one arm to begin with.

Laying his ear against the track, he listened. The distant rumble of the freighter, yet miles away, throbbed up from the heart of the steel rail. There'd be time for a smoke.

He settled back, lit a cigarette, and studied the moon, which had risen into the blackness like an ivory button. Somewhere from out on the prairie, a coyote bayed, a singular and lonely call.

Hook thought about the prisoner, a man trapped in the heart of his enemy's land. He probably didn't speak the language, or if he did, his accent would be a sure giveaway. He'd most likely be wearing a prisoner uniform, and he'd be short of money. Even if he made it out of here, where would he go? Like the corporal said, a thousand miles lay between him and any coast or border he'd care to choose.

So, he would be desperate and dangerous and prone to making bad judgments. Hook, on the other hand, knew this territory well. Most of all he knew the railroad, how it worked and didn't work. If he had to go up against a man like Fleischer, this would be the place he'd choose. All these factors should work to his advantage, providing he didn't screw up, something that he did on a regular basis.

When he saw the light break on the horizon, Hook dashed his smoke and moved back into the brush. The steamer chugged up the grade. She couldn't be doing more than ten miles an hour. Black smoke and steam drifted over the moon, and the ground trembled beneath his feet. When the engine passed by, he could smell the heat and see the engineer's cigarette.

From what he could tell, the train hauled live cattle. Cattle cars were easy to hop, having ladders and open slats, but once aboard, there were damn few places to hide. If Fleischer had made the hop, he probably hunkered on the top, which worked fine until it turned cold or rained, and then a man could freeze stiff as a carp.

Hook waited for the caboose. If he missed the railing, the hunt would end before it started. Once, in Albuquerque, he'd thrown his suitcase aboard an open-door grainer, stumbled on a spike, and watched as everything he owned rode off to Barstow.

When the Alva lights broke from behind the caboose, Hook moved up next to the tracks, looking for the caboose railing. At the last second, he spotted it, stepped in, and grabbed hold. The caboose catapulted him into the air, and he swung about, catching his prosthesis underneath the railing and pulling himself aboard.

He pushed against the caboose wall and rubbed his shoulder. He tried the door, but the brakeman had locked it. The train topped the grade and picked up speed. The clack of the wheels turned to chatter as the train sped into the prairie. Behind him, the lights of Alva flickered and then disappeared in the night.

He'd have to work his way along the top, which exposed him more than he preferred. If Fleischer had a weapon, there'd be damn few places for cover. He waited until the train had gained full speed, too fast for a sane man to bail, and then he climbed his way up the ladder.

The cars ahead rolled and warped like a giant snake, each gap between them a death trap just waiting for a misstep. The wind sucked the breath from his nostrils and the moisture from his eyes.

When they banked into a curve, smoke rode down the line like a black tornado. He held his sleeve over his face and closed his eyes until they'd come about once again. Scooting forward, he stopped, listened, moved again. Fleischer could be anywhere, between the cars or on the side, dangling from the slats.

The engineer gave her full throttle as they charged into the night. Hook hung on against being swept over the side. Working to the end of the car, he lowered himself down to the Janney coupler, the ties flickering beneath him. He hauled himself over by the grab bar. To fall here would end a man's troubles in a heartbeat. The train slowed momentarily as they passed over a crossing, her whistle wailing, her bell clanging.

When Hook pulled himself over the top of the car, he spotted Fleischer down line. He lay flat, his head buried in his elbow against the driving wind. Hook eased along the top of the car, his eye trained on Fleischer, who was so busy he'd failed to notice Hook. Inch by inch Hook wormed his way forward. Drawing his weapon now would be useless, what with the cars pitching and rolling like ships at sea.

Suddenly Fleischer spotted Hook over his shoulder. He scrambled to the end of the car. Looking back again, he paused and then leaped through the air, landing on the next car. Hook stood, but the wind slid him sideways. He dropped to all fours and worked his way forward. The gap between the cars changed with each roll and pitch of the track. He might make it, but then again he might not.

It occurred to him that since Fleischer had no place to go anyway, crossing over on the coupler would be a lot less stressful. By the time Hook got over, Fleischer stood at the end of the lead car with naught ahead but the engine. The moon lit the "PW" on his back, and his hair fluttered in the wind. Hook pulled his side-arm.

"Surrender," he yelled. "Down on your belly."

Fleischer looked back and then out into the prairie. The train tore through the night, the engine stack boiling black smoke into the sky.

"The end of the line," Hook said, leveling his sidearm. "There's no place to go."

Fleischer edged to the side of the car, looking over.

"Don't do it, you dumb bastard," Hook yelled. "You'll never make it."

Fleischer moved closer, glanced back at Hook, and jumped.

"Goddang it," Hook said.

Holstering his sidearm, he stepped to the side of the car, shook his head, closed his eyes, and leaped into the blackness after him.

# 12

By THE TIME Hook figured out where he'd landed, the freighter had already chugged off into the distance. The sagebrush had taken its share of hide. He brushed the dirt from his clothes and examined the scratches that covered his arms. The wound over his eye had opened, and blood trickled down his cheek.

Climbing out of the brush, he dropped down on a knee to listen. He heard nothing but the faint hoot of an owl. Fleischer couldn't be far away if he had survived the jump. One thing was certain, if he ever got another chance, he aimed to shoot him on sight. Any man who would bail off a freighter at cruise speed has no business living.

Hook followed the brush down to a ravine where a small creek wound through its center. Moonlight reflected in the water, and frogs croaked from the reeds.

He studied the bank, finding fresh prints leading off downstream. Unfortunately, Fleischer had survived the jump. Hook reached for a cigarette but decided against it at the last second. The smell of tobacco smoke was unmistakable, and this son of a bitch just might be crazy enough to attack, sidearm or no sidearm.

He walked downstream, following the tracks as best he could. Dawn had edged onto the horizon by the time he came upon the farmhouse, an old bungalow with wood smoke curling out of the chimney. A black and tan coon dog lay on the front porch, and he lifted his nose in the air as Hook approached.

Hook unholstered his weapon and moved to the window. Inside, an old man and woman lay on the floor, bound and gagged with pillowcases.

Hook stepped over the hound and eased into the house. When he found no one, he untied the old man and his wife, showing them his badge.

The old man rubbed his wrists. "We've been invaded by the goddang Germans," he said. "Mom here like to have died of fright. Me, too, if you've got to know. That feller had a look in his eye what turned your blood to ice."

"Where did he go?" Hook asked.

"Which way is Germany?" he said. "Thing is, the bastard took my Johnny Pop, drove her off like he'd been doing so his whole life."

"Hook finished untying the old lady and helped her up. "Your Johnny Pop?"

"You ain't a German, too, are you?" the old man asked.

"I'm a railroad bull," Hook said.

"Jeez," he said. "Some days a man ought stay in bed."

"You going to tell me or not? I'm running a little behind here."

"My John Deere tractor, two-cylinder Johnny Pop. That German cranked her up, and off he went. Shouldn't be too hard tracking a goddang Johnny Pop even for a yard dog."

"I need a vehicle," he said.

"Pulled the motor out of my Ford over there under the tree.

The old wheat truck is out there in the barn. You figure the railroad's good for it?"

"You've got my word," Hook said.

"I was hoping for a tad more than that," the old man said.

"I've got a twenty-dollar bill here. In the meantime, maybe you could call the county sheriff."

"Oh, sure, sure," he said. "Keep her under forty, or she heats up. Once she heats up, well then, it's just too goddang bad."

The ole coon dog watched on as Hook worked at the door handle of the wheat truck. The cab smelled of dust and grease, and a pair of work gloves had been thrown on the dash. The glass in the speedometer had long since disappeared, and there was a hole where the radio had once been.

He goosed the choke, pumped the foot feed a dozen times, and cranked her over. Smoke filled the shed as the truck churned to life. Hook fished around for reverse and backed her out. The old man and his wife watched from the porch as he pulled down the drive.

At the end of the drive, he found where the tractor had crossed the road and gone through an open gate into the field. Fleischer had taken the shortcut, probably straight over to the section line. Hook didn't know much about Johnny Pops, but they ought be a damn sight slower than a truck. With luck he might still be able to catch him by going around. He gave a wave back as he pulled off down the road. Smoke and dust boiled up through the floorboard as he drove away.

Just as he made the corner at the section line, he spotted Fleischer across the field like a green dinosaur. The flywheel spun on the side of the Johnny, and puffs of blue smoke shot upward from the exhaust. Fleischer saw him just as he came out of the gate. Hook floorboarded the truck.

As he pulled up behind the tractor, Fleischer suddenly turned. Only then did Hook see the revolver in his hand. The slug smacked through the windshield and embedded itself in the seat, only inches from Hook's shoulder.

"Damn it," he said, slamming on the brake.

When he looked up, Fleischer had wheeled the Johnny Pop around and was headed straight for him. Hook crammed the shift into reverse. Looking in the side mirror, he guided the truck backward down the road as she roared and coughed and inched along at walking speed. When he dared look again, the Johnny Pop had come up only inches from his front fender. He could smell the kerosene from her exhaust and hear the *thump thump* of her engine. Fleischer stood and leveled his weapon straight at him. Hook ducked just as Fleischer fired. This time the windshield shattered into a million crystals.

Hook's ears rang as he struggled to get to his sidearm. But by then the Johnny Pop had caught the front fender of the truck, shoving it sideways in the road. Hook's head cracked against the steering wheel, and lights flashed behind his eyes.

Shaking it off, he unholstered his weapon and crawled out the passenger door, dropping behind the front wheel for cover. Only then did he realize that the Johnny Pop had lumbered off into the adjacent field.

From down the road rose the wail of a siren. Hook wiped the blood from his eye to see the flashing red lights of the county sheriff's patrol. The sheriff pulled up alongside Hook and rolled down his window.

"What the hell is going on?" he asked.

"I'm a railroad bull," Hook said. "There's a German escapee on a tractor headed across that field. He's armed."

The sheriff grinned, flakes of tobacco stuck between his teeth. "You shittin' me?"

"He can handle that Johnny Pop like a panzer tank," Hook said, "and he isn't too bad with that pistol, either."

"Yeah?" the sheriff said. "Well I got a 303 high-powered rifle ought stop the son of a bitch. Climb in."

Hook jumped in, and the sheriff spun off. "We'll catch him at the county line," he said.

Hook steadied himself against the dash as they roared off.

"You might want to consider what you're going to do with him after you catch him," Hook said.

"There he is," the sheriff said, pointing down the road. "I'll drive up alongside, and you put a slug in his head."

Fleischer looked back over his shoulder as the sheriff's car approached. He spun the wheel, and the Johnny Pop dipped into the grader ditch, up the other side, and through a barbed-wire fence. Broken wire whizzed about like razor blades as the Johnny Pop trudged off across the field, dragging posts and debris behind her.

"I'll be jacked," the sheriff said, turning the car around. "I can't go in that field, she'll bog down sure. We'll catch him a mile over."

Sure enough, just as they came around the corner, the tractor pulled out of the field and onto the road ahead of them.

"I've got an idea," Hook said. "Get on by him. Drop me off when you get below the hill where he can't see. Go on another mile and pull across the road."

"You're nuts," he said, gunning the patrol car.

Fleischer looked down at them as they shot by, his jaw rippling.

"Mind if I use your 303?" Hook asked.

"Anyone you want me to notify?"

"Pull over here," Hook said.

The sheriff skidded to a stop, and Hook bailed out. Rolling down the ditch, he searched for cover, finding it behind a cedar stump. The *pop pop* of the tractor echoed in the valley, and the red lights of the patrol flashed down the road.

He checked the safety on the 303 and laid the barrel in the

crotch of the stump. With luck Fleischer would be too busy watching the patrol car to notice him. If he didn't, then he was face-to-face with a Johnny Pop and a German panzer commander. Maybe he should have told the sheriff to notify Eddie Preston, who would no doubt be delighted with the news of his demise.

When the tractor topped the hill, Fleischer's eyes were locked on the lights of the patrol car ahead. The gearbox growled as the Johnny Pop gained speed down the hill. Hook leveled the 303 in on Fleischer. From here, he could blow the bastard's head off.

He cocked the bolt and shot at the front tire of the Johnny Pop. The air rushed from the tire, screaming like a steam whistle. Fleischer struggled to hold her steady, but the front wheels slid to the side, pushing a wave of dirt ahead of them. The Johnny Pop thumped and churned and thumped a final time before coming to a stop.

Hook stepped out from behind the stump, his rifle trained on Fleischer. "Throw down the weapon," he said.

Fleischer hesitated and then threw his pistol into the dirt. Hook cuffed him and signaled for the sheriff.

"You're lucky to be alive, Fleischer," Hook said.

"As are you," Fleischer said.

"How you figure on getting back to Germany on a Johnny Pop?"

"We defeat you here or there," he said. "No matter."

"Don't you know you're in the middle of America?"

Fleischer looked down his nose with eyes cold as winter.

"The American is soft, and he is greedy," he said. "In the end he defeats himself."

The county sheriff took Fleischer into custody, agreeing to deliver him to Major Foreman. Hook called Division about the damage to the wheat truck and the front tire of the Johnny Pop, which sent Eddie Preston into a rage about the high cost of security.

Hook caught the next train back to Alva. When he got to his caboose, he looked in the mirror. There were bits of sagebrush still stuck in his hair. He lay down in his bunk and let the weariness sweep over him.

Maybe Spark *had* been in cahoots with the Germans and maybe not. But this much Hook knew for certain: if those other five thousand prisoners out there were as tough and smart as Fleischer, that prisoner-of-war camp was a bomb just waiting to explode.

# 13

Runt could still smell rain in the air when he went out to do the chores, no more than a sprinkle that had settled the dust. The sun bobbed over the horizon, and Ma's chickens darted like madmen into the hoards of baby grasshoppers that had appeared overnight.

Ma had smiled with Friday's pay, and with the stick of bologna he'd bought at the camp canteen. Essie and Billy Joe gorged on the chocolate bars he'd brought home, licking the wrappers clean, looking up at him with grins big as day.

Shorty snorted and danced from one foot to the other as he put lard on her sore tit. Just as he finished up, she swatted him across the face with a tail full of cockleburs.

"You ole bitch," he said, slugging her in the ribs, holding his fingers against the sting.

After milking and separating, he fed the hogs, his foot kicked up on the fence while he watched them eat their mash. By the time chores were finished, the wind swept in from the southwest, a dust devil on its crest, twisting down the road.

Standing at the stove, Ma stirred the bits of bologna into the gravy.

"Don't seem right, them Nazis eating better than my kids," she said.

"We could use a rain," he said, slipping off his barn shoes.

"We could always use a rain," she said, adding a dash of flour to the gravy.

"Well, if we don't get rain in April, we ain't going to get rain at all. That much I know."

"Them kids are still in bed, and that thunder pot ain't been taken care of. It's Essie's turn, but she's too highfalutin' to carry a thunder pot, though she ain't too highfalutin' to use one."

"It's Saturday. Let her sleep."

Setting his plate in front of him, she sat down in her chair and watched the chickens out the window as they scrambled for grass-hoppers.

"Mighty good biscuits," he said, washing them down with coffee.

"That ole hen's goin' in the pot," she said. "She ain't laid but one egg all week, and then she broke it getting off the nest."

"I'm going over to see Simmons this morning. Maybe he'll trade out a couple of them Rhode Island hens. After that I'm making a delivery to Hook Runyon at the elevator siding."

"A far piece, ain't it?"

Polishing his plate, Runt pushed it aside and lit a cigarette.

"He's the railroad yard dog. I figure it like Sheriff Donley's char-ity. It's just one of them things. I'll catch a northbound over at Four Corners."

Picking up his plate, she dropped it into the wash pan and then leaned on an elbow to ease her back.

"What about Essie? She ain't done her chores."

"I'll take it out. It's plenty warm enough to use the outhouse from here on anyhow. I'd check for black widders before I used it, though."

Ma looked at him over her shoulder. "I heard that Bill Stillson sported a brand-new army coat down at the pool hall. Said he found it throwed off one of them troop trains. Right there in the bar ditch like providence itself."

"Bill Stillson's had considerable luck in his life. You remember when he found all that copper wire down at the county shed, don't you?"

"Well, it's a feeling, Runt. A man ought keep his eyes peeled when it comes to the government."

"Don't you worry," he said, winking at her. "I'll be careful."


On his way to the still, he stopped in a thicket of sumac near the creek, as was his habit, to listen, to gauge the quiet, to make certain that no one followed. His pa had taught him that. "A man gets caught on his way *to* the still, not after he's there," he always said.

As he started to leave, he spotted a slash of red in the weeds. Kneeling, he parted the grass. The rooster's bloody comb lay on the ground, the pile of feathers, the smudge of grease in the dirt.

Cutting across the field, he worked his way up Dead Man Creek. At the bend, he lit a cigarette and thought about the rooster, how he'd watched him over the weeks, how each morning he'd grown braver, ranging a little farther from the house even though he knew the coyotes were out there. If a hundred feet was safe, then why not a hundred and one, or a hundred and two? Why not an inch, he supposed, if no more? It was, after all, but an inch. "Ole fool," he said to himself, ducking into the draw.

The bramble provided shade and cool, and the treetops whispered high above in the wind. Runt kicked the leaves aside with his foot as he walked, looking for his granddaddy's shine. It wasn't the money that interested him, though it would bring a right fair price, of that he had no doubt. It wasn't the money, but something more, something of those who'd gone before, something of them reaching out to him from the earth.

At the mouth of the gypsum cave he made certain there were no tracks in the damp soil and that the fishing string he'd stretched across the opening remained intact. In the cool of the cave he checked the sugar and meal for rat tracks. He had enough sugar for a half batch, no more, but now with cash in his pocket, he could buy supplies, if he could find them. What with the war, supplies were getting more difficult to find.

Wiping the dust from the jars, he held them to the light before packing them in a tow sack. On the way out of the cave, he stretched the string back over the entrance and checked the position of the sun, time enough to swing by the Simmons's place before catching the northbound to the elevator siding.


Leaning against the wall of the cattle car, he watched the landscape rush by. It had taken a quart more than he'd planned to pry his hens loose from Simmons. But they were young layers and safe from the ax, unless they had a bad week, of course, in which case nothing would save them from Ma's wrath. In any event, Simmons had agreed to carrying them over himself, saving Runt a trip back to the house. 'Course, knowing Simmons the way he did, he'd find an excuse to get a start on his shine.

After the train topped the hill, gathering speed on the run into Alva, Runt hung his legs out the door and watched the ties flicker between his feet. Cattle cars were not his choice for riding, what with their open slats. A man could freeze solid in the wind. 'Course, on a day such as this, it mattered not at all.

The smell of smoke and heat rode down the length of the train as they took a curve, and on the horizon, a Favor Oil truck labored up the hill, its dust plume drifting into the blue of the sky.

As they passed Camp Alva, Runt could see the reefer cars lined up on the spur, disgorging their cargoes of fresh fruits and vegetables. A soccer game was in full swing in the compound, the American flag flapping in the breeze. His week at the camp had been much easier than he'd figured.

Corporal Schubert had showed him around, answered his questions whenever he asked. Schubert, being a quiet sort, kept to himself most of the time, always caught up in his own thoughts. But who wouldn't be, he supposed, locked up in a foreign country.

Beyond that, they left him to his own devices. No more was expected of him than to make certain the raisins were not pilfered for the making of wine. No one talked to him, even those who could, and so he spent the days alone. As a kid whose legs were nearly as short as his arms, he'd learned to handle being alone.

In the distance he could see Favor Mansion, its chimneys and turrets against the sky, and the grain elevators like the smokestacks of a colossal ship.

Gathering up his tow sack, he prepared to jump. Another stumble like last time, and he'd go home empty-handed. As the train slowed for the curve, he bailed, hitting the ground at a trot, swinging into the cottonwoods that grew rank on the banks of a slough near the bridge. The stink of gas drifted in from the slough, and raw sewage ran from a pipe. Next to the pipe someone had dug a grave and made a marker of wood, B. G. HASS, SOLDAT, 1945, carved in its face. Runt supposed it to be the new cemetery for Camp Alva.

Hook, dressed in Levi's and T-shirt, opened the door of the caboose. There was a sunburn ring where the prosthesis ended on his stump.

"Hello, Runt," he said, slipping on a shirt. "I'm just cleaning up."

"Brought you some goods," Runt said, setting the tow sack inside the door. "Frenchy said you might be running short."

"Make yourself at home while I finish up here."

Looking for a place to sit among the books, Runt slid down the wall, lighting a cigarette as he waited.

"Here's a button on the floor, Hook," he said, tossing it onto the bed.

"Thanks," Hook said, slipping on the prosthesis. "I been out to the Hopkins auction this morning up by the county well."

"I went to school with the Hopkins girl," Runt said. "She used to wear a bandaner around her neck with Vicks smeared in it to stave off the croup." Squashing out his cigarette on the heel of his boot, he dropped the butt into the cuff of his pants. "No mistakin' Charlotte Hopkins downwind."

Runt rummaged through the books. "You got more books than the county library," he said, flipping through the pages. "What you do with them all?"

Sitting down on the bed, Hook tied his shoes while Runt watched on in fascination.

"Well, I read them for one thing. Lots of folks read books, and I collect them, too."

"Jake Barnsdall collects Prince Albert cans," he said.

"That a fact?"

"And string, too. He's got a string ball the size of a watermelon. You got to wonder why a man wants a ball of string."

"I bought a 1920 first edition of Evans's *Sleeping Beauty* at the auction, twenty-five cents. It's right there, illustrated, too. I found it in a box of old Monkey Ward catalogs. It's like detective work, like finding a jewel in the middle of the desert. You just never know."

Picking up the book, Runt thumbed through the pages.

"Hell, it ain't even a growed-up book. You should've kept the catalogs, least they come in handy in the outhouse."

Shaking his head, Hook retrieved a jar of shine out of the tow sack, holding it up to the light.

"What I owe you?"

"No charge to the railroad."

Taking money from his billfold, Hook handed it to him. "This isn't Sheriff Donley's charity. All the same to you, I'll pay out."

"Have it your way," he said, standing up. "I best be on my way. You need more, just send word with Frenchy."

"Have a drink with me, Runt."

"I can't sell it and drink it both."

Taking down a couple of glasses from the shelf, Hook blew the dust out of them. "You afraid to drink your own busthead?"

"What you think happened to these legs?" he asked, looking down at his feet. "Shine blew 'em off right at the knees."

"Same thing happened to this arm," Hook said, "but some things are worth a body part or two."

"Well, maybe I will. One for the road. Now that I've got a paying job, I reckon I can take a time-out."

"Sit over here at the table," Hook said, unscrewing the lid on the jar, taking a whiff, waiting for his eyes to clear.

The table was a board hinged to the wall, cluttered with old *Posts*, an ashtray reeking with butts, a box of cornstarch—smooth as silk and cheap—that he used on his prosthesis to keep it from irritating his stump. There was a Bugler cigarette-rolling machine that he could never get to work, a sack of Bugler tobacco and papers still sitting on top of the machine. A copy of Hemingway's *For Whom the Bell Tolls* propped up the window.

Scooting up to the table, Runt waited while Hook poured them each a shot.

"Here's to missing body parts," Hook said, "which isn't so bad, given we still have the most important one."

"If not the least used," Runt said, taking a sip, letting the liquid roll across his tongue. "Could use a tad more juniper, don't you think?"

"Elixir of the gods," Hook said, pouring himself another.

"It ain't right I drink up all your liquor, Hook."

"Look, it's been a hell of a week. I been jumping off moving trains and chasing Germans on John Deere tractors. If it's all the same to you, I'd as soon not drink alone. Besides, there's rats out here big as kangaroos. If I should happen to get down, which occurs with some regularity when I drink Runt Wallace popskull, they might carry me off, feed me to their young."

A warm breeze, with its smell of wheat and dust from the elevator, swept through the screen door of the caboose. Cottonwood fluff from the slough gathered in the screen like flakes of snow, and a crow tramped across the roof looking for grasshoppers impaled on the vents. When the wind came down the tracks and into the elevators, it lifted and moaned like the sobbing of a woman.

"Don't let it be said I left a friend to fend for his life," Runt said, his nose already fuzzy with moonshine.

"I hear you're working out at Camp Alva," Hook said.

"I'm the new assistant baker."

"The hell you say?"

"Mostly I watch the bakery inventory and whistle Dixie. It's the easiest job I ever had."

Having topped off their drinks, Hook lit a cigarette and picked up the book.

"You read Hemingway?"

"I been meaning to," Runt said.

"You got to wonder why God fancies sons of bitches, don't you? Right there is no man's friend, a fellow you couldn't trust with your sister, hell, with your mule, a man so talented it makes you want to cry. He dashes from war to war with his head stuck in the air like a flushed quail, and without so much as a scratch, making a million dollars in the process. Then someone like Spark Dugan comes along, a guy with nothing in the world but an old shack under the trestle and a bucket full of coal, and he winds up under the wheels of a reefer car. Where's the justice in that?"

Taking the book, Runt turned it over, examining it as one might a stick of dynamite or a snake. For a little man, Runt's shoulders were powerful, his hands veined, his fingers thick as sucker rods. Setting it down, he held out his glass for Hook to refill, drinking it, placing the glass on top of the book.

"My rooster's been working his way over to the creek for two weeks now, a little farther each day, strutting around, crowing, flapping his wings like the king of the world. Well, this morning I found him, no more than a grease spot and a pile of feathers, and now some other rooster's taken his place. I figure it's that way for all of us sooner or later, something waiting down on the creek."

Taking another drink, Hook steadied himself against the table. The crow had flown down to the step of the caboose and pecked at cotton fluff on the screen. Turning its head sideways, it watched Hook, its eyes the color of ink.

"Most folks figure Spark Dugan crawled under that reefer and went to sleep. They figure there's no reason to look any further," Hook said. "Most folks didn't know Spark Dugan. I've seen him drunk, and I've seen him sober, mostly drunk, and I never knew him to sleep under no railroad car, especially no reefer waiting to be iced."

An image of Spark Dugan's crumpled body flashed through Hook's mind.

"Maybe he did. Who can be sure? The thing is, he lay on his back like he was facing the train when it came at him. There was damn little blood, too." Taking a sip of his drink, Hook watched the crow. "I know this sounds crazy, but he had no fear on his face. No fear at all."

"Spark Dugan be a happy feller," Runt said. "He had his shack, his coal stove, and a weekly supply of Runt Wallace shine. I'd say that's about as near to heaven as a man can get."

"You can't be happy with a reefer car cutting your arm off and scraping out your backside down the track. How can you be sleeping through that? Besides, there wasn't enough left of him to see if he'd been stabbed or shot or hung by the neck, and there was a hell of a bunch of people out there that night, too, that deck foreman, Ross Ague, for one. And a whole crew of German POWs working on the ice deck. Nobody saw or heard a thing. To top it off, Spark's coal bucket had scattered down the other track."

"What reason would there be for someone killing poor ole Spark Dugan?" Runt asked.

Hook rolled up the loose sleeve on his shirt. "You see this eye?"

"Kind of hard to miss, though I hadn't planned on bringing it up."

"I took a trip out to Spark Dugan's shack, taking a look around, and found a rucksack full of military clothes. Maybe Spark had been doing a little black-marketing, or maybe he traded for the clothes for himself. Anyway, before I left, a couple of boys worked me over. They fed me a little dirt. Thing is, they didn't take my money, or even my P.38. They took only the rucksack and the clothes."

"You think they killed Spark Dugan over a rucksack full of clothes?"

"I made a trip out to Camp Alva and had a talk with Major Foreman. Seems he doesn't know anything about black-marketing. And then I had the pleasure of meeting Colonel Hoffmann while there. Seems he doesn't know anything about black-marketing, either."

Putting a paper in the rubber sheet on the Bugler rolling machine, Runt sprinkled in some tobacco and then ran the roller over the top.

"Look at that," he said, sticking the cigarette in the corner of his mouth. "Yeah, I've seen Hoffmann. He's the ranking German officer for the whole camp. Those prisoners dribble their pants when he comes into the mess."

"A cold-eyed son of a bitch," Hook said.

"Hell," Runt said, sucking on the cigarette, "you got the tension set too tight on this machine. You ain't tamping corner posts, you know."

Checking the contents of the mason jar, Hook freshened their drinks.

"I've seen eyes like Hoffmann's before, men who would gut you out for coffee change," he said.

Taking out his pocketknife, Runt adjusted a screw on the machine and rolled another cigarette.

"There," he said, lighting it, "just like store-bought."

Hook tried to focus on Runt's cigarette, but it drifted off.

"Why'd those boys jump me? Who sent them?"

"I ain't much on figuring. If I was, I'd be figuring how to get Hugh Favor to adopt me," Runt said.

"If Spark Dugan had taken up black-marketing, someone would have to be getting the supplies to him. There wasn't anyone there that night, except the graveyard shift, and the prisoner work crew. All of them were up on the ice deck."

"Are you sure?"

Hook propped his chin in his hand as he thought. "There was Joe, the operator down at the depot, and that Favor Oil truck, I guess."

"Oil truck?"

"Yeah, picking up a load of drill bits. Joe said they were regulars, that they'd signed in and signed out just like always."

"I best be getting home, Hook. I'll miss the southbound if I don't get on the road."

Hook poured Runt another drink. "The southbound's always late. Just as well have one more."

Afterward, they shot rats, or, more accurately, shot *at* rats in the elevator shafts with Hook's P.38. A ricochet spun a piece of concrete into Hook's lip, and it bled onto the front of his shirt, so they decided to sample the second quart of shine to take away the pain and the possibility of infection.

After that, they smoked some more Buglers, and Runt sang his rendition of "Amazing Grace," which, according to Hook, was not nearly so good as the Holy Roller preacher and stood no chance of getting anybody out of the bowels of hell, especially someone as intractable as Spark Dugan.

By the time they'd worked halfway to the bottom of the second quart, Hook decided to take Runt out for chicken-fried steak at the Corner Cafe. In as much as they got lost down on Main, it became a long walk, and then they had to stop at the courthouse to pee.

At the Corner Cafe, they sat in the front booth, where they could watch the comings and goings on the town square. No sooner had their steaks been served than Hook noticed two men sitting at the back booth. Even under the fog of Runt Wallace shine, he could make out the white beard of the tall one, the ball cap on the table, and the walking stick propped against the wall in the hallway leading to the bathroom.

Pushing his plate aside, he said, "Runt, I believe those two boys back there are the same who visited me at Spark Dugan's shack."

Runt stopped midair with his fork. "Aw, I'm starved clean to death. Maybe it could wait until after I eat this chicken fry?"

Hook slid out of the booth and made his way to the back. Runt lay down his fork, shaking his head as he climbed out behind him.

The waitress watched from the cash register, her pencil stuck behind her ear.

"I know you boys from somewhere?" Hook asked, leaning onto their table.

The bearded one looked up. Gravy clung to his beard, and his nose had swollen to the size of a fall turnip. Runt stepped up beside Hook, his arms dangling at his sides like a spider. The odor of fried onions and urine hung in the hallway, and dishes clattered from back in the kitchen.

"Can't say as you do," the short one said, putting on his ball cap. "Maybe you ought go back to your booth before someone takes off your other arm."

"Maybe you ought answer the question," Hook said, heat rising in his neck.

"We came for the freak show," the bearded one said, "the one-arm freak show."

"A one-arm yard dog and a no-leg midget show," the short one said, grinning.

When the bearded one started to rise, Hook sighed and slammed his elbow into his upturned face. The man fell forward onto the table with a thud, his water spilling into his plate, his silverware clattering onto the floor. A tooth dangled on a string from his mouth, and a blood bubble grew from the slot between his teeth.

Hook prepared to give the short one a taste of the same, but Runt had already seized his wrists, pinning his palms against the table. The short one glanced up at Hook, and then at Runt. "Let go," he said, his fingers turning red, but Runt didn't respond, the force of his grip closing in like a hydraulic jack.

"What were you doing out to Spark Dugan's shack?" Hook asked. "Why did you jump me?"

The veins in the short one's eyes bulged, and his breath turned shallow and rapid. "Go to hell," he said.

The bearded one moaned from his nap on the table, his nose and mouth an indistinguishable mass.

Hook looked over at Runt, who upped the pressure. Perspiration broke on his prey's forehead, and his lip quivered, water gathering in his eyes. Suddenly, he jerked back hard to free himself from the death hold, but it was useless. No one broke Runt Wallace's trap once snared.

"Let me loose, or I'll kill you!" the man said, blubbering.

Runt concentrated, not looking at Hook, or at the man struggling in his trap, or at the bearded one who blew froth from the gap in his teeth.

First, the short one's hands turned purple, the color of a bruise, then black and shiny. He dropped his chin on the table, his nostrils flaring, his eyes rolling white.

"We was sent," he said, finally, moaning.

"Who sent you?"

"I don't know."

The bones and ligaments in his wrists crackled, and he drooled, nodding his head that he was ready to talk.

"Who sent you," Hook asked again, "and why?"

"It was always dark," he said, groaning, "under the ice deck at night. This guy would bring the supplies just before shift change. We'd sell them and meet the same time the following week."

"We?"

"Me and Toad there, and Spark Dugan."

"So Spark Dugan got in your way, going to turn you in? Or maybe he got greedy, so you had to kill him?"

"No. No. We didn't kill anyone. When Spark Dugan got hisself run over, they said to clean out his shack before anyone came poking around, that if we didn't, we might all go to jail for black-marketing. We hadn't figured on you getting there so soon."

"And who sent you?" Hook asked again.

Runt bore down, and blood pooled under his prey's fingernails.

"We never saw, I tell you. It was dark under that deck, and he always kept his head covered."

"I don't believe you."

"I swear to God. Make him let me go. He's crushing my arms."

"And what about the truck?"

"I don't know anything about any truck, and the guy never used names. We just sold a few clothes, tools, sometimes food, and there were no lack of takers."

"The guard?"

"No. It was a Kraut, I think. His English was good, and sometimes he would put the money in his pocket and climb up the steps of the ice deck on his hands like a goddamn acrobat."

"Who are you kidding?"

"I swear, like he didn't give a damn who saw him. Make him let me go, now. Please."

Hook looked back into the cafe. The place had emptied of customers, and the waitress stood at the cash register, her hand covering her mouth.

"Let him go," Hook said.

When Runt released him, he stood, his eyes burning with rage, and he shoved Runt away. "I'll kill the both of you," he said, his voice quivering.

Picking up the walking stick, Hook chucked it like a Geronimo spear right between his eyes, and the man spilled into the cigar butts, dirty napkins, and chewing-gum wrappers on the floor. Blood dripped from off his nose, and his brow dangled from over his eye like a brown caterpillar.

"Must be all talked out," Runt said. "You going to call the sheriff?"

"Black-marketing's not my worry, Runt, and I can't see any reason why these boys would kill Spark Dugan. Besides, I filled out enough reports for Sheriff Donley this week."

"What do we do now?"

"Come soon, I'm going to have a visit with a Favor Oil truck driver. In the meantime, we're going to finish our steaks, and then we're going back to the caboose. I've committed lots of sins in my life, but abandoning a jug of Runt Wallace shine hasn't been one of them."

Hook waved his hat and waited as Frenchy brought the switch engine to a stop.

"What the hell you doing?" he asked, leaning out of the cab, "looking for the Dalton gang?"

"I'm putting Runt Wallace in that grain car back there."

"What you do, read him to death with them goddang books?"

"Set him off at Four Corners, Frenchy."

"It's against the law. This ain't no goddang passenger train, you know."

"Prop him up so he can be spotted. And be careful," he said, waving his hat as he made off down the tracks. "Anything happens to that boy, it's a mighty cold world for the both of us."

# 14

MAJOR FOREMAN, THIS is Dr. Reina Kaplan," Amanda said, "from the Special Projects Division."

The major stood behind his desk, his gray eyes leveled at Reina, his expression as indifferent as army issue.

"Doctor," he said. "It is *Doctor*?"

"That's right," Reina said, glancing over at Amanda. "Ph.D., literature."

"Thank you, Amanda. That will be all for now," he said.

Nodding, Amanda closed the door behind her, with some reluctance, Reina thought.

"Well, Dr. Kaplan, did you make arrangements for a place to stay? We do have quarters in the temporary barracks."

"Still pending," she said. "I'll know by tonight."

Clicking his pencil against his teeth, he looked her over—the suit, the glasses, the hair, thick as fleece, gathered in a bun on the back of her head.

"And, so, you're here to educate our clientele, are you?"

"Yes," she said. "The reeducation program is to go public. When all these prisoners go home, and they will, America is going to want some assurance that they've been exposed to, let's say, a different way of life."

Major Foreman took out his handkerchief, his top lip quivering with a sneeze.

"Doctor," he said, dabbing at the end of his nose, folding the handkerchief, slipping it back in his pocket, "you realize that we are not talking about graduate students here? This is a prisoner-of-war camp; moreover, it's maximum security and contains the most hardened Nazis. We've only recently had an escape attempt."

"But many of them are educated," she said. Reina's head whirled a little, and she leaned against the chair.

"Would you mind if I sit down? It's been a long week."

"Of course," he said. "Something to drink?"

"No, thank you," she said, rubbing her head. "Has anyone ever combusted from eating chicken-fried steak?"

"Only if consumed with the local thump whiskey."

"Well, no, I passed on that at least," she said, taking a deep breath. "Look, you must know that I'm no threat to the way things have been done in the past, or to you. This reeducation program is quite innocuous when you think about it, a few courses in English, a library, perhaps a newsletter."

"I hope it's more readable than *Der Ruf*," he said. "There's not a half-dozen prisoners in the whole of the camp who can understand it."

"But your clients," she said, "as you refer to them, are in need of the most reform and have the greatest potential for influencing their own government when they return."

"And are the most resistant. I assure you."

From outside, the cadence rose as the prisoners drilled up and down the street. The smell of effluent wafted in from somewhere, and her stomach lurched.

"This is a program they'll have to earn. Participants will be required to pay scrip to take course work and to buy materials. Books will be selected with care, of course, and for maximum effect, but it is education, not propaganda, at least not in the normal sense. Some of these men may be monsters, but they're bright. The brighter the individual, the more curiosity there is, the more curiosity, the more interest in theoretical debate. It's the most competent who can entertain alternatives, don't you see? Only the feeble-minded are unequivocal."

Taking out his handkerchief again, he covered his nose, his eyes shut as if to sneeze. When he didn't, he said, "I don't like it. It won't work."

"Yes," she said. "I thought as much."

Reaching into the green cabinet, he asked, "Do you know what's in this file?"

"I don't believe I do."

"These are the rules of the Geneva Convention. And this file here, Red Cross, this one, the Swiss Legation. There's not a day goes by I don't have to placate these people, and believe me, that's not an easy job." When she started to say something, he held up his hand. "Let me finish here. I also have the army to please. To top it off, the local drunk gets himself run over by a reefer car, and the railroad yard dog accuses me of being in the black-marketing business.

"Then, of course, we have the guards, who probably *are* in the black-marketing business, a menagerie of battle-fatigued veterans, rejects, mental defects, and alcoholics."

"Look, Major—."

"I'm not finished. There are the locals, too, you see, convinced that Hitler's hiding out there in the hills just waiting to take over the town. They're angry because of the food rations, and the unions are angry because of the cheap labor. There's the prisoners, angry because they aren't able to butcher what little's left of the free world, and then there's me, angry because I can't see the end of any of it in my lifetime.

"Oh, and then you show up with your theories and intellectual games, the good doctor who's persuaded that I don't have a clue as to how to run a prisoner-of-war camp." Sneezing into his hand, he shook his head. "To top it off, the goddamn wind never stops blowing."

"I understand your position," she said, holding her stomach, "and how you might perceive my presence here as a threat to your authority, but now you need to understand my position. I am here to do a job, to expose these prisoners to as many alternatives as I can before they are sent back to Germany. I'd prefer to do it with your assistance, but I intend to do it either way. If you have objections, please file them with the Provost Marshal General. He's the one who ordered me out here."

Major Foreman took off his glasses and dabbed at the sweat that had gathered under his eyes.

"Very well," he said. "I'll expect you to do nothing to jeopardize security or to interfere with the military operation of this camp."

"Fair enough. Now, where will my office be? And I'll need a facility for the library."

After putting the files back in the cabinet, he drummed his fingers on the top, his back to her.

"There's the old toolshed," he said, not turning around, "over by the mess. That should serve well for both. It will take some renovation, but then that's your business, isn't it?"

After clearing security, Reina met Amanda for lunch at the front door of the headquarters. The guard watched her from his tower, his tommy gun jutting from the window. Dust drifted across the compound, and tumbleweeds pressed against the security fence. Row upon row of tar-papered barracks lined the streets, waiting and empty, their windows blinking in the sun.

No life existed, except the beat from the parade field and the shadow of a cloud that swept down the street.

The silence, the void, and the distances emptied her, snuffed away her breath, pried at her fingers as she hung from the precipice.

Amanda slipped her purse over her shoulder as she came out the door and covered her eyes against the glare of the sun. How did she keep such white skin in this place? Reina wondered.

"Hi," Amanda said. "You look a little green. Are you up to lunch?"

"As long as it isn't chicken-fried steak," Reina said.

"They eat better in here than we do out there," she said. "If we hurry, we can eat before the prisoners get there."

A small man at the back of the mess watched them as they entered. The cooks, with their impossible English, pointed at the trays of food and smiled back at the women as they made their way down the line. In the end, Reina took a baked potato and a glass of milk, foregoing the streusel to ward off any protest from her stomach.

Amanda introduced her to the others at the front table, country girls who nodded, eyeing her with curiosity.

"Who's the little guy with the red hair?" Reina asked, taking her plate off the tray.

"A local," Amanda said. "Runt Wallace is his name. He's working bakery, I think."

"The food looks wonderful."

"It's the best part about this job," Amanda said. "By the way, what did you say to Major Foreman? He's been in a foul mood ever since you left."

"His foul mood is a permanent feature, I would guess," Reina said. "Apparently, he views me as some kind of threat to his manhood."

"What manhood?" Amanda said, smiling. "Did he assign you an office?"

"The toolshed."

"The toolshed? You mean the old one?"

"So it seems."

"Oh, my. I don't think it's much of a place. It was here before they built the camp. They were going to tear it down, I thought."

Pushing back her plate, Reina let her stomach settle for a moment.

"It will do for a start. There's plenty of labor available to fix it up. If he puts up too much of a fuss, I'll have the Office of the Provost Marshal General give him a call. I'm sure the major would like to make colonel before retirement."

Still holding her fork at her mouth, Amanda looked over at Reina.

"You could do that?"

"Sure I could, and he's in for a surprise if he thinks that I won't." Searching through her purse, she said, "Is smoking permitted in here?"

"Ah, no," Amanda said, finishing her bite, looking around to make certain no one had overheard. "Nobody ever crosses Major Foreman. He has the final say about everything around here."

"Well, darlin', things are a fixin' to change. By the by, do you know that boy over there is watching you?"

Glancing over her shoulder, Amanda shrugged, her face blushing.

"No he isn't."

"Well, maybe you're right. Listen, I'm going outside for a smoke and then over to take a look at my new office."

"Walk where the towers can see you," Amanda said, pausing. "It helps, if you know what I mean."

"Thanks," she said. "I do know what you mean."


On the steps of the mess, Reina lit a cigarette and held her face to the sun. The long train trip, the decision she'd made about Robert, even the encounter with Major Foreman had taken their toll, and she wished for some time to sort things out. Still, better to be busy, she supposed, than to sit around feeling sorry for herself.

When she saw the prisoners forming rank at the end of the street, she snuffed out her cigarette, fieldstripping it as she had seen the soldiers do, and made her way down the steps of the mess.

A German colonel approached, touching his braided hat, his glasses thick, his eyes the color of cobalt, like bottomless pools of ice, and her blood thickened under his gaze. He smelled of leather and tobacco when he passed, and his eyes burned on her back as she walked away.

The shed stood at the end of the street, and a good deal farther from the other buildings than she'd been led to believe. It was but one room. The building had been covered in tar paper and lath like the other buildings, but it leaned precariously on its foundation. The door was unlocked, and she eased it open, waiting for her eyes to adjust to the darkness.

A workbench bearing the scars of hammers and saws occupied one end of the room. Too heavy to move easily, the bench had been left nailed to the studs of the open wall. A box-leg vise had been bolted to its top, a spiderweb shimmering from its handle. When she pushed the door open wide, a spider scrambled up a thread and disappeared into the wall. The smell of grease lifted in the heat of the room, and a ray of sunshine shot through a hole in the roof.

"Thanks, you bastard," she said to herself, bumping the window up with the heel of her hand.

A breeze rushed in, fresh and cool in the stale room, and she could smell a distant rain. Turning about, she took stock. There were bookshelves to be built, and the room needed curtains for the two windows, a desk, a chair, a filing cabinet to index the books. There might be just enough room for a reading table against the north wall. A single light hung from the center of the room, its empty socket occupied by a mud dauber, and an electrical plug had been installed under the switch at the door.

She stepped back outside, pulled the door closed behind her, and sat down on the front steps. From here, she could see the railroad spur, the grain elevators in town, the trees that shrouded Favor Mansion. Taking out her notepad, she made a list of items. At some point she'd have to order books and magazines through the mail and arrange for an English instructor, but all that would come in time.

Amanda waited at the gate, her coat slung over her arm.

"Hi," she said, waving her hand. "Guess what? Major Foreman received a call this afternoon from a Major Dunfield, Special Projects Division. Now Foreman has given us the staff car for the duration, and he's scheduled a work crew to renovate the shed. On top of that, my father called, and Mr. Favor has agreed to let you stay in the carriage house, no charge."

"Major Dunfield believes in fattening up his Christians before feeding them to the lions," Reina said.

"I'm sorry?"

"Oh, nothing," she said. "It's just New York cynicism. I'm pleased that you and I will have the chance to become friends."

As they pulled onto the road, a cloud gathered on the horizon, dark and promising with rain. Lightning ripped from its belly, and thunder rumbled across the prairie. But even as it darkened, it moved into the distance, the sunset marshaling colors into the sky.

Reina watched Camp Alva disappear in her side mirror. Leaning her head back, she took a deep breath. For now, maybe she wasn't doing so badly. She had a place to work, a place to live, and she'd held her ground in a fashion with the indomitable Major Foreman.

# 15

Hook PULLED HIMSELF from the bunk, his mouth tasting of the gutter. With head thumping, he brushed his teeth and donned clean clothes. "You dumb bastard," he said to himself, checking the cut over his eye in the mirror.

It took him awhile to locate his camera, and then as he was about to leave he discovered that there were no bullets in his P.38. Touching the cut in his lip, he shook his head. With luck, he and Runt hadn't killed anyone during their hunt for elevator rats.

When he stepped out on the porch, the sun cut like glass shards, and the smell of the slough settled like mud in his lungs. He could hear the northbound pulling Four Corners. It would be Frenchy with the work train. Not anxious to visit, he headed toward town, the wind warm at his back, the zing of locusts rising and falling from the reaches of the cottonwood grove.

It wasn't so far to the Corner Cafe, given sobriety and the advantages of a direct route. Breakfast was still being served when he pulled himself onto the bar stool. The waitress slid him a menu and cocked her hands on her hips.

"You want me to call an ambulance, hon?" she asked, smiling.

"How about a cup of coffee?"

"Coffee it is, and we've got biscuits and gravy for breakfast?"

Looking over the menu, he pushed it back to her. "Coffee," he said, again.

"Say," she said, filling his cup, "ain't you the one in here with that little sawed-off guy last night?"

Sipping his coffee, he looked up at her through the steam.

"I don't think so," he said. "Must of been some other dumb bastard."

"No," she said, flipping her hand at him. "It was you. I remember the . . . oh, well, you know."

"Don't worry about it," he said, reaching for her apron string with the prosthesis. "Most folks don't forget something like this. I sure as hell don't."

"Boy," she said, "did you see the way that little guy held that feller to the table like his hands were nailed down?"

"It had sort of slipped my mind," he said, lighting a cigarette.

Scratching out a ticket, she laid it on the counter.

"Well, they had it coming, that's for sure. There's trouble every time those boys come through the door."

"I'm sorry about the disturbance," Hook said. "I guess we had a little too much to drink."

"Listen, hon," she said, winking, "you had more than a little too much, but you and that shorty kid can come in here anytime you've a notion, drunk or sober, far as I'm concerned."

Draining his coffee, he squashed out his cigarette and then counted out the coins.

"There *is* something you could do for me."

"What's that, hon?" she asked, lifting her brows.

"How do you get to the Favor Oil sheds from here?"

"Just east of town," she said. "Straight down that road. You can't miss them. They're the biggest buildings around, 'cept maybe the elevators."

"How far you figure it is?"

"I don't know, hon," she said, shrugging. "A mile maybe."

"Thanks," he said. "I'll take you up on that breakfast some other time."

The sheds were open bays, each capable of housing a Favor truck. A fence encircled the compound, and a man sat in the gate shack checking off numbers as the trucks came and went.

"This is Favor Oil property," he said, looking up from his clipboard. "No one's allowed beyond this point."

"I'd like to talk to one of your drivers," Hook said.

"You'll have to wait 'til he's off duty, mister," he said. "Only employees are allowed beyond this point."

Taking out his badge, Hook stuck it though the window.

"I'm the railroad agent," he said. "One of your trucks might have been in the Waynoka yards the night Spark Dugan bought it. I want to talk to your driver, that's all, to find out if he saw anything unusual."

Swinging around in his chair, the man said, "That badge don't mean nothing off railroad property."

"Maybe not," Hook said, tucking the badge back into his pocket, "but I can go get the county sheriff and a search warrant if you'd prefer. Of course we'd have to shut this place down for a week going through all the records, searching every truck, checking your gate files."

"Look, mister, I don't want no trouble. Every time something happens in these shops, Mr. Favor takes it right out of my ass."

"No trouble," he said. "Now, why don't you give me the name of the driver who made the Waynoka run?"

Reaching into a box, he pulled out a file, mumbling to himself as he ran his finger down the side of the page.

"Roy Bench, over in shed twelve. Roy's got a real short fuse, mister."

"Thanks," Hook said over his shoulder. "I'll try not to light it."

Roy Bench had his head under the hood of the truck, a crescent wrench dangling from his hip pocket. When Hook cleared his throat, Bench peeked out from under his arm.

"The office is over in shed one," he said, turning back to the engine.

"You Roy Bench?"

Taking another look under his arm, Bench turned, pushing back his hat. His hands were black, and he had a smear of grease across his forehead. A button had worked open on his shirt, and his cigarettes were squashed from leaning over the fender of the truck.

"Who wants to know?"

"My name's Hook Runyon, Special Agent for the railroad," he said. "Spark Dugan met up with a reefer car in the Waynoka yards the other night. He didn't come out of it so well."

Bench shook a bent cigarette out of the pack, cupping it with greasy hands as he lit it.

"Come a standoff between man and a reefer, the reefer wins every time. Ain't much give to a reefer, is there? What's it to do with me?"

"Your truck had signed in at the yards that night. Thought you might have seen or heard something."

A Favor Oil truck rolled by the door, the smell of dust and diesel drifting into the bay. Leaning against his truck, Bench took out the crescent, rolling the jaws open and then closed again. Smoke crawled up his face, and he squinted up an eye.

"I just pick up loads," he said, "and keep my nose out of other people's business. I didn't see nothing or hear nothing."

"Maybe you could tell me what you were picking up that night?"

"Look, mister, I just drive a truck. You want to know Favor Oil business, you'll have to talk to Mister Favor. Now, I got work to do," he said, turning back to his engine.

"Thanks for your help," Hook said, checking the truck number as he made his way out the door.


The sun bore down on Hook as he walked down the tracks toward the caboose. At this rate, he needed to get a car or a different job. In a way, he welcomed the walk, the dust, even the throb in his head. Maybe it was due penance for the bouts with Runt's shine. Once, no more than adventures, the bouts had turned sinister somewhere along the line, nagging and demanding. But they filled him, at least for the moment, against the emptiness that had grown within him. Still, he didn't trust the feeling altogether. In the past he'd made his own calls, but now he wasn't so sure.

Sitting down on the tracks, he lit a cigarette. Creosote oozed from the ties, and the rails shimmered. To his left a driveway twisted into a stand of trees, and above them stood the limestone chimneys of Favor Mansion.

This Spark Dugan thing had begun to eat on him. Why hadn't anyone heard or seen anything that night? Why wasn't he allowed to talk with the prisoner labor crew? Why hadn't Ross Ague, the night foreman, checked things out before moving the cars? Why had they ignored standard procedure? Why did Spark Dugan wind up on his back, and why hadn't he screamed out? And what was so damn secret about Favor Oil freight, anyway?

He understood that no one cared about Spark Dugan or a few stolen clothes, not the railroad, not Sheriff Donley, not the army itself. Maybe he was getting soft in the head from too much shine, just like Spark Dugan. Maybe someday they'd find Hook Runyon in a bloody ball under a reefer car, too, but if they did, he hoped that someone would at least ask why. Maybe, in the final analysis, he just didn't like the way things smelled.

Slipping the camera from around his neck, he focused in on the tracks and clicked off a picture. Rising, he dusted off his britches and rolled up the next frame. What the hell, he'd just have to find out what old man Favor had to say.

Standing at the front door of the big house, Hook checked himself in the reflection of the glass.

From his vantage, he could see the gardens below, the limestone walls, the wrought-iron gates, floral repeats of pineapples and clumps of grapes, all assembled with hand-forged collars and rivets.

Marble statues stood their posts with uplifted arms, or with children in tow, or with flutes at play. Banks of tulips and crocuses cropped from their beds of black soil, and sprinklers clicked like giant insects, mist gathering and drifting like fog over the gardens. Robins scratched from under the arbors, stretching worms from the water-laden soil, and the scent of lilacs hung like perfume in the dampness of the oasis.

For a moment, Hook hesitated before knocking, small and insignificant in the opulence about him. When the door opened, he resisted the urge to turn and leave.

"Yes?" the butler asked, peering through the crack in the door.

"Is Mr. Favor in, please?"

Opening the door wider, he examined Hook. "May I ask who's calling?"

"My name is Hook Runyon. I'm Special Agent with the railroad," he said.

"Is this an official visit?"

"It won't take but a moment."

"Please wait," the butler said, closing the door.

Hook fumbled at the pack of cigarettes and studied the carvings on the mahogany door. From above the limestone archway, a gargoyle watched him, its nostrils flared, its eyes evil, its forked tail looped over a shoulder.

When the door opened, the butler said, "Mr. Favor will see you. Please wait in the foyer."

The foyer smelled of wood and wax, and light from the stained-glass windows scattered on the floor. When his eyes adjusted, he could see the terrazzo tile, the intricately designed dome of the foyer, the Italian-marble fireplace, big enough for a man to stand in.

Paintings in gilded frames were scattered about the room. Next to the double doors leading into the inner sanctum hung a large oil painting of a little girl, her face and arms lifted to clouds that swirled black and tumultuous above her.

When the doors swung open, a smallish man stepped through them, dressed in suit and tie. He wore rimless glasses that magnified the intensity of his eyes. Dark brows slanted inward like the gargoyle above the doorway. Void of disposition, his mouth maintained but a slit, all expression having been concentrated in the severity of his eyes.

"Mr. Runyon," he said, crossing the room, not offering his hand, "what is it that the railroad needs of me?"

"Sorry to bother you at home, Mr. Favor, but we had a man killed at the ice plant the other night."

"Spark Dugan, I believe."

"That's right."

"I heard, of course. A tragedy to be sure, but an avoidable one, I believe. Mr. Dugan's penchant for alcohol was well known. We make our beds, and we sleep in them. Isn't that the saying?"

"One of your trucks happened to be in the yards."

"That's a strong possibility. We send trucks to the yards frequently."

"Could you tell me what it was doing there that particular night?"

Walking to the painting of the little girl, Hugh Favor stood looking up at it, his hands folded behind him.

"I should think that would be a question for the driver or the gate man at the sheds."

"Both were reluctant to answer my questions. That's why I'm here."

"Yes," he said, turning, locking his eyes on Hook. "Sometimes one's employees can be overly zealous. Fact is, I don't know what they were picking up; however, I can tell you what is typically shipped in by rail."

"Let's start with that, if you don't mind."

"Chemicals, drill bits, drill stem, cable, earth-moving equipment, an occasional truck ordered directly from the plant."

"I see," Hook said, "and no one reported seeing anything unusual?"

"No one, though it's rare that my truck drivers report directly to me about anything so trivial. Will that be all?"

"Sorry to have bothered you, Mr. Favor."

"I hope I am of some help. Can you find your way out?"

"Yes, thank you."

"Good day, then," he said, disappearing through the double doors.

At the gate, Hook spotted a small house tucked away in the trees. A staff car from Camp Alva was parked in front, trunk open, and a woman knelt on the driveway.

Cutting through the hedge that separated the cottage from the grounds, he approached.

"Are you okay?" he asked.

"Oh my God," she said, holding her hand against her chest. "You scared the life out of me."

Her hands were white and delicate, lacking the ravages of manual labor. Her nose turned as perfectly as a teacup handle, and her lips were full, almost pouting, but she easily moved into a smile. She wore small silver rings clasped to her ears and a matching chain. Her dress and shoes were of the same lavender color, and he could have enclosed his hands around her small waist. She smelled of cloves and soap, and a blush the color of peach colored her throat.

"Sorry, miss."

"My books," she said.

"Let me help."

Gathering them up, she heaped them into his arms, ignoring the prosthesis.

"You new to the area?" he asked.

"You might say," she said. She cut her words, a Yankee clip, edgy with attitude even as she smiled up at him. "The backseat is full, as you can see."

"That we can manage," he said, carrying them around.

"My name is Reina Kaplan," she said, "Dr. Reina Kaplan. I'm starting a reeducation program at Camp Alva."

"Most folks around here are still working on their first education," he said, "if at all."

"Thank you for your assistance, Mr. . . . ."

"Hook," he said, closing the trunk lid. "Hook Runyon."

"I think that a mother would not call her son Hook."

"It's Walter, or used to be."

"Yes, Walter. That's much better," she said, adjusting one of the silver earrings clasped to her ear. "I'm going to Camp Alva. Could I drop you off somewhere?"

"You wouldn't mind?"

"I'm a bit shaky with the driving thing, but then, where better to practice than out here in the middle of nowhere?"

"Exactly," he said, opening the door.

As they drove down the drive, he offered her a cigarette, lighting it as she negotiated the curve with both hands.

"So, Walter, do you work for Mr. Favor?"

Resting his prosthesis out the window, Hook lit his cigarette.

"Take the first left. It's the courthouse on the east side of the square, if that would be okay." Taking a drag, he watched the mansion move behind the trees. "I'm an agent for the railroad, a bull, a yard dog to those who love us the most. We've had some trouble in the Waynoka yards, and I've been checking on a few things with Mr. Favor."

"Ah, a Mr. Spark Dugan, I understand."

"How do you know that?"

"Seems everyone knows everything about what goes on around here, especially something as horrific as Spark Dugan's demise. To be exact, Amanda Roswell told me. Amanda's father is Mr. Favor's chauffeur, you see. They live in the carriage house.

"In any case, I should think Mr. Favor is a nice man. He's offered me the back room in the carriage house for the duration of my stay and at rather affordable rates. I'm most grateful, of course, though I've yet to meet him personally. Is he reclusive, do you think?"

"Reclusive but not shy would be my guess."

"What does a railroad bull do? It all sounds so masculine and daring."

"It's most often neither. There's lots of bums on the rails these days, and they like their mischief. For a guy like me, though, it's a good job," he said, holding up the prosthesis, "until something like the Spark Dugan case comes along at least.

"I live in a caboose over at the elevators. There's lots of moving from place to place as you might guess, which suits me, and a little time for poking around, which suits me again."

When they stopped at the tracks, Hook braced himself against the dash.

"Sorry," she said, squashing her cigarette out in the tray. "I told you I'm a bit rusty."

"Turn here," he said. "The courthouse is just over there."

"No one lives in a caboose. You're putting me on, right?"

"Yeah, I know, but it gives me a place to live and work up and down the line. It serves me pretty well, with a few exceptions, like when trains roar by my window at sixty miles an hour in the middle of the night, or Spark Dugan quits delivering coal for my stove, or Ross Ague decides to move the caboose to a new location."

Pulling into the courthouse, she searched for neutral with the gearshift.

"Listen," she said, looking over her shoulder, "if you ever want a title to read, I'll see what I can do, though I'm sure it's against all kinds of regulations."

"How about Werfel's *The Song of Bernadette*?" he asked.

She looked at him. "That's amazing. How did you know that we chose that as one of our titles?"

"He's a German exile, isn't he? Perfect for reeducation of the Nazis, I should think."

"Aren't we informed, though," she said.

"Yes," he said. "Besides, I saw it on the backseat."

"Oh, you," she said, flashing a smile.

Sliding out of the car, he leaned in, "Thanks for the lift, Dr. Kaplan. Perhaps I'll see you around."

Standing at the steps, he watched as she lurched through the intersection and disappeared around the corner.


He located the pay phone under the stairwell in the courthouse. He searched his pockets for coins. Spending good money for a call to

Eddie Preston irked him, but it was better than a trip back to the depot to use the company phone.

"Eddie Preston," the voice said on the other end of the line.

"Eddie, this is Hook Runyon."

"What now, Runyon?"

"Listen, it looks like our boy, Spark Dugan, might have been involved in some black-marketing over at the prisoner-of-war camp here."

"That's an army problem, isn't it?"

"A railcar killed him, remember?"

"Were the two linked? Did one thing have to do with the other?"

"I can't be sure, but they were probably making contact under the ice deck."

"That's pretty weak. How about your getting back on the job? My desk is stacked with reports of pickpockets running out of Kansas City."

"I want you to check something out for me."

"Goddang it, Runyon, I'm the supervisor. You're the agent. You're supposed to check shit out for *me*."

"I want you to check the lading receipt on a Favor Oil car that was sided in the yards the night Spark Dugan was killed."

"You can't go picking a fight with Favor Oil. They're a hell of a big customer, and the old man carries a lot of weight in the state."

"It's just a call."

"I don't want my ass on the line with this."

"Call me here at the courthouse," he said, reading off the number. "I don't have a phone in my office."


When the call came, Hook snuffed out his cigarette in the bucket of sand provided at the door of the phone booth and picked up the receiver.

"What did you find out, Eddie?"

"Drill bits, drill bits for an oil company. Maybe we ought to run 'em in, you think? We can't have shit like that going on."

"Drill bits? That's it?"

"Thing is, the load wasn't picked up until a few days later."

"There was no pickup that night?"

"Looks that way."

"The truck left the yards empty?"

"Listen, did you get those journal boxes checked out over at Four Corners? Those goddamn bums been pulling packing out the bushings for starting up their fires. You know what a hotbox costs the company?"

"Thanks, Eddie," he said, hanging up.

From the courthouse, Hook took a heading on the elevators that rose from the horizon. In spite of the rats, he liked the caboose at the edge of town, a book, a quiet evening. He thought of Janet, her memory rushing back out of nowhere. An icy pain crawled up his arm or what was left of his arm. Maybe it was just as well Spark didn't have such things to bear. A lost arm would have changed Spark forever, made him pitiable and less than what he had once been.

Shaking it off, he struck out for the elevators, the sun fuming with oranges and pinks at his back. The week had taken its toll, and the day had much to ponder. But of this much he could be certain: Dr. Reina Kaplan hadn't seen the last of Walter Runyon, not if he had anything to do with it.

# 16

AFTER BUYING A few groceries, Reina and Amanda drove back to Favor Mansion. The limousine sat in the driveway of the cottage.

"Daddy's home," Amanda said. "Would you like to come in?"

"Thank you," Reina said, "but if it's all the same to you, I'm going to my room to rest. It's been a hectic day."

"Good night then," she said. "I'll see you in the morning."

Taking the flagstone path that led around the house, Reina unlocked her door. The room was hot, with its lingering, vacant smell. She opened the window, slipped off her shoes, and put the groceries in the refrigerator. Too tired to eat, she lay down on the bed, the warm breeze fluttering the lace curtain against her feet. Locusts zinged from the elms that encircled the grounds.

Weariness swept her, and she dozed, waking as the sun quivered on the horizon. The day had taken its toll, as had many things in her life—Robert, the move, the war itself.

As she watched the sun sink, she thought of Robert, of his affair, of his indifference to the pain he'd caused. How different he'd become from the man she'd met this morning, the yard dog with his look of the road, with his prosthesis and quiet certainty. A man like him did not preen at the mirror, or worry about the shine of his shoes, but if a man like him were unfaithful, it would be serious indeed, a grave wound, a decision considered and conscious and without absolution.

Rising, she worked awhile putting clothes and toiletries away, arranging a few of her favorite books on the shelf above the bed. But as evening fell, she grew restless, deciding that a walk might ease the headache that mounted at her temples. She slipped on her shoes and moved into the evening balm.

The smell of moisture hung in the air, and when lightning flashed in a distant cloud, she waited for its rumble, for its promise of rain. Somewhere in the evening a killdeer called, frantic, and the first sliver of moon bobbed onto the horizon. Leaning against the limestone wall, she could feel the warmth of the sun leeching from its mass and could see the marble statues beyond, like ghosts in the twilight of the Favor gardens.

Something compelled her to climb the wall, the call of Eden, the mystery of the unknown, the thrill of transgression. Lowering herself, she waited as the moon broke above the trees, silver and silent in the sky. The scent of lilac and plum infused the evening, and from the tops of the elms, an owl hooted. "Who?" it asked, with singular authority, and a tingle raced down her back.

Making her way down the path, she stopped at the statues, Carrara marbles as soft and ivory as the moonlight, bronzes with patinas of green, kneeling children, winged angels, and fat-cheeked cherubs. Kneeling at a pool, she touched the water, watching the ripples race across its surface. Thunder rumbled once more, farther away now.

"What are you doing?" a voice asked from behind.

"Oh," she said, nearly spilling into the pool.

"What are you doing in my garden?" he asked again.

Peering into the darkness, she searched for his face.

"I'm sorry," she said. "I'm Dr. Reina Kaplan. I'm staying in the cottage."

Stepping from the shadows, he tapped his walking stick against the paving stone as one might at a stray dog.

"I didn't ask *who* you were, Dr. Kaplan," he said, his glasses reflecting in the moonlight. "I asked *what* you are doing in my garden?"

"I'm really very sorry," she said, standing.

"My gardens are private," he said, "and heavily guarded."

"It's unforgivable of me, I know," she said, "but I was just drawn. It happened before I realized."

"Please follow me," he said, turning up the path.

When they arrived at the gate, Reina took her first good look at Hugh Favor. He had the demeanor of power and money about him, someone who knew what he wanted and how to obtain it. He would have been rather attractive had not his ambitions hardened him. Like the statues in his gardens, he looked out onto the world with blank, cold eyes.

"I'm very sorry," she said again, "for abusing your hospitality. I have a minor in art history and have just never been able to resist beautiful things. I would not have harmed your garden, I promise."

"Clean the mud off your shoes, and I will invite you in. If you're to frequent my garden, I should be able to identify you."

"Oh," she said. "I think I landed in your crocuses."

"Yes," he said. "This way."

Reina's chin dropped at the splendor around her, the exquisite stained glass, the Italian marble, the carved mahogany paneling. A Renoir hung on the wall, and a Matisse next to the fireplace, of those she could be certain, and an enormous oil of a little girl caught up in a storm. Draperies of velvet hung from the windows, and chairs with carved backs, a dozen perhaps, were placed around a banquet table just off the foyer. A bar with crystal decanters and glasses stood within serving distance of the table.

"It's splendid," she said, turning in a circle, taking it in.

"Do you by chance belong to the temperance union?"

"I would as soon belong to the Luftwaffe," she said.

"Would you care for a drink then?"

"That would be lovely."

"Brandy?"

"Yes, please."

Pouring their glasses, he handed one to her. "To secret gardens."

"And forgiving hosts," she said, tasting the brandy, expensive, mellowed with age and care.

"So," he said, dropping a hand into his pocket, "you are a lover of the arts?"

"As are you," she said, "a Matisse there, and a Renoir. I can't believe my eyes."

"Yes, but then these are for my guests. My private collection is beyond those doors."

"You are a collector?"

Taking a sip of brandy, he looked up at the painting of the little girl.

"My collection is world-class, and I've put it together one painting at a time."

Walking to the window, he looked down on the garden, and she realized that's how he'd spotted her, the moonlight, the vantage from the window.

"I collected what I could, prints at first, then crude paintings by unknown artists, and then one day a masterpiece."

"It's a passion," she said, "a craving?"

Sipping his drink, he turned. "Yes," he said. "Consuming. Most people don't understand, you see. They think of it as investment, or of cornering the market, or of waiting for the right moment to sell. It's none of that, of course, nothing so crass as that.

"Piece by piece I built my collection, each time trading up, making sacrifices, increasing their quality. A collection is more than the sum of its parts. There are the paintings, of course, but there's also the power of the collection as a whole. That's where I come in. That's my contribution.

"As my business grew, so did my ability to have only the best, but so did my understanding of what constituted the best. Today, my collection is unparalleled. I own some of the finest paintings in the world. It's the only thing that matters to me."

Setting her glass on the table, she looked up at the oil of the little girl. "This one," she said, "so sad?"

"I've let your glass go empty," he said, refilling it. Handing it to her, he looked up at the painting, "It's called *The Relinquished*, one of my few commissions."

"Someday I would love to see your collection."

Walking to the fireplace, he fell silent, and she knew that once again she'd trespassed into forbidden territory.

"My collection is closed to the public," he said. "I've found them ignorant—worse, lazy and unappreciative. Suffering fools has never been a long suit of mine, Dr. Kaplan."

Feeling her ears burning, Reina set down her drink.

"I shouldn't have asked," she said. "I'm sorry. Now, I think I should go. Thank you for sharing your cottage with me. I was not looking forward to staying in temporary barracks, and I do apologize for trespassing in your garden. It won't happen again."

"Please," he said, "forgive my hesitancy. Your knowledge of art deserves an exception. I would be delighted to show you my collection."

"I think I've intruded far too much already," she said.

"Now, if you will follow me," he said.

Their footsteps echoed in the immensity of Favor's mansion as she followed him up the winding staircase, past chandeliers, clusters of brass and crystal, tapestries of burgundy with reds and golds, vases of alabaster and cloisonné.

When he opened the door to the gallery, Reina covered her mouth in amazement. Hundreds of pictures adorned the walls, some small and discreet, others towering and spectacular, but each remarkable and distinctive in its mastery. At each painting, she stopped, breathless and humbled by the quality and celebrity of the collection.

There was Botticelli's *Primavera,* Rembrandt's *Portrait of Saskia* and one of his Madonna and child works, the familial similitude pure and above reproach. There was no one of consequence in the art world who was not represented in Favor's magnificent effort: Cézanne, Van Gogh, Raphael, and Matisse. An entire wall had been dedicated to Picasso, and yet another to Renoir. Another room featured Degas, Vermeer, and Goya. Beyond that, sculptures of marble, bronze, and terra cotta, all exquisite and worthy of an evening in themselves.

Favor led her through the exhibit, his talk fevered, his knowledge encyclopedic, and when at last they had finished, she felt as if she might collapse.

Standing at the front door, saturated and giddy with excitement, she shook his hand.

"Thank you, Mr. Favor. An unforgettable experience."

"I've enjoyed sharing my collection with someone of your knowledge. You have my permission to use my gardens for your pleasure. Good night," he said.


Too excited to sleep, Reina lay in her bed as the moon arched across the sky. The thunder had retreated, the smell of rain had faded, and somewhere along the line, her headache had disappeared. As the moon edged below the elms, the curtains furled and whispered in the stillness of her room. Turning on her side, she watched the light from the darkness of Favor's mansion blink through the limbs like a beacon, not for sailors or ships at sea but for a man lost and adrift in the storms of his obsession.

# 17

As RUNT APPROACHED the gates of Camp Alva, he hummed "Amazing Grace." He couldn't remember the last time he'd heard it, but the tune had stuck in his head. Walking across the compound of Camp Alva, he could see the roof patches on the new library, and he thought of Amanda, of how close she would be to him each day now, where he could feel the heat of her body, smell her fragrance.

They'd barely spoken, but he'd hardly slept, thinking of her, of the way she looked at him, paying no mind to his size or afflictions.

But the POW camp had affected him. A spell had been cast, and evil reigned. This much Runt knew: something lurked among the Germans, he could feel it, something waiting down at the creek. His foreboding had deepened as the days passed.

When he walked into the bakery and saw Corporal Schubert busy at the ovens, his spirits lifted.

"Good morning," he said, hanging his hat on the rack behind the door.

"Morning," Corporal Schubert said. "There's an order of lard to be inventoried."

"Right," Runt said, picking up his clipboard, pausing.

Corporal Schubert turned back to his work without looking up.

Runt counted out the cans of lard, entering the total in his book. On the spur of the moment, he decided to check the supply inventory before leaving. It would save him time at the end of the day. When he got to the flour, he came up three hundred pounds short. He counted the bags again, and again he came up short.

After locking the door, he went to the kitchen to work on the pots and pans that had built up from the morning bake. A knot gathered in the pit of his stomach as he debated what to do. Not much flour was missing, hardly any considering the amount they went through in a week's time, but the responsibility for the inventory fell to him. There were only two people besides him with keys to the bakery supply, the duty guard and Corporal Schubert.

At break, he went to the footbridge to wait for Schubert. Each day they met there for a smoke, but today he did not come. Returning early to the kitchen, Runt washed the last of the pots, with time enough left over to scrub the floor.

At noon Corporal Schubert stepped to the door, concern on his face.

"Runt," he said, "there's a problem at the loading dock. Please come."

"Sure," Runt said, drying his hands.

When Schubert rolled the door back on the reefer car, the stench washed over them, putrid and thick in the heat. Runt's stomach lurched.

"Jesus," he said.

"Cabbage," Corporal Schubert said, "at one time."

Taking out his handkerchief, Runt covered his face, his eyes tearing from the gases as he leaned into the car. The load sagged in the heat, and what were once cabbages were now lumps of slime, black and festering in the car. Working his way in, Runt put his hand against the ice-bunker wall.

"It's warm," he said. "The whole load's lost."

"These things happen," Corporal Schubert said, pushing his bangs from his eyes

"We'll have to bury it," Runt said. "I'll report it to the duty guard. Guess it's between the army and the railroad now."

"I'll get men," Schubert said.

Once the prisoners were at work shoveling the mess into a truck, Runt and Corporal Schubert walked back to the bakery. A wind blew down the road, dust stinging their eyes. Neither of them spoke.

High overhead, turkey buzzards circled in confusion over the stench that rose from Camp Alva.

"We've missed lunch," Runt said. "You have time for a smoke? The pots are done, and the shade don't last long this time of day."

"Yes," Corporal Schubert said, looking about.

They sat in the shade of the footbridge, a small structure spanning a shallow drainage ditch, built under the mistaken belief that someday it would rain.

"Have one of mine," Runt said, slipping a cigarette from his pack. "They're store-bought Luckys."

They sat in silence as they smoked. Corporal Schubert was younger than what Runt had first thought.

Pulling his knees into his arms, Corporal Schubert took a drag off his cigarette.

"Your country reminds me of Africa," he said, "the sun, the winds that blow without reason. My country is green and cool with mountains and rains that fall with ease. But I think I am meant to die in the desert."

"You care to talk about what's going on?" Runt asked.

Shaking his head, Schubert took another drag off his cigarette, studying the buzzards that floated like specks in the blue.

"At least you have no sand fleas here," he said. "In Africa they are a torment."

"I've brothers in the war," Runt said. "It's downright strange, ain't it, with me and you smoking and talking like neighbors over the fence."

"I was in the *Panzerdivision*," Corporal Schubert said, "but late in the battle when there was little left but destroyed tanks and bodies in the sand." Moving into the shade, he rubbed at his arms, looking out onto the prairie beyond the compound fence. "Corpses do not decay on the desert. The fluids are leeched away until there is only leather and bone, mummies who grin and wait beneath the sands."

"But then you are a soldier," Runt said, "something I could never be."

"There is a darkness in soldiers that comes from killing and never goes away. Be glad that darkness has not entered your heart."

"But at least you are out of it now," Runt said.

"Many here have not seen the destruction that has happened to the Third Reich. They blame those of us who were left for losing the battles. They cannot know. They cannot accept it."

In the distance, a train whistle blew, with its sound of mourning and sorrow. Corporal Schubert listened, looking away.

Snuffing out his cigarette, Runt looked at him. "Are you a Nazi, Schubert?" he asked.

Locking his fingers about his knees, he shook his head.

"My 'Heil Hitler' had too much exuberance for the Americans, so I was branded a Nazi and sent here. But I am a German soldier, a national like your brothers." The sun had moved once again, and Schubert leaned into the shade. "Colonel Hoffmann says it's our duty to be ready for liberation when the Führer comes. He does not understand that the Führer has abandoned us, that German soldiers now starve on the battlefield even as they await the enemy. Germany is doomed, but one could never say such things here and live."

Leaning back on the bridge, Runt squared the bill of his hat, studying Corporal Schubert.

"Thing is," Runt said, "I took inventory early this morning since I was already at it, you see. There's three hundred pounds of flour missing. I wouldn't bring it up at all, but I'm the one who's responsible for the inventory. If I didn't know better, I might think it went the way of the black market."

Corporal Schubert lowered his eyes and clinched his arms over his chest. A hot breeze swept across the yard, and an empty bean can clattered down the drainage ditch.

"I burned up half the morning bake. I'm accountable for the shortage."

"But I'm supposed to report missing inventory."

"Sometimes soldiers must do what they are ordered to do. To defy orders can be dangerous. This is an American prison camp, but it is still the German army. Leave this alone."

Standing, Runt buried his hands in his back pockets. "Well, who's to say? I've had plenty of accidents in my time. A plug of chewing tobacco fell out of my pocket into a batch of shine once. Pa scratched his head for a week wondering how he cooked up such a fine shade of corn. I never did say, and no one ever died from it, not that I know of at least."

Climbing up the embankment, Corporal Schubert turned at the top.

"There are many things can happen to a man in here, even to his family at home. Remember this, my friend."

# 18

WHEN SOMEONE KNOCKED, Hook tossed his book into the pile and slipped on his shoes. What the hell was there about Sunday mornings that always brought trouble?

He opened the door to find Dr. Reina Kaplan standing there, a book in her hand. She wore blue jeans, a khaki shirt with the tail out, and a white ball cap. The first two buttons of her shirt were open, revealing the white drift of her breasts.

"For heaven's sake," she said, "you really do live in a caboose."

"Dr. Kaplan," he said.

"*Reina*, if you don't mind. *Doctor* is a bit formal, isn't it, with me on your step and you standing there half-dressed?"

"Oh, sorry. I thought you were an elevator rat," he said. "I caught one working the hinges off the screen door last night."

"I'm not that species of rat, and if you don't invite me in, my reputation is going to be ruined."

"Come into my den. I'll get dressed."

"If you must," she said, smiling, her black eyes snapping.

When she stepped past him, he could smell her perfume.

Hook cleared a chair of books. "I'll fix the coffee."

"Here," she said, looking about at the stacks, "just what you need, another book."

"Ah, *Bernadette*."

"I knew you must be anxious to read a book about a Catholic saint written by an Austrian Jew," she said.

Pouring water into the coffeepot, he set it on the kerosene burner. When he lit it, black soot floated in the air.

"I like people who keep their word," he said. "Werfel has that distinction."

"Yes," she said, "and good reading for our prisoners at Camp Alva."

Sitting down, he started to button his shirt, a task that took considerable concentration without the help of his pincher.

"Here," she said, picking up the prosthesis from where he'd tossed it next to the bed, "aren't you supposed to wear this thing?"

"I'll do it later."

"That's ridiculous. Put it on."

Turning away, he slipped on the harness, buttoning up his shirt.

"There, decent and whole once more."

Locking her eyes on his, she said, "Let's get this out of the way."

"Get what out of the way?"

"This business about your arm."

Shrugging, he said, "My girlfriend was driving. I left the arm behind in the wreckage."

"That's not what I mean."

"Turns out she had a squeamish streak," he said.

"You have a cigarette?"

"Sure," he said, shaking one out of the pack for her.

"A light, too, if you don't mind?"

"Oh, yeah."

Blowing the smoke away, she crossed her legs and leaned forward on her elbow.

"Here's how it is. I don't give a damn about your arm one way or the other, so you can just get over it."

"You're pretty tough, aren't you?"

"If I have to be."

"So now you can understand why I clutched up a little with your driving the other day."

"Even I was a little nervous about my driving the other day," she said.

He took the water off the stove, scooping coffee into the pot, blowing it down as it threatened to overflow. The aroma filled the caboose.

"Got to wait for the grounds to settle out," he said, filling the cups. "There. Now I have a question for you."

"And what's that?" she asked, cocking her head.

"Kaplan is a Jewish name, isn't it?"

Her eyes narrowed, and she glanced up at him. "That would be correct. Why would you ask?"

"Because I don't give a damn one way or the other, so you can just get over that one, too."

"Yeah?"

"Yeah."

"Done," she said. "I don't suppose you have anything to eat?"

"I don't think so. No, wait a minute. I have a few eggs. 'Course, they may be hatched out by now."

"In which case we can have chicken," she said, searching for a pan. "Break them in that saucer, first, however, if you will?"

When the eggs were scrambled, she served them up, freshening their coffee.

"It's been awhile since I've had a beautiful woman serve me breakfast," he said, pulling up to the table.

"It's been awhile since you had any woman serve you breakfast, beautiful or otherwise, so just don't get used to it."

Afterward, they sat on the floor of the caboose going through his books, Reina looking at each with care, stacking them according to category and author.

"I'll never be able to find anything," he said.

"I'm impressed. You have some very nice titles, and we haven't even been through those under the bed yet. How did you acquire all these?"

"The rare ones don't show up out here in the sticks that often, but when they do, no one has the slightest idea of their value, so they're cheap enough for even a scrounger like me. Pretty soon I'm going to need more room. Maybe the divisional supervisor will hook up a freight car for me."

"Your collection is focused and distinctive and in total disarray," she said. "But I'm impressed, nonetheless. How did you learn about all this?"

"A little hunger for something beyond myself, I guess, a little madness, too."

Lying down on the bed, Reina propped her head on her hand.

"Would you consider selling these books?"

"No," he said.

"I thought not. You're the second man I've come across that loves his collection more than money, or anything else. Quite a coincidence, I'd say."

"I love my collection more than money," he said. "I don't love it more than anything, however."

"Hugh Favor showed me his private art collection the other night. It's world-class, one of the finest I've ever seen, and I've haunted many a museum in my day. There was Cranach, Rembrandt, Cézanne, and others I can't even remember. The collection is quite incredible."

Reaching for his camera, Hook leaned against the wall of the caboose, studying the light in her eyes.

"Hold," he said, taking a picture. "There, I have proof that a beautiful woman not only cooked my breakfast but ended up in my bed."

"I'll cook your goose," she said, tossing a pillow at him.

Picking up the copy of *Bernadette*, he thumbed through it.

"Runt knows a fellow who collects Prince Albert cans," he said. "What Hugh Favor does is a million miles and a million dollars from what either of us does. It's not the same thing."

"But the compulsion must be. It's the same passion, isn't it?"

"Hey, want to throw rocks at elevator rats?"

"Answer me, Walter."

"I started collecting this stuff after I lost my arm. I'm forty now and still at it. I had this emptiness that needed to be filled. These books served that purpose, I suppose, just a hobby to keep me from going crazy. Of course, now I can't stop. I'd betray my country this day for a mint copy of London's *Star Rover*. It's pathetic, really."

"Exactly," she said, sitting up on the edge of the bed. "Maybe that's why Hugh Favor spends millions on those paintings. Maybe he's a man possessed, a man driven and alone."

"Or maybe it's just a tax deduction," he said.

"Stop it. He came very close to throwing me out of his house when I asked to see his collection."

"So why did he show it to you?"

"Feminine wiles," she said, looking up at him. "He simply found me irresistible."

"I can understand that. But I'll bet Hugh Favor never invited you to throw rocks at elevator rats?"

"No, but then I've done that plenty of times. In fact, I've thrown rocks with some of the most distinguished rock throwers in the country."

"Yeah, well come on. I'll show you rats. There's one in the west elevator big enough to saddle."

When Hook pushed open the door of the elevator, its creak echoed in the darkness of the towers. A shaft of light bled from the opening of the door and onto the floor. The smell of wheat, of dust, and of rat droppings hung in the staleness. Reina took hold of his arm, her breath against his shoulder. Turning on his flashlight, he scanned the darkness, the pit where the truckloads of wheat were dumped, the augers, the chains, the ropes, the one-man lift, no more than an open platform that ascended into the heights of the concrete shafts. Dust shrouded everything, as still and undisturbed as a tomb.

"There," he said, pointing to the eyes, red as blood under the glare of his light. "You first."

When Reina threw her rock, the rat scurried from its hiding place, its tail curled behind, cutting back at the last moment to run between her feet.

"Oh, God!" she screamed, dancing.

"You missed him," Hook said, laughing.

"Get me out of here right now, Walter Runyon."

Helping her out the door, he slipped his arm around her shoulder.

"You did great, but the rat hunting doesn't get good until dark. How about a walk instead?"

"I'm not crazy about your local pastime," she said, wiping the dust off her clothes.

"Hunting elevator rats is best done after a quart of Runt Wallace shine," he said. "It's simply not proper work for the sober."

"Or the sane," she said. "I'm just glad we didn't run into that one with the saddle."

The afternoon warmed as they walked the right of way, the smell of sage sweeping in from the prairie. Even with the lack of rain, green sprouts of grass reached for the sun. In the distance the whistle of Frenchy's work train rose and fell. Sometimes, if the winds were right, the whistle could be heard from as far away as the Four Corners grade. Side by side they walked, secure in their silence, like an old married couple with uncertainties long since resolved.

Kneeling, Reina picked up a handful of dirt, letting it sift through her fingers.

"The earth is red, as if God had abandoned it still raw and unfinished."

"There's many a farmer would agree with that," he said.

Frenchy's train rumbled under their feet as it broke in the distance, black smoke boiling against the horizon. Like some primeval beast, it drove toward them, its light sweeping, its bell clanging, its drivers gleaming in the sun. When it passed by, Frenchy waved from the cab, his cigar stuck between his teeth.

Reina waved back, her arm looped through Hook's.

At the curve, the gun towers of Camp Alva cropped into view, austere against the blue of the sky.

"Let's stop here," she said.

"There's shade over there," he said. "We'll take a rest before we head back."

Sitting under an elm, they smoked a cigarette and listened to a squirrel bark at them from the highest branches.

Hooking her hands behind her head, she leaned back on the tree trunk, her breasts lifting under her khaki shirt.

"How is the investigation coming?" she asked.

Hook looked down the rails that struck into the prairie with the precision of a surgeon's scalpel.

"Spark Dugan didn't take up much room in this world, you know, slipping around, picking up a little coal here and there. He had this loyalty about him, something you don't see that often anymore.

"Once, a sound woke me early in the morning, and when I looked out the window, there was Spark Dugan filling my coal box, his old hat pulled down over his ears, his breath rising in the chill. He never once asked anything back. Not once. Doesn't seem right he should have to die like he did."

"And you don't think he died in an accident?"

Leaning against the tree next to her, he studied the gun towers of the camp.

"It's a feeling most of all, I suppose, though there's some things that don't fit."

"Like what?"

"Like the *way* he died, for example. Spark Dugan knew those yards better than anyone. He lived in them most his life. They say he could call an engine number by the sound of her stroke as far away as Four Corners. Why would a man like that crawl under a sided reefer car and go to sleep?"

"Amanda told me about what happened at the Corner Cafe with you and Runt Wallace. I must say that you have the whole town in a stir."

"I found black-market contraband in Spark Dugan's shack. Those two boys caught up with me and tried to run me off. Damn near succeeded, too."

"Maybe they killed Spark Dugan and were out to kill you? Have you thought about that?"

"Oh, indeed I have, but they're small-time operators, as I see it, making a few bucks to buy a jug of wine. Men like that have it in them to kill you, but only if they're cornered or scared. But they don't plan the next hour of their lives. It doesn't fit."

"So you think someone planned Spark Dugan's death?"

"There's a feel to an accident, especially a rail accident. I've seen plenty of them to know. You can smell the terror, see it in the victims' faces, those final, awful moments as they realize what horror awaits them.

"It didn't feel that way with Spark Dugan. I couldn't see the fear, you know. And why was there no blood? Why was he facing the car when he went under? Why didn't he scream? With all the people who were there, why didn't someone see him, and why didn't the line get checked before they moved the engine?"

"I see what you're saying."

"And that Favor Oil truck sitting in the yards. Why didn't it pick up its intended freight, and why was Roy Bench, the driver, so unhappy about me showing up at the Favor sheds?"

Pausing, he looked in the direction of Favor Mansion. From here, he could see the chimneys just beyond the trees that encircled the grounds.

"Did you know that Hugh Favor has an infant daughter buried in the cemetery?" he asked.

"No. He didn't mention anything about it."

"Well, he does, just a few days old when she died. I saw the headstone next to Spark Dugan's grave. You never know what's been in a man's life, do you?"

"Have you talked to Major Foreman about the black-marketing?" she asked. "We had problems like that at Fort Kearney, too. Turned out to be an inside deal. In the end, it has to be, you know."

"I talked to him and to Colonel Hoffmann. Both denied it, of course."

Reina rubbed at the tops of her legs as she thought.

"Are you familiar with the zone of the interior?"

"Yes," he said. "I've been duly warned."

"I've heard that the zones are sometimes used to punish a soldier who gets out of line," she said. "Or that the prisoners just use it to see who has the most courage. They say some commit suicide by stepping over the line one day. In the end, it's pretty hard to know which.

"I can't be certain that sort of thing happens here, I suppose, but I've seen how the men freeze in Hoffmann's presence." Taking off a shoe, she poured sand from it and slipped it back on. "He turns my blood to ice. It's a feeling I've never experienced before."

"He looks right through you with those blue eyes," he said.

Drawing her knees into her arms, she looked off at the gun towers. Sunlight sprinkled across her shoulders, and she touched a finger against the fullness of her mouth, as if to stop a tremble or a sigh.

"I sometimes can see Major Foreman watching from his window," she said. "It's almost as if he is a prisoner, too."

"I'm sorry they've given you such a hard time out there," he said.

"So, where do you go from here with the investigation?"

"I don't know. There's no logical reason, other than the black-marketing stuff, for someone to want to kill an ole coal picker like Spark Dugan. I'm a little too close to the case, I think. Maybe it was just an accident like they say. The divisional supervisor thinks so, and he's raising hell to close out the investigation. If I can't establish a motive, I'm not going to be able to keep it open much longer."

On the way back they walked arm in arm, the sun warm on their shoulders. The fragrance of plum trees with their ivory blossoms filled the air, and redbuds shot from the pale green of early spring. A falcon watched them from atop a telegraph pole like a sentinel.

"I know so little about you, Walter," Reina said. "Did you grow up out here?"

"El Paso," he said.

"What of your family?"

"Both of my parents are gone now. My father walked off one day, and my mother committed suicide over it."

"I'm sorry."

"Suicide doesn't end with a death. It goes on for generations, they say. Then I lost this arm in an accident. I went a little crazy after that, riding the rails, drinking too much, getting in trouble with the law. I managed to pull out of most of it. There's nothing at the bottom when you get there but the bottom."

When he fell silent, she said, "You seem well-adjusted to me."

"I think pretty straight most of the time," he said. "You either lay down and die or you just keep on keeping on. It's the same two choices in the end."

"A man jilted me," she said, "a public humiliation, so I ran."

"Hurt to one's pride is the worst, I guess," he said.

"It's vanity, I suppose, though it seems more," she said.

"What did you do before you came here?"

"I wrote book reviews for *Der Ruf*, a newsletter for the prisoner-of-war camps here in America. It's a place called The Factory out of Fort Kearney. I know it sounds crazy, but that's what I did. I guess I saw it as my contribution to the war effort. I needed to participate, you know. I needed to be a part of this war."

"Yes," he said, tucking his hook into his pocket.

By the time they had walked back to the staff car, the first colors of sunset draped the sky, and the winds had died down for the night.

"I better get back," she said, "before Amanda sends out the law."

"I am the law," he said.

Looking up at him, she smiled, her mouth ripe and inviting. He leaned over and kissed her.

"Wait," she said, catching her breath, holding her hand against his cheek. "I'm a little vulnerable right now."

"There's an auction next Saturday," he said. "Maybe you'd like to go? We might find that London book."

"Maybe," she said.

"Oh, and you'll need to bring the ride unless you want to hop a freighter."

Getting into the car, she started up the engine and let it idle as she thought over his offer.

"Okay," she said. "A little local color couldn't hurt. But hunting elevator rats is out. Is that clear?"

# 19

Hooκ LOADED FILM in his camera under the shade of a hackberry while he waited for Frenchy's switch engine to side a carload of lumber. He'd slept little last night from thinking of Reina, like a schoolboy on his first date. But he liked her, liked her a lot, the way she faced the world with both feet planted. But he also liked her tenderness, the way she looped her arm through his when they walked, the way she laughed at herself, even when under attack from elevator rats. Unlike Janet, she dealt with his handicap for what it was, a missing arm, and so what? "Get over it," she'd said, and so he had.

Janet's allure had been strong in its way, raw and sweaty and compelling, but defective, too, leaving him empty and alone in the end. But Reina, beautiful by any standards, seized him with her intelligence and wit, layers of emotions and wisdom. For hours they'd talked of books, of ideas, and of the ironies of life. As each hour passed, he was more taken with her, the sweetness of her kiss capturing him.

———

The squeal of the switch-engine brakes broke the morning silence as Frenchy leaned out of the cab window.

"Where's that pretty gal was stuck on your arm?" he asked, grinning, pushing back his hat. "Ain't no one told her about the dangers of running with yard dogs?"

Swinging up on the ladder, Hook settled in among the lunch boxes. Frenchy eased the engine forward.

"You don't think I'm going to bring any girl of mine around the likes of you boys, do you?" Hook said.

The smell of heat and smoke filled the cab as the engine moved forward, the clack of the wheels, steel against steel as they gained speed. The fireman checked the boiler, tapping the pressure gauge with a pair of pliers.

"Guess I'd be afraid of losing my gal, too," the fireman said, winking at Frenchy, "around a couple of real working men."

Lighting a cigarette, Hook moved into the open door, the wind warm against his face. In the distance he could see Favor Mansion clean and white against the morning sun.

"Frenchy," he said, "ever see a man run over by a train?"

Scratching at his chin, he said, "Can't say as I have, though most engineers are likely to 'fore it's done. Why you ask?"

"It's a bloody affair with steel against flesh."

Taking out his handkerchief, Frenchy wiped at the sweat that had gathered on his forehead.

"These steam engines can squash a penny thin enough to read a newspaper through. Flesh and bone don't hold against that."

"But bloody, Frenchy. There's lots of blood."

"Hit a Holstein cow at Four Corners one night, doing about fifty with twenty cars of winter wheat in tow. Hell, it rained blood. The world stank with blood. Blood sprayed on the engine light and on the window and on the weeds in the bar ditch. Blood dripped off the cab, and we had to sand the tracks to keep the drivers from slipping when we steamed up."

"I didn't see that much blood with Spark Dugan, not so it mattered. It was like he'd already been set up, like he'd been dead awhile before that reefer ran over him."

Taking out a cigar, Frenchy bit off the end and spit it on the floor.

"You been reading too goddang many books. Spark Dugan's blood turned to shine ten years ago, that's all, and it was pretty damn cold that night as I remember it."

Standing, Hook dusted off his pants. "You're probably right. Let me off at the depot, will you? I need to check in with the operator."

"Goddang it, I ain't your personal limousine, you know?"

"Thanks, Frenchy," he said, swinging down on the ladder. "You boys take a bath, and I might let you meet my girl one of these days."

Laughing, Frenchy waved as they pulled off.

"Hell," he hollered back, "she can't be all that particular, seeing as how she's mixed up with a goddang yard dog."

The depot, of classic Spanish design, sported a red-tile roof and mission windows with crosses encircled above them. Archways led into the reading room and into the Harvey House, where girls dressed in black-and-white dresses, looking like nuns, served breakfast to the passengers. Upstairs were rooms for the train crews, for sleeping, or for nursing hangovers during layovers.

The waiting room itself reminded Hook of a church, with its oak pews worn to a shine from the seats of passengers. At one end a sign designated the bathroom for coloreds, used by the conductor, the only black man within two hundred miles of the depot, at the other end, a whites-only, rank with the urine from constant use.

The smell of cigar hung in the waiting room, and long after the ladies boarded, with their purses, and their plumes, and their high-heeled shoes, sachet lingered with a stale sensuality.

The operator sat in his cage sound asleep, his feet kicked up on the table. The clock pendulum clacked and ticked, and a cigarette butt smoldered in the ashtray.

"The foreman will have your ass for sleeping," Hook said.

Dropping his feet down, Joe rubbed at his face. "Just resting my eyes," he said. "What the hell you want, Hook?"

The telegraph chattered, but Joe ignored it, lighting up a new cigarette.

"Anything from Eddie?" Hook asked.

Digging through a stack of papers, Joe pulled out a message and handed it to him.

"Nothing that you ain't heard before. In the end, I'm the one who catches hell anyway."

"You deserve it," Hook said, "sitting around, sleeping all the time."

"Ain't no one got it softer than a yard dog," he said, "riding up and down the line all day, flaunting his badge, like as if it mattered a damn somewhere in the world."

Honey-locust blossoms hung like white lanterns from the trees, their fragrance rich and sumptuous, and bees hummed in the morning quiet as Hook walked the tracks to the yards. Once there, he cut east to where a line of reefer cars waited for icing. Water dripped from the ice-bunker drains and into the bedding rock, where sparrows dipped and preened in the gathering puddles. Squatting down, he let the water run over his fingers. She ran frigid and icy, and an ache crawled up his arm.

At the ice deck, a crew, garbed in rubber aprons, worked three-hundred-pound cakes of ice down a chute, pulling them along with tongs, guiding them with their knees onto a conveyer. As the blocks were managed into the bunker openings on top of the cars, they were crushed and tamped with iron rods, and handfuls of coarse salt were tossed in to lower the temperature.

As Hook climbed the ladder to the deck, he could see the "PW" letters sewn across the shirts of each of the work crew, and atop one of the cars, a military guard sat with a tommy gun across his lap. Hook recognized him as the guard he'd encountered at the front gate of Camp Alva.

At the far end of the deck, Ross Ague, the night foreman, worked on a pair of ice tongs, looking up through his brows as Hook approached.

"What now, Runyon?" he asked.

"Thought you were the *night* foreman?"

"I'm whatever the railroad wants, night, day, or twenty-four hour, like when them potatoes come up out of Texas. What the hell does it matter to you?"

Putting his foot on the railing, Hook looked down the line of reefers. A row of floodlights hung from the deck railing to light the yards below. From here, he could see the angle cocks of the front five cars, and the undercarriage of the first three. Spark Dugan had been dragged between the second and the third cars and could have easily been seen by anybody watching from this vantage.

"You ice all the cars coming through here?" Hook asked, leaning onto his knee.

"Depends on the icing schedule, don't it?" Ague said, testing the tongs.

"Icing schedule?"

"Most everything comes out of Oceanside, California, already iced, and then again at Winslow. Most are re-iced for the third time right here in the yards, 'cept taters out of Texas, which ain't iced at all until they get here, 'cause they ain't as apt to spoil. This is the biggest plant on the line, and that's why we ain't got time to stand around talking to yard dogs all day."

Taking out a cigarette, Hook turned his back to the breeze before lighting it.

"Each car has its own icing schedule, you say?"

Reaching for a cigar, Ague glanced down at Hook's prosthesis and then slipped the cigar back into his pocket.

"How the hell long you worked for the railroad?"

"Thanks," Hook said, flipping the spent match onto the deck. "It's always a pleasure talking to you."


Even though it was less than a two-mile walk, Hook was tired by the time he reached the graveyard. Juniper trees, planted in the old part of the cemetery, now knurled from time and wind, provided sparse shade from the sun. Over the years their roots had toppled stones and desecrated the sanctity of the coffins below.

It had been only days since Spark Dugan's funeral, but it took Hook two trips up and down the road to locate the grave. The marker had been set, as the digger had promised, brass, with the dates of Spark Dugan's birth and death. The first signs of copper patina grew from beneath the bird droppings that ran down its front. Spark Dugan had died at thirty-seven, younger than Hook by nearly three years, a fact that not only surprised Hook but gathered in the pit of his stomach like a lump of clay. Bermuda grass had claimed the fresh-turned earth of the grave, and a rosebush, planted by the cemetery board, struggled to root.

The little girl's stone next to it leaned as if planted in haste, slight and uncertain like her own brief life. Hook read the inscription again: "Sarah Favor, Our Angel, Born: Jan. 6, 1939, Died: Feb. 10, 1939." Lifting his face, he let the sun shine red through his lids. Why couldn't he let this thing go? What could it matter to anyone anymore? Spark Dugan lay dead in his grave, and nothing could ever change that fact.

When he opened his eyes, Bud Hanson, the digger, stood behind him, his arms folded across his chest.

"Thought you might be dead," he said. "Come to take you back to the shop."

"Not without money down, I figure," Hook said.

"Good point."

"Thanks for the marker. Spark Dugan would've appreciated it."

"Spark Dugan was too dumb to appreciate a marker," he said, "but you paid for it, so you got it."

"You planting someone today," Hook asked, "or just out visiting loved ones?"

"Babe Wilson," he said, pointing his chin, "from out to Belva. Broke her leg in a posthole. Being a widow and all, nobody found her for a week."

"Shame," Hook said.

"Ripe, too," he said, "laying out in the sun like that, and then them cats of hers. She didn't have a damn dime, either. I don't know what I'd do for a living if not for the county burial fund."

Taking a match from his pocket, Hook stuck it in the corner of his mouth.

"Don't suppose you're headed back to town?" he asked.

"Come on. I'm just leaving."

Hanson had parked the hearse in the shade of the cemetery shed. It smelled of flowers and formaldehyde, and a bee buzzed in the back window as they turned down the drive. Hook opened the wing window for air.

"Ever heard of a Sarah Favor?" he asked. "Her stone's back there by Spark Dugan."

Hooking his elbow out the window, the digger twisted his mouth as he thumbed through the years.

"Sure, I remember. I did the pickup on that one. Blowing snow and freezing cold when the call came in. She was Hugh Favor's infant daughter. Smothered in her crib, they said. Got her blankets tangled up, and that was that. The mother went crazy. They put her in the insane asylum over to Fargo."

"She still there?"

"Dead," he said. "Odd thing that funeral, arranged over the phone, and a check sent, but no one came, not a goddang soul, not the mother nor old man Favor either one. I never had another funeral like it, 'cept indigents and such. Me and that Holy Roller preacher held our own that day."

Turning onto the road, they gathered up speed.

"He sang just like he did for Spark Dugan, just me, the preacher, and that baby girl. A damn lonely funeral all right, and I've seen more than a few in my time."

Dust from the road gathered up around them as they pulled to the stop sign.

"Let me out at the drugstore, will you? I've got photographs to pick up," Hook said.

"Thing is," he said, looking over at Hook, "I never understood how that baby died. Some said the mother smothered it herself, being crazy from the get-go, and just couldn't deal with a newborn and with Hugh Favor at the same time." Shrugging, he pulled up to the drugstore. "Who's to say after all these years?"

"Thanks for the lift."

"My pleasure," he said. "Ain't all that often I get passengers who can talk back."

Runt Wallace's pickup had pulled in at the gas station when Hook came out of the drugstore. Runt leaned on the fender, counting out gas coupons for the attendant.

"Hey," Hook said, coming across the street, "you give up hopping trains, have you?"

"Hello, Hook," he said, handing the attendant the coupons.

"Hitching train rides is against the law. Besides, I had this here sugar to pick up. Ma's getting ready for summer canning."

Looking into the pickup bed, Hook shook his head.

"Looks like it's going to be a fair garden season. That's a lot of sugar."

"Ma raises big gardens," he said, "if the rains come."

"Which way you headed?"

"Take you as far as Four Corners if you ain't particular what you ride in."

Opening the door, Hook slid in, pushing aside a can of rusty nails and a pair of fence stretchers.

"Been riding in a hearse all morning," he said. "It wasn't as friendly as this truck, but it was a damn sight cleaner."

Runt grinned, reaching for the clutch, easing the pickup into gear. The engine clattered, and smoke boiled up behind them as they pulled away. Hook could see the road whizzing by through the hole in the floorboard between his feet. Gasoline fumes and oil smoke drifted up, turning the air blue inside the cab.

The dash rattled with junk, a hammer with a broken claw, a left-handed glove, a calendar yellowed with age, a bottle of iodine with its cap missing, empty cigarette packages, fence steeples, screws, bent nails, a bolt with an assortment of nuts and washers on it, a Monkey Ward catalog, its pages curled beyond repair.

Runt peeked over the steering wheel as he negotiated the curve north of town. Shaking out a cigarette, Hook offered him one.

"Thanks," he said, leaning over for Hook's match.

"Don't suppose you got any goods on you?" Hook asked.

"Sorry," he said, drawing on his cigarette. "I could bring some by."

"Sure," Hook said, "when you get a chance."

"You're a friend, Hook, and I'm glad to provide some goods," he said, shaking his head, "but I got to tell you, I shouldn't be drinking with you no more."

The boards on the bridge rattled as they crossed over White Horse Creek. Cockleburs grew in the sand of the dry bed, and sand-plum bushes twisted in a tangle along its shore.

"Why's that?"

"'Cause last time, I woke up at Four Corners eat up by red ants."

"That could happen to anyone, Runt. It's happened to me plenty of times."

"Thing is," he said, "I don't know how I got there."

"It's a shame," Hook said, "when a man can't drink his own shine."

"She's hard enough to make," he said, flipping ashes onto the floor, "without having to drink her, too."

A rabbit dashed out of the trees ahead of them, cut right, and headed straight down the road, its hind legs kicking dust into the air as it struggled to outrun the pickup. Runt honked his horn, and it darted off into the ditch.

"How you liking that new job?" Hook asked.

Shifting into second, Runt made the curve.

"I gained ten pounds," he said. "Never seen so much food in one place. Seems a fool thing, feeding the enemy better than your own."

"Maybe they're fattening them up to butcher," Hook said.

"My hogs been living off mash and blue milk and running the fence for more while them Nazis got everything a man could want. Don't seem right."

"The army's scared of the Geneva Convention," Hook said. "Scared they'll do something to bring harm to our own troops over in Germany."

Pulling over the tracks at Four Corners, Runt shut off the pickup and stared down the road.

"They brought a reefer full of spoiled cabbages in the other day. It stank like death, and we dumped the whole mess in a ditch. We dumped enough to feed a family for five years. It near broke my heart."

From where they sat, Hook could see the hobo camp. It looked deserted. If someone was taking journal packing, they were long since gone, or maybe it was just Eddie's way of discouraging him from the Spark Dugan case.

"Wonder why it spoiled?" he asked.

"Danged if I know. It failed to get iced, I reckon."

"Camp Alva's not too forthcoming about anything, Runt. Least that's been my experience."

Leaning forward onto the steering wheel, Runt shook his head in agreement.

"And it's a tad dangerous, too, if my feelings are right."

"You know Dr. Kaplan?"

"In a fashion," he said. "She's a tough one. They say there's stuff going on in that camp a person might die for—death squads, beatings, chicken bones left in the bunks as warnings to traitors. It's a deep river, running dark and silent, and all that Major Foreman does is look out his window like he ain't got a care in the world." Starting his pickup, Runt waited for a moment before speaking. "Sometimes I can't sleep nights for thinking on it. If it wasn't for the kids, I'd just go back to selling goods and raising hogs."

"Do you know *The Song of Bernadette*, Runt?"

"I know 'Amazing Grace,'" he said. "Why?"

Slapping him on the shoulder, Hook said, "Sometimes a man just has to keep the faith, my friend, no matter what. Thanks for the ride."

That night in the caboose, Hook scrambled up the last of the eggs, seasoning them with hot sauce that had turned the color of dishwater. When darkness fell, he lit the lantern, thumbing through *The Song of Bernadette*. He thought of Reina and about how she laughed, how her laughter bubbled up like springwater, and about how smart and how beautiful she was, and how, beneath it all, she was tough as a rawhide saddle.

Outside, thunder rumbled, and a gust of wind rocked the caboose. When lightning flashed, the room froze in a fluorescent glow, and rain swept across the roof. Taking the photographs from the packet, he tossed them one by one onto the table. The thunder rumbled again, but distant this time, the promise of rain fading.

He came across the photo of Spark Dugan under the reefer car, his severed arm, his crumpled body, and another taken from farther back, the seal on the door, the upturned coal bucket on the next track. He'd taken a third picture of the work crew on the ice deck, the floodlights still on from the night shift. He could just make out a military policeman standing next to the chute.

At the bottom of the stack he discovered a close shot of the belly of the reefer, taken as he'd backed from under the car with the smell of death in his nose. Then it came to him, with the distant rumble of thunder, and he held the photograph to the light. He could see no water dripping from the ice-bunker drains. There were no puddles of melting ice. Ague had said a load of cabbage, that's what he'd said, cabbages for Camp Alva, and cabbages took ice.

Maybe she'd carried something other than vegetables, or maybe the drains were plugged, or maybe Ague didn't know shit about anything. One thing sure, freshly iced cabbages didn't spoil on a run as short as the Camp Alva spur.

# 20

Hook sat straight up in his bed, his heart pounding, as the passenger train sped down the track. Lying back down, he pulled the covers over his shoulders only to bare his feet to the morning chill. Determined to sleep, he drew his knees up and dropped his arm over his eyes. No sooner had he drifted off than a gnat set up a whine in his ear.

"Damn," he said, tossing aside the covers.

Given the burgeoning stacks of books, he scarcely had room to stand, so he sat on the edge of the bed to dress. Shivering, he slipped on the prosthesis and then checked the coal box under the steps just in case someone had thought to deliver coal. Empty, of course, except for rat droppings and the telltale slime of a nocturnal slug.

After setting the coffee water on the kerosene burner, he lit his cigarette on the flame, his lungs recoiling, sending him into coughing frenzy.

Pouring a cup of coffee, he checked his watch. There were still a couple of hours before Reina would be arriving. He'd thought of nothing else. Standing on the wrong rung of the social ladder had made him all too aware that the rung was not far from the bottom. Reina was educated, polished, from New York City. That didn't mesh with a yard dog, a hick, a drifter with a drifter's job. To top it off, he was an arm short and too fond of shine. What could a woman like Reina see in a rogue like him?

By the time the staff car pulled up to the caboose, he'd swept the floor, made his bed, and blazed a trail through the labyrinth of books. When he opened the door, Reina, dressed in Levi's and a denim shirt, beamed back at him.

"Morning, Deputy," she said, cocking her hand on her waist. "I'm turning myself in."

"Why, howdy, ma'am," he said. "I be fixin' to go out and kiss my horse good mornin'."

"Maybe you could kiss me instead?"

"Why, yes, ma'am," he said, kissing her upturned mouth. "Deputy Walter Runyon never abandons a damsel in distress."

"Go get your spurs on, Deputy, because I left the staff car running."

Retrieving his hat, he followed her to the car, her figure manifest in the cut of the Levi's. She drove while he followed the map, reading the sale-bill items aloud between turns in the road.

"Here's a 1937 McCormick binder," he said, "complete with canvasses and a season's binder twine. It's just what you been looking for, I think."

"Oh, dear," she said, "a 1937 just won't do. I believe it a bad year all around."

"Well," he said, "I've learned never to doubt your taste."

"Seriously, Walter, how does this all go?"

"It's a story repeated every spring out here. The aging farmer dies over the winter—bad heart or such. The wife, suffering from poor eyesight and weak bones, can no longer manage, so she sells off the sum total of their lives. With the money, she buys a frame house in town, trades in the pickup on a five-year-old Buick, plants irises in the backyard, and finishes her life out among strangers."

Locking her dark eyes onto his, she studied him over her shoulder.

"How depressing."

"Especially to see one's life stacked on the back of a hay wagon."

"Then why do you go?"

Turning on the radio, he ran the dial up and then back again before shutting it off.

"Even among the most humble lies a desire for something beyond hard work and frugality, a collection of hatpins or linens, well-read books of faraway places, daffodils planted in a tractor tire. It may not be much as the world goes, but it's there, a flash of beauty, a treasure to be found among the machinery and hand tools."

Turning onto the dirt road, she leaned forward as she eased the car over a low-water bridge.

"There's a soft touch behind all that yard-dog toughness," she said.

"Turn here," he said, "half-mile east now."

"A teddy bear."

"Looking for a bargain, that's all, Miss New York know-it-all."

Reaching over, she touched his knee.

"I like that in a man," she said.


Pickups stretched down the bar ditch for a quarter mile, and the call of the auctioneer echoed from among the outbuildings. People gathered about, bewitched by the low and whoop of his call. Tables from the kitchen and dining room had been placed in the yard, stacked with miscellaneous items—utensils, glassware, boxes of shells, an old cream can, a wheelchair, a tricycle with one wheel missing.

The hay trailer had been reserved for tools, shovels, hammers, garden hoes, open-end wrenches, boxes of nuts and bolts, gaskets, and rolls of barbed wire. Men gathered around a collection of rifles, holding them to their shoulders as they laughed and talked. A hum rose from the crowd, an air of excitement in the possibilities that lay ahead, of the bargain that might yet be found.

Reina and Hook wandered from table to table, debating the function of the items as they picked through the boxes. Under the hay wagon, Hook discovered a box of books.

"Here," he said, sliding it out, "the family library."

The books smelled of mildew, and a daddy longlegs clambered across his hand when he reached into the box. He found a dozen *National Geographic* magazines, their edges chewed away by rodents; a couple of *Reader's Digest* magazines; a half dozen Louis L'Amours, the pages crumbling with age.

"Not exactly the Huntington Library," she said, her hand on his shoulder.

"Readers are a rare breed in these parts," he said.

"If this is typical, then what's the point, or do you just like to rummage through junk?"

Dumping the remainder of the box onto the ground, he retrieved two books, spotted with mud-dauber nests, their covers dark with the grime of passing years.

"This, my dear," he said, handling them as if they were infants, gently opening one to the title page, "is Roald Amundsen's *South Pole*, 1912, both volumes here, too, first editions, with illustration and maps. They're beauties, aren't they?"

"They're rather old."

"That's the point—and becoming more rare by the second. They'll make a great addition to my collection."

"What now?"

Putting the books on the bottom of the box, he refilled it, sliding it back under the hay wagon.

"Now we wait."

The sun climbed high overhead as the auctioneer came to the box. Reina watched the intensity in Hook's face, like a warrior preparing for battle. The auctioneer started the bid at five dollars. When there were no takers, he dropped it to two, and then one. Again no takers, and he shook his head at the sad lot who stood before him.

"Who will give me fifty cents then," he said, "a year's worth of reading for fifty cents. Surely upstanding folks like yourselves ain't against getting an education." Hook held up his card. "Sold!" the auctioneer yelped. "Number twenty-four, for fifty cents, a man of low morals and high learnin'."

As the auctioneer moved on down the line, Reina looked over and smiled. "You ought to be ashamed," she said.

Picking up the box, Hook locked his good arm under the flaps to keep them from giving way.

"How about a hot dog?" he asked. "I'm starved after all this high-stake dealing."

"Okay," she said, "but you pay, cheapskate."

After buying a couple of dogs and colas from the quilting-club table, they made their way to the shade of a locust grove not far from the house. Sitting under a tree, they ate their dogs while they looked through their treasures.

"It's a rush," he said. "There's something about it."

Taking a bite of her hot dog, she said, "I could see it in your face."

"It's not greed, if that's what you're thinking. I don't know what it is, but I do know it's not that."

"Hey," she said, examining her hot dog, "is this pork?"

Peeling back the wrapper, he looked at his dog. "Why?"

"Because I'm Jewish, and we don't eat pork."

"Then it must be beef because I saw you eating it."

"Oh," she said, taking another bite. "I thought so."

Afterward, they smoked and listened to a woodpecker chisel away somewhere in the grove. Locust blossoms hung, pregnant with nectar, their smell sweet in the heat of the day. Reina leaned against his shoulder, and his groin stirred.

"How is the investigation going?" she asked, settling in against him.

"Slow," he said. "Eddie Preston's going to have my hide if I don't wind it up soon."

"Maybe it's time. I mean, maybe there's nothing there. It's not worth losing your job over."

Taking her hand, he studied it, delicate and smooth and perfect, a hand spared the abuse of hardship and poverty, the shame of trading bits of coal for food.

Turning onto his side, he said, "You know those reefer cars are sealed at the point of origin. The seal on that car had not been broken. I checked it myself. The only time those reefers stop is for icing. According to Runt, the camp's getting spoiled vegetables right along." He paused to light a cigarette. "The other day when I was looking at some pictures I took of the scene, I discovered that the bunker drains were dry on the reefer car that killed Spark Dugan."

Reina buried her hot-dog wrapper in the sand as she thought.

"None of it makes any sense to me," she said. "I think I better stick to literary theory."

Locust blossoms drifted down from the treetops. Picking them up, he held them in the palm of his hand.

"I stopped by the cemetery to see if the marker had been placed for Spark Dugan. I ran into Bud Hanson there."

"Hanson?"

"Yeah, the digger, you know, the funeral director. He told me that he made the run the night Sarah Favor died, Hugh Favor's little girl. No one came to the funeral, no one but him and the Holy Roller preacher. Why wouldn't the Favors have attended their own daughter's funeral?"

Shrugging, Reina said, "Like you say, you never know what's going on in people's lives. Maybe there were extenuating circumstances."

"Maybe," he said. "What can be so important that you don't go to your own daughter's funeral?"

"Something drives a man like Hugh Favor, Walter, that much I know, something that the rest of us don't understand."

"But enough about my case," he said. "How about you?"

Reina stood, strolling to the edge of the locust grove, looking down on the buildings below. The auctioneer's voice drifted up on the wind.

"The library is open now, though our collection is limited," she said. "Amanda has taken charge of that. She's quite competent, you know, and a class in English is being taught twice a week. It's very popular. Some of the prisoners have started a camp paper, the editorials of which are quite revealing about what's going on in the camp. Major Foreman balked at the film-study proposal, though, until he received a call from the Office of the Provost Marshal General. Hollywood's coming to Camp Alva."

Walking back, she knelt in the sand next to him.

"But it's a painful time for me. I'm no longer certain I believe in what I'm doing."

Pulling her down beside him, he slipped his arm about her shoulder, her body warm against him.

"What's wrong, Reina?"

"The Germans are losing the war. I guess everyone knows that, everyone except the POWs, of course."

"That's what they say," he said.

"I've been receiving reports from Major Dunfield back at The Factory. As you know, it's our job to prepare these prisoners to return to society after the war is over, to provide an opportunity for them to see how a democracy works."

"Sounds noble to me."

"He's sent photographs, pictures to be posted in the camp for the Germans to see. They will be made available to the public soon. They are of concentration camps in Dachau, Auschwitz, Kraków, and others as well, Buchenwald, and Belzec, God knows where, photographs of Jews being slaughtered like cattle, of babies, of little girls holding their mothers' hands as they walk to their deaths, of old men and women, too blind and starved to even know they are about to die, surrounded by machine-gun nests.

"There are thousands of them, naked, emaciated, and heartbreaking. Like frightened deer they crowd together, these skeletons with enormous eyes, with their bellies swollen. Without looking at their genitals, I can't tell if they are men or women, only bones and skin, closer to death than to life, no more than a flicker from the grave."

"Why would they do such a thing?" he asked.

"I can't know," she said. "I can't know. The shame is too great for humanity to bear, too obscene and cruel. When I look at those young POWs, I wonder what will become of us, into what darkness we have gone? If it's of man, it's of us, too, of you and me."

Pulling her close, he held her tight. "You can't take on the sins of others. In the end, it's only you and what you've done that matters."

"One report lists property taken under the auspices of the German Chamber of Culture, page after page, property stolen from the Jews, everything they had, taken as they were executed or sent to the concentration camps.

"Monuments officers are finding it in caves and in mines and in the basements of cathedrals. Goebbels himself has shipped much of it to Switzerland for selling on the open market: jewelry, gold, coins, paintings, rare books, tapestries, many from the Rothschild collection, they think. They've even looted the bells from the churches and the gold from the mouths of their victims."

"But who would buy such things and from these people?"

"I don't know."

Turning her about, he kissed her forehead. "Makes the death of one man seem a little trivial."

"Spark Dugan's life had value, too," she said, "and there's got to be justice somewhere in this world."

Reina shut off the lights of the staff car and waited while Hook gathered up his books and set them on the steps of the caboose. A breeze had rolled in from the south, laden with moisture, and the last of the sunset faded in sprays of orange. An owl hooted from the recesses of the elevators as it waited for darkness.

Coming back, Hook leaned against the car door.

"It's been a long time since I've enjoyed a day like this," he said.

Turning off the engine, she laid her hand on his. "I didn't mean to burden you about the photographs and all that. It's just that I don't have many people to talk to out here."

"Maybe you'd care to stay awhile?"

Flecks of orange danced in her eyes as sunset faded. "Yes," she said. "How about a coffee?"

"Come on," he said, opening the door. "I'll even wash the pot."

After lighting the lantern, Hook made coffee and opened the windows of the caboose to let in the evening. From somewhere high in the elevators, the owl hooted again. The smell of locust blossoms and sage settled into the valley, and frogs croaked down at the slough.

Sitting among the books, Hook read a few paragraphs under the lamplight from his new acquisitions. He loved the way they fit his hand, their weight and smell, the way the words rose from the page. He loved owning them, to make them his own. Reina listened, focused on his words.

"There's nothing I like better than being read to by the right person," she said. "It's like having your back rubbed by someone you love."

Gathering her into his arms, he said, "I do a fair job at that, too."

Lifting onto her toes, she kissed him, falling into him.

He blew out the lantern and took her hand, guiding her to the bed. Stretching onto her stomach, Reina sighed. He massaged her neck with gentle strokes, and then her shoulders, the length of her arms. He kneaded the palms of her hands and the joints of her fingers and the hollows of her elbows. Moaning, she sank into the pillow.

"I want your touch against my flesh," she whispered, lifting her shirt.

He trailed his fingers along the span of her back, the curve of her hips, carved and white as marble, tracing her backbone, each segment with the tips of his fingers. He kissed the nape of her neck where the sassy curls were unkempt and wild and buried his face in the cup of her shoulder, inhaling her fragrance, her pulse tripping against his lips.

"Reina," he said, to hear her name, to make it real, to connect to this creature beneath him.

"Take off the prosthesis," she said, removing her shirt, cupping her breasts in her hands. "I want you warm and alive."

"You're certain?"

"Yes," she said.

Slipping off the prosthesis, he laid it aside, watching as she removed her clothes, the feline curve of her hips; the round of her stomach, fecund and ripe; the duskiness between her thighs, sensual and enigmatic. Her breathing was shallow, rapid, like a rabbit, and her smell that of earth, of turned fields, of dust and primordial heat. When she touched him, he groaned with her touch's extravagance.

"Walter," she said, her voice husky, viscous, her hand pressed in the small of his back.

Above them, the moon arched through the inky sky, its light spilling onto the caboose below.

# 21

A DUST DEVIL twisted across the yard, chicken feathers and bits of grass spiraling like demented spirits. Runt ducked his head and held on to his hat as he walked the path to the barn to milk Shorty. He smelled rain in the air, the smell of dust laden with moisture, but still far away and unsettled. Even though the summer had yet to arrive, the sun rose with audacity, the promise of a hot day, a promise seldom broken in this country.

Shorty greeted him with a snort, working her head into the stanchion to await her morning feed. Only a few weeks' fresh, she suffered from lack of green grass, her bag shriveling, her milk blue with the absence of cream. The butterfat had dropped, and hauling her milk to the creamery for tests would be futile if things didn't improve. Without cream money coming in, there would be little enough for gas and for sugar. The Camp Alva job would be all that stood between them and hard times.

After separating it, he mixed the milk into the mash for the hogs. Holding them at bay with a stick, he poured it into their trough. It smelled of sour and of whiskey as the hogs slurped and rooted their way from one end of the trough to the other. Perhaps he should butcher one to cut down on the feed and provide Ma with much-needed pork. Lighting a cigarette, he studied their backs, debating which carried the best ham, the best side of bacon.

By the time he got back to the house, Ma worked at the stove, sweat glistening on her forehead as she slid baking-powder biscuits into the oven.

"We're getting low on coffee," she said without looking up. "Maybe you could pick up a tin on your way home?"

Slipping off his boots, he set them behind the door and took up his place at the table.

"If I get done in time," he said. "I got to stop by Hook Runyon's on the way home. I'll be taking the pickup to work."

"There's eggs this morning."

"No, thanks, Ma. Biscuits and coffee will do. I need to carry some sugar up Dead Man Creek before work."

"Them Rhode Islands know how to lay an egg," she said. "Maybe Simmons would be trading a few more?"

"I'll check on it."

Taking the biscuits out of the oven, she dropped a couple on his plate, then blew on the tips of her fingers. She pulled up a chair and watched the chickens scratch under the lilacs. She bobbed her foot the way she so often did.

"Bess Hendricks said there has been some trouble at the Corner Café," she said.

Daubing sweet butter on his biscuits, Runt took a bite, squinting his eyes against the sun that had popped into the window.

"What's that got to do with me?"

"You ain't drinking that shine, are you? You know what it did to your pa."

"Bess Hendricks is a nosy ole bitch," he said, "and got her own no-good son to look after."

"Hush, Runt," she said. "Essie will hear you."

"Well, it's the truth."

Getting up, she poured him a cup of coffee, then topped off her own cup.

"She said you and Hook Runyon had been seen at the Corner Café drunk as lords."

Brushing the flour off his hands, Runt took a swig of coffee.

"We had a few drinks, I reckon," he said. "Anyway, those boys banged Hook up pretty good down at Spark Dugan's shack. I figure they had it coming."

Sitting down, she studied him for a moment, dabbing her apron across her forehead.

"I don't want you drinking with Hook Runyon no more. I want you to promise me. I don't want you ending up like Spark Dugan, no more'n roadkill scattered up and down the tracks. And all the time them Nazis up on the ice deck eating their sack lunches and drawing their wages. You can't tell me, not when the world's gone crazy."

"I'm a growed man and can take care of myself. Besides, no one knows what happened to Spark Dugan. He could've gone to sleep on them tracks. No one knows, not even you."

"And I could get a call from the queen for high tea, but it ain't likely, not today at least. Now, I want you to promise."

"I ain't just one of your laying hens."

"Promise me, Runt, so I can hear it."

He pushed back his chair, slipped on his boots, and stuck his hat on his head.

"I promise I won't drink with Hook Runyon no more, goddang it," he said, slamming the door behind him.

With a sack of sugar on his shoulder, he made his way along the slow drift of Dead Man Creek. The sun warmed his face, and a turtle dove cooed from the upper branches of a cottonwood. Its song stirred lonesome as death in the morning, and from behind, the hogs squealed over the last of the mash. A warm breeze rushed in with its smells of sage and sunflowers, and the bawl of a lost calf drifted from beyond the hills.

At the grove, he stopped for a breather and to look for his grand-daddy's shine. Scraping away the leaves with his foot, he looked for signs of anything buried, a hollow perhaps, or a stake driven to mark the spot.

Finding nothing, he settled against a tree to wait a spell, to listen to the morning, to listen for the telltale crack of twigs or the flight of blackbirds that watered down at the creek. A man could get set upon just here in these last few yards. Better to wait quietly for a while to make certain.

Not having to hop the northbound gave him an hour's jump on the morning, a luxury he'd nearly forgotten since the war. Pushing back his hat, he lit a cigarette and closed his eyes. Amanda's face came to him, her gentle smile, the ivory of her skin. Her voice puddled like mercury when she laughed and settled into him, filling him with ease, and he could smell her scent like the freshness of dawn. And her touch that tingled up his arm when her fingers brushed his hand at the tray station.

If only he had the courage to talk to her, to tell her of his feelings, to tell her how he'd thought of little else but her since they'd met. They'd talked some before, to exchange pleasantries, to debate the war or to complain about Major Foreman, but never alone, never without the presence of the others. Snuffing out his cigarette, he buried it in the sand and loaded the sugar onto his shoulder.

After checking to make certain the fishing line had not been broken, he looked for any tracks that may have been left in the sand at the base of the ravine.

Once in the cave, he waited for his eyes to adjust to the dimness before covering the sugar sack with a washtub to protect it as best as he could against rodents and dampness.

Afterward, he retrieved a quart of shine from the store, wrapping it in a tow sack. What with Hook's willingness to spring for the shine, there would be cash for Ma's coffee and a little leftover for sweets for Billy Joe and Essie. On his way back down the ravine to Dead Man Creek, he picked up his pace. If he hurried, there would just be time to stop by and make amends with Ma before leaving for Camp Alva.

Marino watched him from the guard tower as Runt trudged his way across the compound. Goosebumps raced down Runt's arms, and he rubbed them away with his hand. From the soccer field, the voices of the prisoners rose in disagreement, and far off, the bark of cadence from the drill pad, precise and cold as machine-gun fire.

Halfway across, he spotted Amanda as she unlocked the door to the library, her knee bracing an armload of books that threatened to fall. Just as he got there, the books spilled into the dirt at her feet.

"Oh, dear," she said. "I hope I haven't ruined them. Dr. Kaplan will have me in the guardhouse."

Gathering them up, Runt blew the dust from the covers as he stacked them on his arm.

"I'll carry them in for you."

"Oh, don't bother," she said. "I'm sure you have work to do."

"It's no bother," he said, slipping the last one under his chin. "There ain't much going on over there except for standing around."

"Well, okay," she said, opening the door. "Just set them on that table."

After putting the books down, Runt took in the library. So close were the stacks that he could barely turn.

"It's more than a man could read in a lifetime," he said.

"Dr. Kaplan has read them all," Amanda said, looking about, "and others as well."

Running his fingers across the spines of the books, Runt shook his head.

"It's more than a man can fathom, like climbing a mountain a hundred miles high."

"And some of the prisoners have read nearly as many. There are some very bright men here."

Hooking his hands in his pockets, Runt studied his feet.

"Reading ain't something I took up," he said. "Just dumb, you know."

Spiking her hand on her waist, she squinted her eyes at him.

"Don't you talk like that, Runt Wallace. Just because you haven't done much reading doesn't make you dumb. It makes you ignorant, that's all."

"I'd as soon be dumb as ignorant," he said.

Smiling, Amanda sat down, looking at the titles, arranging the books into stacks.

"Ignorant doesn't mean you can't. It means you haven't or you won't."

"Seems a mighty fine line to me."

"Well, it isn't, and you can call me Amanda, if you please."

Runt looked out the window. He could see Marino clearly from here, his hat cocked, his tommy across his lap, his finger working at something elusive in his nose.

"I've always been taken with the name Amanda."

Smiling, she pushed a book onto the shelf. "No you haven't. You're just making that up."

"It's a name what melts on your tongue," he said, "like a pat of butter."

Falling silent for a moment, she said, "Runt Wallace, I do believe you're a romantic."

"Is that the same as ignorant?" he asked.

"Well, in a way," she said, laughing. "It's a matter of believing something in spite of all evidence to the contrary."

"Had a dog once," he said, "believed he could suck eggs even with my pa's 410 stuck in his ear. I figure he might have been a romantic."

"Or ignorant," she said.

Handing her a book, he shrugged. "Dumb, I'd say."

Outside, the cadence grew louder as the prisoners marched in for roll call, a ritual executed two times a day, the beat of jackboots, the yelp of alien names into the prairie stillness, the click of Hoffmann's heels as he inspected the soldiers.

"Thanks for helping me with the books," Amanda said.

At the door, Runt paused. The beat of his heart drowned out the cadence from the compound as he turned.

"Amanda," he said, "I ain't much to look at, and I might be a tad ignorant like you say, but I'm a hard worker and hold up my end of things best I can."

Amanda laid her hand on her throat, lowering her eyes.

"What are you saying?"

"Well, I was thinking," he said, staring at the doorknob. "I mean, might we go out sometime, you know, to the Corner Cafe or something?" Putting his hat on, he shrugged. "But just 'cause I was thinking it don't make it so. I mean, a pretty girl like yourself has to be careful, and folks might wonder, might talk. I'm used to it, having growed up this way, but I could see where it could be hard for a person like yourself."

"You promise to behave? You know things didn't go so well last time you went to the Corner Cafe."

"Oh, that," he said, ducking his head. "Ma made me promise not to drink with Hook Runyon no more. She's afraid I'll wind up like Spark Dugan. Ma thinks the Nazis killed Spark Dugan, but then she thinks they been stealing our chickens out of our barn, too. It's a fear comes from Cinch and Rollins fighting Germans. I guess she's ignorant that way."

"I'd love to have dinner with you."

"You would?"

"Yes. When?"

"Saturday?"

Turning back to her books, she said, "See you then."

He couldn't remember crossing the compound, or washing the stack of bread pans, or taking the inventory. So blinded was he that he missed lunch altogether, not realizing that everyone had gone until he returned the pans to the bakery. By midafternoon his head had cleared, and the reality of Amanda's approval settled into him with a warm glow.

At break time, he pilfered a pie apple and a handful of pecans from Supply, eating them in the shade of the footbridge. The sun hung in the blue sky.

Corporal Schubert ducked his head under the bridge, "May I join you?" he asked.

Flipping the apple core into the drain, Runt reached for his cigarettes, offering one to Corporal Schubert.

"Have a smoke?"

"Thanks," he said, crawling under. "It's quiet here."

"Suits me," Runt said, lighting Schubert's cigarette and then his own. "Them guards peering down my neck all day wears thin after awhile, and I ain't even a prisoner."

Corporal Schubert drew on his cigarette, his hand cupped against the wind. The front of his shirt was covered with flour. Drawing his knees into his arms, he dropped his head as if deep in thought. A ladybug clambered across his hand, testing its wings before lifting away.

"Runt," he said, without looking up, "you ever think about dying?"

Leaning on an elbow, Runt drummed his fingers against his skull.

"I think on it sometimes," he said. "I figure it's not something I want to do."

Corporal Schubert looked up at him, his eyes the color of turquoise, the exact color of a ring Runt saw once down at Rawland's pawnshop.

"It's too bad we didn't know each other before this war," he said.

Squashing his cigarette out on the bottom of his shoe, Runt nodded.

"I would've liked that just fine. I ain't had that many friends in my day."

"Did you know that there's a prisoner cemetery here, a place not so far away?"

Runt nodded. "Down by the slough."

Pinching off the coal of his cigarette, Corporal Schubert field-stripped the butt, scattering the tobacco into the wind.

"Where the effluent dumps into the Salt Fork River. I've been there on burial detail. It's a lonely place. Someday no one will know they're there. No one will come to their graves." Encircling his knees with his arms, he leaned forward. "If I was to die, maybe you'd come, show your kids where the German soldier you once knew is buried. Maybe you'd come and smoke a cigarette."

"One day this war's going to end," Runt said.

Climbing from under the bridge, Corporal Schubert leaned back in.

"You're right about that, and I hope you're there to see it, my friend."

Runt watched Corporal Schubert climb the steps two at a time to the dock. At the top, he turned.

"Hey," he called, "did you know I'm a champion gymnast back in Germany?"

"Yeah, and I was a ballerina before I took this here prison-cook job," Runt said, laughing.

Lifting onto his hands, Corporal Schubert walked across the

dock, waving his feet in the air as he disappeared through the bakery door.

Even though the order that rose from the compound was in German, Runt recognized it. No matter how hard the day or how hot the sun, the roll call came at the same exact time and with the same exact precision. Colonel Hoffmann, his hands clasped at his back, walked the tattered lines, stopping at each prisoner, examining him at length for violations.

Hanging up his apron, Runt made one last check of the inventory. The bakery was empty, as he knew it would be. Checking inventory was easier after the building cleared for formation.

What with Amanda's accepting his invitation, it had been a good day, and he whistled as he finished up the inventory check. He looked forward to quitting time, a quick stop over at Hook Runyon's, and then a date coming up with the most beautiful girl in all of the county.

Hook stood at the door, an unlit cigarette in his mouth.

"Come on in, Runt," he said.

"Figured you might be running low," Runt said, holding out the shine.

"Set it on the table and help yourself to a glass. You look like you need it."

Pulling up a chair, he said, "Thanks the same, Hook."

Hook opened the shine and poured himself a shot, holding it up to the light before taking a sip.

"Quality. What I owe you?"

"I ain't one for charging the law for goods."

Taking out a bill, Hook slipped it into Runt's shirt pocket.

"I pay my way, Runt. You know that."

Pouring tobacco in the Bugler machine, Runt rolled a cigarette. Old *National Geographic* magazines, *Reader's Digest*s, and Louis L'Amour books littered the table. An ashtray and an empty glass with lipstick on its rim sat on a stack of photographs.

Taking a sip of shine, Hook looked out the window. An elevator rat dashed from the doorway and into the tumbleweeds that grew along the siding. From atop the elevator, an owl watched on, its head cocked.

Taking a drink of the shine, Hook held up his cup. "Sure you won't have a short one? I'm buying."

"No thanks," he said. "I got things to do, Hook."

Runt picked up the photographs that Hook had brought home, flipping through them, tossing them onto the table one by one. His stomach knotted at the picture of the severed arm against the tracks, its fingers curled, and then the one of Spark Dugan's crumpled body. He found a photo of Spark's coal bucket. He found one with the car number, RD 32, showing and another with the door seal still secured. One photo showed the ice-bunker drains and the bits of bone and flesh that had been crushed away under the wheel carriage. Another was of the ice deck, the flood lamps like bursts of fire in the morning darkness.

"I appreciate the cash, Hook. It's hard times out to the farm," he said, "what with Pa gone like he is and with Cinch and Rollins fighting Germans over to Africa. My regular customers have cut back on goods, and the grass is dried up with the drought. Essie and Billy Joe got more needs than before, too, now that they're getting older."

Pulling at his lip, Runt studied the last photo, shaking his finger at it.

"I'll be," he said. "See that one there, that one up on the ice deck?"

Taking the photo, Hook held it to the light. "Is that a man walking on his hands?"

"That's Corporal Schubert. I watched him do that this very day on the bakery loading dock."

"You certain it's Schubert?"

"He's the only German I know walks on his hands. 'Course, there's a good many Germans I ain't met yet."

Hook took a hard pull at the shine and watched the owl dip through the sky, plucking the elevator rat from the tumbleweeds with its talons, banking away on the warm currents that rose from the valley floor.

"The soldier peddling black-market goods under the ice deck walked on his hands, Runt. You remember?"

Runt sprinkled tobacco in the Bugler, rolling himself a cigarette, tucking it behind his ear.

"I found three hundred pounds of flour missing the other day on inventory check," he said. "Corporal Schubert told me he burned a batch of bread. You can't help but wonder."

Hook sipped the shine, letting its warmth roll over him. "You care to hire out your pickup? Come along as my driver while I chase down a few details? I couldn't pay much, but I think I could get the railroad to kick in for expenses, if you'd be willing to wait for the paperwork to go through."

Stacking the photographs to the side, Runt donned his hat.

"Sure. I could do that."

"Good. Come by Sunday as soon as you can get loose. Now, how about a shot of this busthead before you go? It's sure to warm your heart and stiffen your shorts."

"Got myself a date with Amanda Roswell, and she's a sight prettier than you, meaning no offense. Anyways, last time I drank busthead with you, I got put upon by elevator rats, two crooks, and a plague of red ants. I reckon there's easier ways of spending the time," he said, smiling, as he closed the door behind him.

# 22

MA WRAPPED THE tablecloth around Runt's neck and combed back his hair.

"I swear," she said. "Where you get all these red curls?"

"If you don't know, who would?" Runt said.

She whacked him on the shoulder and ran the clippers up the side of his head. "Shame on you, Runt Wallace."

"Don't cut it too high, Ma."

Picking up the scissors and comb, she thinned out some of the mop that hung over his eyes and let the clumps fall into his lap.

"Since when did you get so particular about haircuts?" she said.

"A man's got a right to look best he can. It's good for his career."

Billy Joe scooted down the kitchen cabinet and looked up at Runt.

"Pretty is as pretty does," he said.

"I ain't licked you yet this week," Runt said. "Maybe it's time."

Billy Joe grinned and pulled the hair on Runt's leg.

"Ouch," he said. "Hurry up, Ma. I got to go cut me a switch."

"Hold still, Runt, 'fore you lose an ear."

Essie wiped off the last dish, lifted on her toes, and slid it into the cabinet.

"I hear he's got a girlfriend, Ma."

Ma stopped cutting. "Who?"

"Runt," she said. "Bab Ringle said everyone knows."

"Be quiet, Essie," Runt said. "Or you'll be next for a lickin'."

Ma walked around and looked at Runt. "Is that a fact?"

"It's a black lie. You just shut up, Essie."

"Ain't, either," Essie said. "Bab said Harold Beasley saw you talking to Amanda Roswell at the POW camp, your eyeballs hanging out all goggle-eyed like a sick calf."

"Bab Ringle's got a green wrist from wearing a copper bracelet, and she ain't even got arthritis," Runt said.

Ma hooked her hand under Runt's chin to level his head. "You been hanging around that girl, Runt?"

"No, I ain't been hanging around no girl."

Ma finished clipping up the back of his neck and blew the loose hair off his shoulders.

"I saw you laying out them new overalls, and I figure they ain't for advancing your career as a prison cook, neither."

"Well, what if they ain't?" he said. "A man's got a right to a little privacy."

"Who is this Amanda?"

"She works in the camp library. I went to grade school with her before the war came along."

"There," Ma said, rolling the hair up in the cloth. "You look a sight better if I do say so."

"We're going to the Corner Cafe today," he said. "I'll be needing the truck for a while."

"Runt's got a girlfriend. Runt's got a girlfriend," Billy Joe said.

"You hush. You want to carry out the pot all week?" Ma said.

Billy Joe slipped out the door, poked his head back and around, and stuck out his tongue behind Ma's back.

Essie dried off her hands and looped the dish towel through the cabinet pull.

"Her daddy works for old man Favor," she said. "They live in a mansion."

"That would be two trips in one week with the truck," Ma said.

"I got a cash job now, and I'm doing a little extra work for Hook," Runt said.

When Runt came out, he was wearing his new overalls. He'd slicked back his hair and smelled of Colgate Aftershave Talc. Ma had Essie braiding up the latest batch of wool rags while she stitched in the rug.

"I'll be back soon," Runt said.

Ma slipped the needle and thread into her dress collar.

"Runt, I got something needs to be said. I wouldn't say it did I not think it important."

Runt pulled up a chair. "Okay, Ma," he said.

"You know what an Okie is, don't you?"

"I guess everybody knows that."

"People don't call you that because of where you live. It's what they think you are. Well, maybe that *is* what we are. Maybe you ought to know that because a good many folk look down on it."

"Amanda says that we all got smarts and that folks knowing how to survive is a thing to be proud of."

"You take a hard look in the mirror. Ask yourself what you see. Now, I wouldn't hurt you for the world, but others will. Do you know what I'm saying?"

"I've looked in that mirror plenty," he said. "I guess I know better than anyone what looks back. But Amanda don't see what I see, and she don't see what you see."

"I hope you're right, Runt."

"Take Hook Runyon," he said. "No one talks about him, how his arm's gone, and he ain't got nothing but a hook now. No one says he ain't the best goddang yard dog in the country. If they do say it, it's only once."

"You keep a little aside for yourself. Keep a little against the world, and those who would break your heart."

Runt walked to the window and looked out. "You think Hook Runyon keeps a little against the world, Ma?" he asked.

Ma took out her needle and slid it through the rug with a sweep of her hand.

Runt grubbed out the pickup, tossing the hammer with the broken claw in the back and throwing a rubber mat over the hole in the floor. As he pulled out of the yard, he waved at Ma, Billy Joe, and Essie, all sitting on the front porch. Billy Joe grinned and waved, but Ma wiped at her eyes with her dress tail before going back into the house.

About a mile down the road, he pulled over and gathered up a handful of wild daisies that grew in abundance near the creek. Though the blossoms were small, they were bright as snow and smelled of the wild.

When he pulled into the drive of Favor's mansion, his heart ticked up like a wound clock. Trees lined the road, towering up into the sky, and the mansion loomed ahead. His old pickup rattled and smoked and hitched along, a broken-down old wreck no better than himself. Maybe Ma had been right. Maybe a man ought know where he belonged.

The Favor limousine sat in front of the cottage, a mile-long Cadillac as big as Hanson's meat wagon. Runt pulled alongside it and shut off his engine. She loped a couple times and settled out. He wiped his palms on his overalls and gathered up the daisies. A honey bee clambered out of a blossom and buzzed off toward Favor's gardens.

He rang the doorbell and stepped back. A man with a bald pate answered the door. He lacked the tan of the men Runt knew, the look of the field and of backbreaking work.

"Yes?" he said.

"Miss Amanda Roswell," Runt said.

The man turned. "Amanda, there's a deliveryman here with flowers."

"Oh, hi, Runt," Amanda said, stepping to the door. Her black hair shimmered like oil on water, and her eyes snapped like matches.

"Daddy this is Runt Wallace. He works out at the camp. We're going to go over to the Corner Cafe."

"Do something with these flowers," her daddy said.

Amanda took the flowers from Runt. Her hands were small like a child's hands and as white as marble.

"They smell wonderful," she said, burying her nose in them.

"Sit down, Mr. Wallace," her father said. "Tell me, what you do at the camp?"

"I'm in the bakery," he said. "They've got food enough out there to make a man cry."

"*Runt?*" he said. "A peculiar name."

"Yes, sir," Runt said, looking at his shoes. He could see a clop of cow manure stuck against the heel. He put his foot down. "I guess it might be, hearing it for the first time and all. Days go by, and I hardly notice it myself."

"How is it you came by such a name?"

"I was the smallest of the litter, you might say. Ma always said I'm damn lucky someone didn't pinch my head off."

Her father looked over at Amanda, who had arranged the daisies in an amber vase.

"My brothers are fighting Germans in the war," Runt said. "I stayed home to take care of chores and the family. They said a man with my legs couldn't run fast enough, but I can run like a mustang when I need. I beat Jacob Saul's bull to the front porch by a length."

"Come on, Runt," Amanda said. "Let's go before the Saturday crowd."

"I don't mean to be impertinent," Amanda's father said, "but exactly what are your intentions?"

Runt looked over at Amanda. "Well, I intend to have the liver and onions. They're half-price on the weekend, but Amanda can have anything she wants."

Her father turned and rolled his eyes.

"We better go," Amanda said, opening the door.

"Perhaps I should take you in the limo." her father said.

"No," Amanda said. "We're going in Runt's pickup. I'll see you later."

After they'd eaten, they drove out by the POW camp to watch the prisoners playing soccer. Amanda rolled her window down and let the wind lift her hair.

"Don't pay any attention to my father," she said. "He's very protective."

"Oh, I don't blame him for nothing," he said. "I sometimes laugh at myself."

Amanda looked in her purse for her lipstick. Adjusting his mirror, she drew the tube over her lips with a painter's stroke.

Dropping it back into her purse, she turned and said, "Don't talk about yourself that way, Runt. I don't like it.

"I'd like to meet your family," she said. "It's a pretty day. Why don't we drive out there?"

He glanced over at her. The sun flashed in her eyes, and she smiled, a smile so sweet that he could hardly breathe.

"Amanda, I think you're about as nice a person as I've ever known and as pretty as pretty, too. But I don't know. I mean, what would your father say and . . ."

"I don't think this has anything to do with my father," she said.

Runt looked out into the prairie. "You see," he said, "my family's had to get by. I mean what with Cinch and Rollins gone and then the Depression. There's just Ma and me and the kids. Sometimes we can't do . . . sometimes we can't always buy the things to make it so nice."

"What do you think of me, Runt Wallace?" she asked. "I don't judge a person by what he has or doesn't have."

"I don't mean nothing against you, Amanda. It's just the way of things."

"Well?" she said.

Runt fixed his mirror and glanced over at her. She looked at him for his answer.

"It's a fair ride out there," he said.


When Runt pulled into the yard, Essie and Billy Joe came climbing down from the cottonwood that grew on the creek bank. Ma stepped to the screen door, which hung a little loose where the doorframe had given way. Her face darkened when she saw Runt wasn't alone.

Amanda slid out and slipped her arm through his. "Don't forget to introduce me," she said.

Ma stood at the stove, the needle and thread still in her dress collar, her hair spilled across her eyes.

"Ma, this is Amanda Roswell," Runt said. "We came home to meet you and the kids."

Ma brushed the front of her dress and pushed the hair back out of her eyes.

"Land's sake," she said. "I'd have put on a clean dress."

"I love your farm," Amanda said. "You can see clear to Kansas out here."

Ma nodded. "Sometimes on a summer night the stars near poke you in the eye."

Essie and Billy Joe busted through the door. Billy Joe had his boots on the wrong feet, and both of Essie's knees were covered with mud.

"This here is Billy Joe," Runt said, "and Essie there. She'll be graduating out of the eighth pretty soon."

"Hello, Billy Joe. Hello, Essie," Amanda said. "I love your hair."

Essie ran her fingers through her hair. "It's not nearly so red as Runt's," she said.

"But like a girl's," Amanda said, smiling.

Essie locked her fingers behind her back. "Runt's is the color of barn paint," she said.

"Exactly what I thought, too," Amanda said. "Yours is more like a ruby ring I had once."

"Mine's the color of a carrot," Billy Joe said.

"But you got your ma's eyes," Amanda said.

Billy Joe smiled and glanced over at his ma's eyes. "The color of a bluejay," he said.

"Exactly."

"Could we walk your place, Runt?" Amanda asked.

"It's just an ole farm," he said.

"I'd like to see it."

"Well, we could go down Dead Man Creek. It's cool there this time of year."

Billy Joe sat down on the floor to switch his boots.

"I'll show you my hideout," he said. "Ain't no girl ever seen it before."

"You kids stay here," Ma said. "Go feed the chickens."

"Aw, Ma," Billy Joe said.

"Get," she said. "Then come back here."

Runt and Amanda walked the creek, jumping over where it narrowed. Amanda followed behind as he held branches back so they wouldn't swat her in the face. He showed her where the muscadine climbed nearly to the top of a tree and where the coyotes had polished the bones of the ole milk cow that died after ingesting a hunk of barbed wire. They sat on the bank in the shade and watched a crawdad poke its head out of its mud castle. Runt could feel the heat of her leg against his.

"Your dad made shine on this place, didn't he?" she asked. "Maybe in these very woods where there's lots of good water."

Runt's face flushed. "It's a hardscrabble farm," he said.

"I always heard that no man made better."

"Sometimes pride in work is all a man has," he said.

Amanda slipped her hand into his. "You remember that when you talk to my father, Runt. You remember that and understand."

He turned her hand over, so white and soft against the brown and callus of his own hand.

"What do you mean?"

"My mother left my dad for another man when I was little," she said. "It nearly broke him. He grew kind of cold and hard after that. Sometimes when he looks at me even now, I can tell he's thinking of her."

Runt looked up the canyon to where the gypsum cave lay hidden in the bushes. He helped Amanda to her feet.

"We better go back," he said. "It will be dark by the time you get home."

"Runt," she said, taking his arm. "Sometimes I say more than I should."

"Ma says there are times a man has to set a little aside so he can go on and face things. Maybe it's his way of settin' a little aside from the world. No man will ever hear it from me."

Ma invited Amanda to stay for supper: pancakes, scrambled eggs, and homemade sugar syrup, but Amanda said she had to get on back, said she'd like to come some other day and work on the rag rug. Essie followed at Amanda's heels out to the truck. Runt started up and checked the fuel gauge. There'd be enough to get Amanda home, but he wasn't sure about getting himself back.

"Wait a minute," Amanda said, looking in her purse and then rolling down her window. "Essie," she said. "I just love this new color of lipstick. Have you tried it yet?" Essie shook her head. "Here," she said, "give it a try and let me know what you think. Put just a little on with your finger. A girl as pretty as you has to be careful not to use too much."

Runt pulled into the drive of the Favor cottage. The limo was gone, and the mansion loomed dark and foreboding in the moonlight. He walked Amanda to the door of the cottage. She turned and took his hand.

"I had a wonderful time, Runt," she said. "And the daisies were beautiful."

"Me, too," he said. "And thanks for making Essie feel special. It don't happen so much for her."

Amanda lifted on her toes and kissed him. A tingle shot out his fingers. "Good night," she said.

Runt drove home with the gas gauge bouncing on empty. He'd stop at the gas well near Four Corners and steal a little drip. Sometimes it had water or oil in it, which fouled up the plugs.

Tomorrow he had to deal with Hook's business, a task that could turn dangerous from what he'd been hearing. But tonight nothing could dampen his spirits. Tonight he could walk to the end of the earth or catch a thousand Germans without so much as a care.

# 23

Hook SAT ON the steps of the caboose nursing a cup of coffee when Runt pulled in. Dust bellowed up from the wheels and drifted off down the tracks. Tossing the last of the coffee into the dirt, Hook eased up, waiting for the whirl in his head to subside.

"Whoa," Runt said, propping his elbow out the window. "Is there still time for an ambulance or you just want me to call the digger?"

"I want you to stop making busthead out of kerosene," Hook said, opening the pickup door.

Easing the shift into neutral, Runt waited as Hook climbed in.

"You ain't supposed to drink the whole dang quart at once. It's sipping whiskey, like rare brandy, you know."

Hook looked up through his brows as he settled in.

"It has to be swilled with branch water to keep your heart from stalling, you outlaw."

Double-clutching into first, Runt circled around the elevator and out onto the road. After waiting for Hook to light a cigarette, he shoved open the wing window and rested his foot on the clutch pedal. Dust seeped in and drifted up the columns of light that struck through the window.

"I smell drip gas," Hook said.

"No, sir," Runt said. "That's against the law."

"And it might freeze up your engine, too, just in case you didn't know."

"We can drive around all day if you want," Runt said. "But maybe you could say where we are going."

"Waynoka yards," Hook said, rubbing at his whiskers, "if you think this rattletrap will make it."

"Beats hopping the southbound and listening to Frenchy's fishing stories, don't it?"

As they drove past the Favor carriage house, each fell silent in his own thoughts.

"How did that date go last night?" Hook asked, as the house disappeared behind them.

Slowing for the track crossing, Runt shifted into second. Blue smoke boiled from the exhaust when he dropped it into high.

"Spent Ma's coffee money," he said. "And then took Amanda out to the farm. This morning at breakfast Ma threatened to kill me and feed me to the hogs. Said she'd sell the both of them for a pound of good coffee and forget I was ever born. On top of that I forgot to check on them Rhode Island Reds. Guess that date near cost me my life."

"What's a Rhode Island Red?"

Frowning, Runt looked over at him. "Well it sure ain't the capital of the United States."

"What is it then?" Hook asked, rubbing at the pain mounting between his eyes.

"It's a chicken what lays brown eggs. Everybody knows that."

"That shine of yours has eaten up all my brain," Hook said, "not to mention my liver."

"You're just ignorant, that's all, 'cause you ain't took time to study chickens."

"Are you going to tell me about your date, or are you going to keep on about Rhode Island chickens all day?"

"I couldn't take my eyes off her the whole time, and when I had to climb up on the footrail to get my change, she didn't laugh or nothing. She just waited quiet as you please with my hat in her hand. I tell you, I ain't never had anyone treat me like a real person before, other than you, or maybe Simmons when he's got a load on."

Slowing down for a pothole, Runt pumped the clutch and spun the steering wheel in his hands.

"And when I took her home, she said she'd really enjoyed herself. And because we wouldn't be able to see each other much at work, maybe we could do it all over again. So, we got another date set up.

"It's a wonder, ain't it," he said, shaking his head, "a bona fide marvel that such a girl could look at me and see something other than what I am. I don't even care 'cause I'm a happy man no matter what happens for the rest of my life."

Pushing a can of nails over, Hook rubbed the fumes from his eyes.

"Don't underestimate your charm. You've winning ways and wisdom for someone breathing drip fumes and drinking that pop-skull his whole life."

At the depot, Hook climbed out, slamming the door twice before the latch took. A train idled on the main track, the engine hissing as it waited for the crew change. From the windows, passengers watched on at the world outside.

"You want me to come in with you, Hook?"

"Find some shade. I might be awhile."

Inside, Joe, the operator, hunkered over his ledger, his swivel chair slid forward under the desk.

"There are no escapees in here," he said, "'cause they're all riding the trains, which is where yard dogs are supposed to be."

"I need to make a call, Joe, providing I don't disturb your nap."

"It's over there," he said, pointing with his pencil, "and keep it short. I got important calls coming in from Chicago."

"Right," he said, calling up Eddie Preston.

The phone rang twice before Preston came online.

"Security," he said. "Regional Division."

"Eddie, this is Hook Runyon."

A moment passed before he spoke. "Runyon, where the hell are you?"

"Jamaica. Where you think?"

"Where the hell you been? There's more pickpockets than passengers coming out of Kansas City. The Chicago office has chewed my ass into the quick, and it's getting real tiresome. Just when you figure on doing something about it?"

"Soon. I been kind of busy, Eddie. Listen," he said, shifting the phone to the other ear, lighting a cigarette, "I'm putting Runt Wallace on expenses for his truck."

"What the hell you talking about?"

"I need an assistant and a truck for getting around for a few days."

"Goddang it, I'm a Baldwin-Felts graduate with twenty years' experience, and I don't have an assistant."

"A man with your ability doesn't need one. What do you say?"

"You're blowing smoke again, Runyon, and it just ain't going to work."

"Just a few days, and then I'll nail those pickpockets. That's a promise."

"You still working that indigent case? I can smell it from here. I thought I told you to close that out."

"Just a few more days, Eddie. I wouldn't want anything to come back on you. I mean, it needs to be cleaned up. I think there's more here than just an accident, and I wouldn't want it said that the railroad covered it up. The whole thing could come back on Security. It wouldn't be good."

Hook could hear breathing on the other end of the line.

"To the end of the week, you hear," Eddie said. "After that, no more. I want that case filed by the end of the week."

"I'll send the paperwork on Runt Wallace. You're a fine example of the Baldwin-Felts tradition, Eddie. I'll be talking to you."

Swinging around in his chair, Joe put his feet on the desk, locking his fingers behind his head.

"I don't know how you get by with it, Hook. Eddie Preston is the biggest prick in the division, and you lead him around like a pet duck."

"Never underestimate a man's ego, Joe." From the window, Hook watched the passenger train pull out. "Listen, would you mind checking some ice schedules for me?"

"Ice schedules?"

"I need to know what the schedule is for RD 32 out of Oceanside, the one that ran over Spark Dugan."

"Dang it, Hook, I'd have to go back and look it up. I've got a GFX headed in here out of Albuquerque, not to mention a freighter sitting on the siding out to Belva, and you want me to look up an old icing schedule?"

Slapping him on the shoulder, Hook said, "Hell, Joe, a man of your abilities could handle twice that many and never break a sweat."

Joe looked up at him, grinning. "You got yourself another pet duck, you bastard."

"Thanks, Joe."

Pulling a ledger off the shelf, Joe ran his finger down the page.

"Here it is, RD 32, cabbage out of Oceanside, California, destination, Camp Alva spur. Scheduled for re-icing right here, the Way-noka ice plant."

Hook walked to the window. Tracks led off into the yards like strings on a piano. Runt had parked the pickup under the shade of a catalpa, both doors open.

"You mean it came all the way from Oceanside only to be re-iced here for the last twenty miles of the trip?" Hook asked.

"That's what it says," he said, shrugging.

"Do me a favor, will you, Joe?"

"What, another? Ain't you going to bullshit me first?"

"I figure you're above all that."

"I surrender," he said. "What do you want?"

"Look in one of those books of yours and tell me when the next reefer is scheduled for the Camp Alva spur."

Taking down another ledger, Joe flipped through the pages, his glasses sliding onto the end of his nose.

"Here's one, RD 114, cabbage, out of Oceanside, destination, Camp Alva, just a few days off. It's scheduled for the GFX Extra 5003."

"What time?"

"Four in the morning."

"Is she scheduled for re-icing anywhere?"

"At the Waynoka yards. Now, suppose you could go away? I got trains to run."

"I'm on my way, Ducky," he said, pushing Joe's glasses back up on his nose with his finger.

Runt snored under his hat, his leg hanging out the window. Hook pulled the hair on his leg.

"Ouch!" he said, banging his head on the steering wheel. "Why does everyone pull the hair on my leg?"

"Come on, Wallace," Hook said. "You're on railroad time now. Napping is for moonshiners and bureaucrats."

"Thought you'd left town," he said, rubbing his head, "or died."

"Those reefer cars were scheduled for icing right here in the Waynoka yards. It just doesn't make any sense. Why would they ice a reefer twenty miles from its destination, and why would the cabbage spoil before it got there?"

"Them bunker walls were warm," Runt said, "and that cabbage was damn sure spoiled, that much I know."

"Maybe it wasn't iced at the point of origin, Runt. Maybe it came across that desert with no ice at all."

# 24

Taking the checkout box down from the shelf, Reina examined the file cards and sipped at the black coffee she'd scrounged from the mess. The box was stuffed. Camp Alva may have housed the most dangerous Nazis in the war, but they were a well-read lot and ever hungry for more. The demand for new material overwhelmed both Amanda and her and sent the local post office into a tizzy. The English class, too, had filled to capacity, and she'd given serious thought to opening another section on Wednesday nights.

After Amanda came back with the new books, Reina categorized the checkouts by military rank. The officers, as had been the case all along, were doing most of the reading. A tenet among military propagandists held that the educated were the most susceptible to propaganda. The more subtle and complex the presentation, the more effective its course among the bright and the curious. Most of the titles were directed to this very population. As it turned out, mental gaming could be dangerous to one's beliefs. It was certainly proving to be the case at Camp Alva. Her next task would be to group the checkouts by topic to see what interests were represented.

When finished with the cards, she searched out Amanda, who stood on a stool shelving the new titles.

"How many did we get in?" she asked.

"Five," Amanda said, "and a pamphlet entitled *A Brief History of the States.*"

"Sounds exciting," Reina said, pulling up a chair. "I've coffee left over there. Would you like some before things turn busy?"

Amanda poured herself a cup and sat Indian style on the floor, leaning against the shelves, sipping her coffee.

"It will definitely keep me awake," she said, squinting an eye.

Outside, the work trucks lined up at the gate, the clatter of engines, the smell of fumes, the shout of orders as the prisoners climbed aboard for transport to the job sites. As news from the front had grown more grim each day, Reina sensed a change among the prisoners, a melancholy settling into the camp. A crack had opened in the dam, incontrovertible evidence that the war might be lost. Even the most ardent could no longer deny it.

"Have you started the Faulkner book I gave you?" Reina asked.

Setting her cup down, Amanda wiped at her brow. "Whew," she said, "not easily won."

"*As I Lay Dying* is less difficult than some," Reina said. "Faulkner is never easy, though, but good things rarely are."

"It's the lack of direction," Amanda said, "of having to trust that the answer is there somewhere among the words just waiting to be discovered. It's like turning yourself over to a dream, and not always a pleasant one."

"Good insight. It's called stream of consciousness, the proposition that the mind makes associations at a level that is not always concrete or obvious. You see, if that's true, then Faulkner could, theoretically at least, transcend normal levels of communication, and who knows what might lurk in such realms."

"Rather scary when you think about it," Amanda said.

"If it's true. But I suppose that remains to be seen. What surprises me is how quickly these prisoners comprehend the abstraction that Faulkner necessarily brings to the material."

Listening to the trucks pull out, Amanda shrugged. "I think maybe that evil and stupidity are not always the same thing."

"You are a wise girl to be so young."

"Maybe wisdom and age are not the same thing, either," she said, smiling.

"With age you only learn how to wait," Reina said, "and to temper hope with reality."

"I hope enough for everyone," Amanda said.

Reina lifted her brows. "So, when are you going to tell me?"

"Tell you what?"

"I hear that Runt Wallace asked you out for a date."

"Who told you that?"

"Well, just everyone, I guess."

"He's nice," Amanda said, shrugging

"And?"

"We went out, that's all. Talked. I like to talk to him, you know. He makes me feel good."

"Yes?"

"He's sensitive, and he's been hurt a lot in his life. I can understand that. I know about his folks, too, about the moonshine and all. Everyone around here knows, I suppose, but I don't care. They've had to get by best they could, that's all."

Standing, Reina flipped through the new titles, stacking them next to the card catalog.

"Well, not that it matters, but I happen to agree with you, and I think you've made a fine friend in Runt Wallace, although I do wish we could do something about his name."

Flashing a smile, Amanda swirled the dregs in the bottom of her cup.

"And what about you?"

"Me?"

"You and Hook Runyon?"

"What do you mean?"

"Well, just everyone around here knows."

Pulling up to the desk, Reina sat down and folded her hands.

"His voice is gentle, and he makes me feel special, like he's listening to me every second, like nothing is more important than what I'm saying or what I'm feeling at that very moment. There's not many who can do that, who can remove themselves long enough to listen."

"Wow," Amanda said.

"He has this focus, you know, this ability to tune out everything, to center on something."

"Everything a good detective should have, I would think."

"And he laughs easily," Reina said, smiling, "and he hides his arm, not from shame, but to protect other people from their own embarrassment. There's something very brave about him."

"You are taken, without a doubt."

"And he collects books. Can you believe it? Rare books. His caboose is running over with them. And he gives back rubs, too," she said, winking, "memorable back rubs."

"Oh," Amanda said, blushing. "But there is one thing that simply must be addressed."

"And what would that be?"

"His name, actually. Hook? I mean, really."

"Well, the problem has already been addressed, thank you. His name is Walter."

"Yes," Amanda said. "Walter is much better."

"And now that's all settled," Reina said. "We must get these books cataloged before the war ends."

After lunch, Reina read the editorial page of the camp paper, making note of the latest complaint of the prisoners, reading between the lines for innuendo and inference, relying on her own intuition, giving it rein to take her where it wanted to go. Given the proper analysis, the editorial page opened a window into the psyche of the prisoners. Much to the chagrin of the intelligence community, it turned out that the humanities types, like herself, did the best job with this kind of analysis. Much to their chagrin, the military took backseat, and it gave her no small amount of pleasure in the doing.

When Amanda finished checking books, she joined Reina on the front porch of the library, where she was smoking a cigarette. They watched the prisoners play soccer in the nearby field, their bodies glistening with sweat as they yelled, laughed, and argued over the rules.

Squashing out her cigarette, Reina said, "Amanda, I've received a report from Major Dunfield. It was accompanied by some very disturbing photographs."

Looking up, Amanda lifted her brows. "Oh?"

"I had made up my mind not to show them to you just yet, but I think I better. You see, the military has uncovered some pretty horrible things that have taken place, pretty horrible indeed."

Rubbing the sweat from her hands, she began again.

"The Factory has made the decision to show these atrocities to the prisoners. It's a dose of that reality we were talking about, and I guess there's no way of protecting anyone from it anymore, not even you."

"I see. And you have these photos?"

"Yes. The rest will come in the form of newsreel and will be shown to the general population at the appropriate time. Most of it was shot in liberated German concentration camps. It's appalling stuff. To tell you the truth, I'm uncertain what effect it's going to have."

"I think I should know what's going on in any case," Amanda said.

"That's what I've decided as well. Come with me."

Retrieving the report from the desk drawer, she laid out the photos one by one: the mass graves, the stacks of decayed bodies, the emaciated prisoners clinging to one another for support, their eyes haunted and hopeless in a world too ghastly to comprehend.

Amanda covered her mouth with her hand, her face drained of blood.

"It can't be real," she said.

"And these," Reina said, showing her the lists, "page after page of stolen property, pillaged from these very same people, from their homes, from their collections, from their museums. 'Degenerate art' they call it. Look at these: Delacroix, Corot, Millet, Manet, Renoir, Seurat, Picasso. The list goes on and on. All taken under the auspices of Hitler and the Third Reich Chamber of Culture. Most of it went to Switzerland to be smuggled onto the open market.

"Here's the Rothschild collection in Vienna, four thousand of the world's greatest paintings. Gone. All gone. Sold to the highest bidder to support the Linz, Hitler's personal gallery, or to his henchmen, Göring and Goebbels. It's an atrocity second only to the brutal extermination of the owners."

Amanda walked to the window, her arms clamped about her. Outside on the soccer field, the prisoners roared in laughter.

"Surely they will be destroyed," she said.

"They are out there, out there on that soccer field."

"Reina, I'm sorry. It must be especially terrible for you."

"It's nothing compared to what these people have endured. Now, you go on home. I'll finish up here and walk in. It will do me good. We can talk more about this later if you want."

Reina stood at the window and watched Amanda make her way out the front gate. Gathering up the photos, she tossed them into the desk drawer.

When the knock at the door came, she whirled about. A young prisoner stood in the doorway, hat in hand.

"Dr. Kaplan?"

"Yes," she said, her heart thumping. "What is it?"

"There's a call for you at the headquarters building."

"Oh," she said. "Thank you. I'll be right there."

When she reached the office, the secretary drummed her fingers against the desk.

"It's long-distance," she said.

"Would you mind if I take it in private?"

Shrugging, the secretary picked up her purse. "I've finished for the day anyway."

"Thank you," Reina said. "I promise to be brief."

When she'd closed the door, Reina took a deep breath and picked up the phone.

"Dr. Kaplan speaking."

"Reina, this is Robert."

Something heavy dropped inside her. "Robert," she said.

"How are things on the frontier?" he asked.

"What's the matter?"

"I just called to see how you were getting along. I miss you a lot, you know. No one could debate literature like you, Reina."

"The program is coming along fine. There's been some cultural adjustments, but I'm not anything if not tractable."

"You were always a helluva sport."

"Look, I'm on the secretary's phone. Was there something else you wanted?"

"No, no. It's just that I miss you and wish you were here. Why don't you come back, Reina? You and I both know that you're not cut out for that cow-town crap."

Leaning back, Reina listened to Robert's breathing on the other end of the line.

"They fired you?"

"No," he said, pausing. "I quit. It was like being picked to death by chickens."

"So, now you're out of a job."

"It's only temporary. I'll have a job in no time."

"Yes, I'm sure of it. You know what they say about doors closing and opening and all that. Good-bye, Robert, and don't call again," she said, hanging up.


As she walked across the compound, the sun dropped behind the barracks, casting orange into the blue of the prairie sky. Most of the civilians had gone home, and the prisoners gathered at the mess hall for the evening meal.

After locking up the library, she'd walk the distance to Favor Mansion. She'd done it before and found it to be a pleasant experience in the cool of the evening. Robert's call had scrambled her nerves, and she needed something pleasant. Tomorrow she would get a fresh run on things.

A cool breeze lifted the blind on the window of the library as she cleaned the last of the day's work from her desk. Outside, the zing of crickets filled the evening, and the smell of sausage and kraut drifted in from the mess.

A copy of Saroyan's *The Human Comedy* lay on the table. Picking it up, she read an excerpt from the first chapter and was soon in-

volved in the book. When she looked up, the sun had drifted below
the horizon, and shadows stretched across the compound. Laying
the book aside, she rubbed at her eyes. What Saroyan had to say
about war seemed innocent to her now, ingenuous, in the light of
the photos that were in her desk. Still, it was an engaging read and
would serve its purpose with the population.

From somewhere beyond the prison fence, a coyote bayed, its
voice quivering and forlorn in the evening, and from the barracks,
the distant laughter of soldiers.

She smelled his cologne first, and it caused her to turn. From
the shadows of the bookshelves, he stood watching her. The last
of the sunset caught in the lens of his glasses.

"Colonel Hoffmann," she said, standing. "The library is closed."

Locking his hands behind his back, he smiled.

"Surely, you don't think I'm here for your foolish little collection of books, Dr. Kaplan."

"Then why are you here?"

Walking to the window, he stood with his back to her, his fingers interlocked. Even in the dimness of the evening, she could see
the scar that ran from the base of his ear and under his collar.

"I've had a talk with the Swiss Legation about your propaganda
operation here. You are in violation of the Geneva Convention, and
your library will be closed. In the meantime, I would suggest that
you make other arrangements. The Führer does not tolerate degenerate literature, nor those who peddle it."

"The Führer does not run Camp Alva."

Walking over, he leaned onto her desk, lifting his chin until his
eyes locked on to hers. The stink of cologne drenched the room,
draining the oxygen from her lungs, and her head whirled.

"You may hope to be right about that. To be wrong would be a
grave mistake indeed."

Blood rushed into her face, and her ears rang. Reaching into the
drawer, she tossed the photos on the table.

"What audacity to talk of degeneracy in the face of this. How dare you threaten me."

Beyond the prison, the coyote lifted its voice. Colonel Hoffmann picked up the pictures. Studied them. Laid them back down in the exact order he'd picked them up.

"Such things are necessary," he said.

Reina's lip trembled. "You bastard."

Grabbing her, he pulled her to him, his hand digging into the softness of her flesh.

"This is your future," he said, his breath hot and wet against her cheek, "the future of your race."

"I'll have you court-martialed," she said, struggling against his grip.

Pulling her tight against him, he ran his hand up her dress, his fingers of ice and death.

"And we will destroy you," he said, pushing her away, "until the seed of your tribe is no more."

# 25

WHEN HOOK APPROACHED the guard shack, the guard stepped out. A whistle hung about his neck, and his helmet sat cockeyed on his head. He smelled of onion and tobacco, and the signs of missing chevrons were evident on his sleeves.

"State your business," he said.

"I want to see Major Foreman."

"Do you have an appointment?"

"Look," Hook said, "we've been through this routine before. If you insist on an appointment, I shut your little spur down. Times get hard real fast without access to the railroad, and Major Foreman isn't going to like that. Here's my weapon and my pocketknife. I promise not to rile Corporal Marino up there by stepping over his line."

"Anything else?"

The guard scoffed, pushing the sidearm through the window of the guard shack. Opening the gate, he nodded to the tower sentry.

"I'll notify the major's office," he said.

The secretary waved Hook through when he got there, but by the look on her face, Hook knew the major must not be too happy at his arrival.

Major Foreman sat at his desk sifting through a stack of forms. A button on his shirt hung by a single thread over his stomach, and the drink glass on the filing cabinet had the telltale remains of whiskey in the bottom. A board squeaked under Hook's feet, and Major Foreman looked up.

"Well," he said, "if it isn't Special Agent Runyon. Chased down any tractors lately?"

"Lost more prisoners, have you?" he asked.

"Right," he said.

"I'd like to ask a few questions," Hook said.

"You still looking for Spark Dugan's ghost, Runyon?"

"Just a couple of things I needed cleared up. These investigations always take longer than planned."

"Yes, well," he said, sniffing, "I don't know that I have anything to contribute. It seems a railroad matter to me."

"Oh, indeed it is, and I wouldn't bother you at all except for the work party that might have witnessed the whole deal come down."

"There's a good many people I have to answer to, Runyon, the Provost Marshal General, the locals, the Geneva Convention, the Swiss Legation, my own commander. Every church in the country's wanting in to save these bastards' souls. And now, of course, I have the railroad."

Crossing his legs, Hook reached for a cigarette and then remembered the major's objections. Through the window he could see Reina's library, and beyond that, the camp mess.

"You might recall that I found military issue in Spark Dugan's shack."

Rising, the major walked to the file cabinet, turning the empty glass around and around.

"What is it you want? I keep very careful control of supplies around here. I told you that, and since our discussion, I've put a backup check on inventories. These locals put a great deal of pressure on my men. There's bound to be some of that going on."

"I'm sure that's the case, and under most circumstances, I wouldn't be worried about it."

A twitch set up under the major's nose, and he dabbed at it with his handkerchief.

"What do you mean?"

"The problem is that people died, and that's something I can't ignore."

Foreman's face paled, and he sat down. "That had nothing to do with black-marketing, I assure you."

"I have a photo of Corporal Schubert up on the ice deck the night Spark Dugan died. Turns out the German soldier who participated in the little black-marketing scheme under the ice deck could walk on his hands."

"I beg your pardon?"

"You see, Corporal Schubert worked as a professional gymnast back in Germany, a man who could walk on his hands as easily as his feet. Quite a coincidence, isn't it?"

"That's ridiculous."

"All of a sudden the coincidences are a little hard to ignore."

"This is a prisoner-of-war camp, not a prison, and my authority here is limited."

"All I know is that I had a man killed on my turf, and his house has military issue in it. All the while you're sitting behind your desk without a clue, and even if you had a clue, there's nothing you could do about it because you don't want to get involved."

Foreman wiped his forehead with the back of his sleeve. "Mind if I have a drink?" he asked

"Never too early for a drink," Hook said.

Opening the file drawer, he poured himself a drink.

"Would you like one?"

"I'd like one fine."

There were rings of sweat under the major's arms and a tremor in his hand as he poured the drinks. The whiskey would remedy both soon enough.

"I'm going to level with you," Foreman said. "My ass is on the line for losing Fleischer. Another problem I don't need. Maybe there were a few supplies going out here and there at the work sites, nothing big, clothing, groceries.

"Most of it goes to the locals, stuff they can't get anywhere else. Maybe I took a little for myself, just to cut the misery of this goddamn place—nothing big, I swear, nothing to get a man killed over."

Walking to the window, he opened the blinds.

"Corporal Schubert asked to see me. It's unusual for a Kraut to jump the chain of command like that, but he was pretty spooked up. So, I agreed. Things can get rough down there if the wrong guy is crossed.

"At first I thought he had decided to put a little pressure on, to up the take for himself. But the day he came, he kept looking out of this window and talking about how he was just a soldier and how he wanted the war to be over. He didn't say a word about the black-marketing stuff. All the while he keeps looking out this window as if out there the world had just come to an end."

"So what did he want?"

"That's just it. He never did say. Finally, he walked out. Everything I've told you is God's truth."

Rising, Hook finished off his drink. He'd nearly forgotten how smooth good whiskey could be.

"Thanks for the drink."

When Hook got to the door, Major Foreman called after him.

"What are you going to do, Runyon?"

Opening the door, Hook turned. "I'm just a yard dog, but I do know that patience matters in my business. I'm a patient man, Major. See you around."

When Hook rounded the bend, he could see the staff car parked next to the elevator. Reina sat on the front step of the caboose.

"Reina, what are you doing here?" he asked, easing down the grade.

"I asked Amanda for the car so that I might visit. I hope you don't mind."

She held her chin in her hands, and the last rays of sunset glinted in the blackness of her eyes.

"Are you kidding?" he said, taking her hand. "I can't guarantee the condition of my caboose, though. I've been on the go."

"Wait," she said. "I've brought some wine."

"Wine?"

"Yes, wine, you hillbilly."

When she returned with the wine, he unlocked the caboose door, letting her in ahead of him, searching for a match to light the kerosene lantern.

"Sorry about the mess," he said, turning up the wick.

"Sign of a great mind?" she asked.

"Ill breeding."

"Really, you'd think they could get you electricity."

Searching through the cabinet drawer, he came up with a screwdriver and pushed the cork into the bottle.

"About the time they did, I'd be on my way down the track. This way is easier, not to mention cheaper.

"Whoa," he said. "I haven't had wine since I spent the night in a hobo camp in Amarillo. I think it was wine. It might have been in Albuquerque."

"Not French wine, I'd bet," she said, holding out her glass.

"More like early Arkansas."

Sipping on their wine, they watched the sun wobble on the horizon as it melted away. For the longest time neither spoke. Outside, the day cooled, and the frogs down at the river tested their voices for the evening choir.

"It's so quiet here," she said. "You would never know that a war raged, that terrible things were happening to people."

Hook lit a cigarette and listened to the quiet, the distant moo of a cow somewhere beyond the hills. The smell of damp had settled into the valley.

"You're pretty quiet yourself," he said. "Is everything okay?"

She said, "It's just that I sometimes get discouraged with all this business, you know, about the program. Who would have thought that Reina Kaplan would find herself in the middle of the prairie working with a prison full of Nazis. It's ridiculous, isn't it, when you think about it?"

"Not so," he said. "Dr. Reina Kaplan's uprooting evil at its source, in the mind where it sprouts. Kill it there, and it's dead forever. That's noble work."

"I knew I came here for a reason," she said. "And how did your day go?"

"I had the pleasure of talking to your boss, Major Foreman."

"Some day you had."

Outside, the frogs struck up their chorus, and the lantern flickered as a breeze swept through the door.

"Would it surprise you to know that the good major is black-marketing clothing and food supplies to the locals?"

Reina took a drink of wine. A drop clung to her lips. Leaning onto the table, she studied him.

"Are you going to turn him in to the authorities?"

"I haven't decided. There's pretty good evidence that Spark Dugan and Corporal Schubert were both involved in the black-marketing scheme, and with Foreman's blessing. But it doesn't make sense for a man to die over a few clothes, a few sacks of flour."

Walking to the door, Reina looked out into the night. The moon climbed into the blackness and cast her shadow across the floor of the caboose. He could see the curve of her hips and the grace of her back. She presented an irresistible package of beauty, intelligence, and humor, and she was here in his caboose. Who said there were no miracles?

"What about Colonel Hoffmann?" she asked.

"What about him?"

"If he's involved, he could be using it to blackmail Major Foreman."

"It's possible, I suppose."

"Maybe that's why Major Foreman's such a mouse, why he hides in that office of his."

Standing, Hook slipped his arm around her. She smelled of shampoo. Turning, she nuzzled into him, her breath warm against his neck, and his heart ticked up a notch.

"I wasn't going to tell you this," she said, "but I think I better. Colonel Hoffmann paid me a visit in the library today."

"Oh?"

"He threatened to close down my program. He said it constituted a propaganda machine and that the Swiss Legation would not tolerate it."

"He can't do that, can he?"

"I showed him photos from the concentration camps. He said such things were 'necessary,' just like that, like it's necessary to take castor oil, or shots, or go to the dentist." Hook held her close, her tears warm against his cheek. "I was afraid," she said. "For an instant I knew how those poor people in the photographs must have felt."

"They're only words. He can't hurt you. Why don't you stay the night?"

Laying her hand against his cheek, she brushed her lips against his.

"You're a darling, but I'm all right now. And I've lots of things I need to get finished, as do you."

"Okay, if you must, and I promise to clean this place," he said. "The next time you come, you'll be amazed at how orderly I can be."

"Maybe I'll see you this weekend," she said, kissing him.

"There's an auction out on the county-line road," he said. "Lots of books."

"It's a date," she said. "Good night, Walter."

He waited at the door as she pulled away, her car lights fading in the blackness.

Pouring the last glass from the bottle of wine, he smoked a cigarette. The lantern flame flickered, and shadows danced up the walls of the caboose.

He knew Reina to be smart and not easily frightened. What she had said about Colonel Hoffmann and Major Foreman could be right. Colonel Hoffmann's ruthlessness could not be denied any more than Major Foreman's lack of spine. Between them, they presented a dangerous combination. But neither man was stupid, and killing over a petty black-market scheme didn't fit.

Blowing out the lantern, he listened to the frogs, whose chorus had turned frenzied. With a little luck, he could make it to Kansas City and get back before that GFX arrived from Oceanside, California. He had a pretty good idea the schedule the pickpocket worked.

He'd leave Runt out of things for now. When he got back, he'd catch Frenchy's run to the yards. RD 114's destination had been the Camp Alva spur. She'd be filled with cabbage and scheduled for icing. He planned to be there.

# 26

As HOOK TRUDGED back to the caboose, dawn broke in the east. Pink and blue shafts of light shot into the sky, and a thousand sparrows preened on the top rim of the wheat elevator. Hook kicked his foot up on the track and lit a cigarette.

He'd hitched a ride back from Wichita on an old kettle that had turned his kidneys to gelatin. His bones ached, and his eyes burned from lack of sleep. The pickpocket had showed his hand just outside the Wichita stop, lifting an old lady's purse from the seat next to her while she dozed.

Hook waited until they came into Wichita, nabbing him as he stepped from the train. Turned out to be just a kid. He took him downtown and charged him with trespassing. Thirty days in the Wichita jail would make an impression without ruining his life, and it ought to satisfy Eddie's taste for blood.

Just as he approached the caboose, a jeep pulled up, and an army sergeant climbed out. He carried a sidearm, and the insignia on his sleeve looked to be military police.

"Agent Hook Runyon?" he asked.

"That's right," Hook said.

"Mr. Runyon, we got a problem brewing out to the camp. Could you come with me?"

Hook looked at his watch. "Look, Sergeant, I'm a railroad bull, not the local law enforcement. On top of that, I've not had sleep for about forty-eight hours. I'm in no mood to put up with the army or anyone else."

"We're right sorry to bother you, sir, but this is an important matter. We've got a standoff going out to the camp. If it gets out of hand, your railroad might wind up in the middle of things."

"A standoff?"

"Yes, sir. So far at least. It could turn ugly real fast."

Hook looked at the caboose and then at the sergeant. "Okay," he said. "Lead the way."

The sergeant escorted him directly into Major Foreman's office. Foreman hung up the phone and pointed to the chair.

"This better be good," Hook said. "I get real cranky without my nap."

"Look, Runyon," Foreman said. "The shift guard found a German soldier hanging from the front porch of A barracks this morning."

"Suicide?"

"I don't think so," he said, looking out the window. "This soldier had been on the outs with the powers around here."

Hook rubbed the weariness from his face. "Could we get to the point, Major?"

"Frankly, he'd been an informant for us. Over the last six months, we'd gleaned a lot of information from him. Informants are damned hard to come by in this camp because of a little procedure called the kangaroo court."

"You don't think he committed suicide?"

"First of all, most folks don't consider suicide an honorable thing to do. That's especially true for the Germans, so a man wouldn't hang himself in full view of the entire compound. Whoever did this wanted it public as a warning for the others. Second, this guy dangled from a bedsheet ten feet off the ground. How could he have done that without a little help from his friends?"

"Nice guys," Hook said. "But I don't see what this has to do with me."

Foreman sat down at his desk and clasped his hands in front of him.

"Shakedowns are routine after something like this, searching for weapons, contraband, things like that."

"Yeah? Makes sense."

"Fleischer sent out word that this time there would be no shakedown."

"Fleischer?"

"The same," Foreman said. "I wish you'd plugged that bastard when you had the chance."

"Next time I will," he said. "So, what is it you want from me?"

"There's over fourteen hundred POWs in that area. I've sixty-five guards, and most of them have precious little combat experience. We do have tear gas. Unfortunately, we do not have gas masks. Such items are priority for the front. We've weapons, of course, but I can't issue an order to shoot a bunch of POWs. I'd be in Leavenworth for the rest of my life. Those prisoners are more afraid of their officers than they are of our guns.

"I need two things from you," he said. "Make a call to shut down the rail line. If these prisoners go through the fence, I don't want them scattered from here to Chicago."

"Done," Hook said.

"Second, I want you to see if you can talk Fleischer into giving up."

"Me?"

"You've dealt with him before. He's bound to have some respect."

"Something tells me I'm not one of Fleischer's heroes, but if you think it will help. Who else do we have in there?"

"Luckily, the civilians don't come in until seven," Foreman said. "At least we don't have to worry about hostages."

Hook lit a cigarette. "Hand me the phone," he said.

As they gathered outside the gate, the military police grew quiet. They carried only their batons and tear-gas canisters. High in the lookout towers, the guards trained their tommy guns on the barracks. Major Foreman walked the line of men and then back to Hook.

"We are ready," he said.

"I have one question, Major. Where is Hoffmann?"

"Hoffmann's on ice-plant detail in the Waynoka camp this week."

"Their top commander is not here?"

"No," he said.

"Keep your men back as long as possible," Hook said. "I'd suggest you not use that tear gas unless it's absolutely required. Without masks, it could easily backfire. If you have to use it, remember to keep the wind to your back if at all possible.

"I'll see if I can talk Fleischer out of this first. But I can tell you now, my experience has been that Fleischer doesn't scare easily. If you have to advance, I'd advise to keep a few men in reserve. You'll need to secure any prisoners that are taken. I'm not an expert in these matters, Major, but I'd think it wise to give the prisoners a way to siphon off. Don't block them in to where their only choice is to fight. In the end you want this to be resolved with as little bloodshed as possible."

"Yes," he said. "More trouble I don't need."

"Have your troops open up in the middle as they advance and then close in around small groups of prisoners. When your troops have handled those, move forward again the same way. Cordon off any prisoners that funnel into the escape lane. They're out of the mood to fight, or they wouldn't have gone that way to begin with."

"All right," Foreman said.

"If we can nail their officers, the fight's over. Do you agree?"

"Yes," Foreman said.

"I'll raise my hand if the deal falls through, and then it's your turn. This hand," he said, raising his prosthesis.

When Hook stepped through the gate, Fleischer stood on the barrack's porch. Next to him swung the body of the German soldier, his face black with coagulated blood, his tongue protruding from his mouth. Body fluids had wet the front of his uniform, and he turned this way and that with the morning breeze.

Fleischer, in full-dress uniform, stood with his arms folded over his chest. A slow smile spread across his face.

"My one-arm friend," he said. "We meet again. It's too bad the American tractor moves so slowly."

"I see one of your men has chosen to exit our facility his own way," Hook said.

Fleischer looked up at the body. "Yes, an unfortunate decision. Perhaps you'll bury him in the prisoners' cemetery before the sun heats the day?"

"I understand that a shakedown is in order when such a suicide occurs?"

Fleischer walked the length of the porch, then turned and looked at the military police who had filed through the gate behind Hook.

"Yes," he said. "Such has been the practice, but we have grown weary of such imposition. It will no longer be permitted."

Fleischer raised his hand, and prisoners poured out of the barracks behind him, moving into formation in front of the porch. Within moments the lines stretched across the compound.

"You must know that we've weapons trained on you?" Hook said.

Fleischer looked up at the towers. "I believe your name is Runyon, isn't it?"

"Just call me Hook," he said. "Seeing as how we've become such good friends."

"My men are not afraid of your guns. They will obey my orders. We forbid any more intrusions. In any case, you would have to *use* your guns, wouldn't you? I think your Major Foreman lacks the fortitude. The Geneva Convention frowns on mass murder of prisoners."

Hook shook out a cigarette, offering one to Fleischer. Hook lit Fleischer's cigarette and then his own.

"I see," he said. "What I don't understand is why you would force this showdown. A lot of people are bound to get hurt."

Fleischer drew on the cigarette and then studied its end. "Lucky Strike. The American cigarettes are excellent."

"Isn't there something we can do to resolve this?" Hook asked.

Fleischer looked down the line of German soldiers. "Yes," he said. "Tell the major to call off the search."

"That would put you in charge, wouldn't it?" Hook said.

Fleischer smiled.

Hook dropped his cigarette, squashed it out with his foot, and lifted his prosthesis over his head.

From behind, he could hear the yelling of the military police officers as they charged forward, their batons at the ready. Fleischer barked an order, and the German soldiers rushed toward them.

Hook rolled to the side, coming up just under the porch railing. The thud of batons rose from the yard as the MPs clubbed their way into the throng. A German soldier, his jaw set, rushed Hook from the crowd. Hook dropped his shoulder, catching the soldier's midriff. The soldier bellowed as his air rushed away. Bringing his knee up, Hook caught the man square under the chin, the soldier's teeth snapping like a bullwhip.

When Hook chanced a look back, the Germans threatened to overwhelm the guards. That's when he spotted Major Foreman and the line of men who stood at the ready with the tear-gas canisters. Hook checked the wind.

"Gas," he yelled as loudly as he could. "Do it now!"

Foreman gave the order, and tins of gas were lobbed into the battle. Within moments, clouds of tear gas swept the area. Hook, caught in the melee, grabbed his handkerchief and covered his face. Tears filled his eyes. All about him German soldiers gagged and coughed and clawed at their faces. Mucus ran from their noses as they searched for a way to escape, anything to stop the agony. Luckily, Foreman had provided a corridor around the advancing military police, and the prisoners poured into it.

Within moments, the riot had failed. Even as the winds moved the gas away, its bitterness clung in their clothes and in their hair. Hook looked around for Fleischer, who could not be found. Wiping the water from his eyes, he called to Foreman,

"Where did he go?"

Foreman pointed to the mess hall, where Fleischer stood in the doorway, a butcher knife held at Runt Wallace's throat.

# 27

HOOK TURNED TO Foreman, who shook his head and turned up his hands. Fleischer advanced, pushing Runt ahead of him, the knife at Runt's throat.

When he stopped, Hook said, "What is it you want, Fleischer?"

"As before," he said. "No searches, not if you want the cook to see the day."

"I'm okay, Hook," Runt said.

Fleischer slipped the knife an eighth of an inch, and blood oozed from around the blade, dripping into Runt's shirt collar.

"I don't give the orders around here," Hook said.

Fleischer pulled Runt back toward the door. "Tell your major to withdraw. You have half an hour. After that, you will find the American cook in the locker room with the pork bellies."

Fleischer stepped back into the mess hall and closed the door. Hook made his way back to Foreman, who stood beneath the gun tower. The German prisoners had been corralled in the far corner of the compound. Many sat on the ground holding their heads, which had been bloodied from the soldiers' batons. Those who stood did so with their backs to the German soldier, who swung silently at the end of his bedsheet.

"Damn you, Foreman," Hook said. "You told me there were no civilians here."

Foreman shrugged his shoulders. "I didn't know," he said. "Sometimes Wallace comes in early."

"Fleischer wants the search called off," Hook said. "We've got thirty minutes before he kills Runt."

Foreman walked to the compound gate and then back. "I can't do that," he said.

"What?"

"To call off that search would be to surrender this camp to the Germans."

Hook lit a cigarette and looked over at the prisoners. "Appears to me to have been the case for some time now, Foreman."

"They take care of their own," he said. "It's understood. But this is a challenge to my authority. To let Fleischer get by with this is tantamount to surrender."

"He's got my friend in there with a knife at his throat. What are you going to do about that?"

Major Foreman took his handkerchief out of his pocket and dabbed the perspiration off his top lip.

"There's little I can do," he said. "We can't risk another riot. For one thing, there's no more tear gas. I'd have a bloodbath on my hands."

Hook looked around the compound and then up at the gunner's nest.

"Is there any other way into that mess hall?" he asked.

"No," Foreman said. "There's no back entrance, other than the loading dock."

"Loading dock?"

"It opens to the spur. You know, where they unload the box-cars. There's a car of flour out there now."

"Is there a way to get in?"

Foreman thought for a moment. "I don't see how. The boxcars come in flush against the building for unloading."

Hook checked his watch. Fifteen minutes left. "Boxcars have doors on both sides. I can get in on the far side of the car and climb through. With a little luck, maybe I can get in without Fleischer hearing me."

"And if he does?" Foreman asked.

"You're still in charge either way, I guess. Tell your towers to hold their fire while I work my way around to the back of the compound."

Foreman sent men to notify the towers. Hook checked his side-arm before cutting to the north, away from where the prisoners were confined. He glanced back at the towers as he made his way around the compound fence, hoping all the while that they had understood the hold-fire order. Tommy spray at this distance would not leave much for Hanson to bury. The morning sun rose in the east, and the locusts' chant lifted from the elms.

He paused where the spur ran under the fence. The compound had fallen silent, as silent as death. He crawled his way down the track to where the boxcar had been sided against the building. Ducking under the car, he paused, listening for any sounds.

He cut the seal and tugged at the door. It gave, the rollers screech-ing from rust and debris. If the other door had not been opened, there'd be no options left. Hook peeked into the car. Sacks of flour rose nearly to the roof. Pulling himself up, he scaled the sacks and wormed his way in. Sweat dripped into his eyes, and flour clogged his nostrils. Barely able to move forward or backward, he squirmed into the car.

When he spotted the light coming from the storage room on the other side, he dropped his head on his hand and took a deep breath. Now he had to get to Fleischer before time ran out.

He dropped from the car into the supply room and unsheathed his sidearm. If only he could get close enough for a clear shot. A man who would execute one of his own men would not hesitate to take Runt's life.

Pushing himself against the wall, he edged toward the door. Crates of oranges were stacked about, and sides of ham, smelling of smoke, hung from racks.

When he saw Fleischer, he dropped to his knee, quieting his breath. Runt sat in a chair, and Fleischer stood behind him, facing the door. To shoot now would risk killing Runt. To wait too long put him in just as much jeopardy.

Hook took an orange from one of the crates and slipped it into his shirt. With his eyes locked on Fleischer, he kept low as he crept his way through the containers of produce. Fleischer checked his watch and then walked to the window. Hook lay back in the shadows, close now, close enough that he could hear Fleischer's breathing.

Just then, Runt spotted Hook. He looked away and then back again. Hook took the orange from his shirt and showed it to Runt, who acknowledged it with a nod of his head. And then Hook rolled it across the room. Fleischer turned to the sound.

"What the . . ."

But he never finished the sentence. By then the cold barrel of Hook's P.38 lay directly behind his ear. The shot reverberated through the mess hall, and blood sprayed across the window. Fleischer catapulted against the wall and slumped over.

Hook holstered his sidearm and checked the cut on Runt's neck.

"Shaving kind of close nowadays, aren't you?" he said.

Runt stood and tried his legs. "If I ever find my granddaddy's forty-year-old shine, you're first on the list," he said.

"I could use a nip this very minute," Hook said, helping Runt toward the door.

They sent Runt to the hospital in town to get his neck checked out. At first he'd refused treatment, but when Hook threatened to go get his ma, he changed his mind and went in with a guard. Hook followed Major Foreman back to his office and watched him pace behind his desk.

"You should have killed that son of a bitch in Kansas," he said. "Now, I got both a suicide and a shooting on my hands. Command isn't going to be happy about this. They aren't going to be happy at all."

Hook looked down his front, which was covered in white flour.

"You're welcome, Major," he said. "I knew you'd appreciate the fact that you don't have a dead civilian and a full-scale riot on your hands."

"There will be an investigation, you know."

"What would you do, Foreman, just let them kill anyone they want?"

"Why can't these bastards just wait out the war?" he said. "They've got more privileges than I do."

Hook lit a cigarette. Major Foreman started to say something but decided not to.

"You ever had one of these shakedowns before?" Hook asked.

"Of course. They're routine."

"Do you ever find anything?"

"Pilfered food. Potato-skin beer. Pornography. Nothing of consequence."

"Who would you say runs this camp? Other than you, I mean. Who's in charge?"

"Colonel Hoffmann, of course."

"And so Fleischer chose a standoff the day Hoffmann left town?"

"You can't predict these bastards," he said. "I wake up in the night wondering what they've planned next."

Hook walked to the window. Reina and Amanda were just arriving for work.

"I need to get home now," he said.

"I'll have a guard drive you," Major Foreman said.

"Thanks, but Dr. Kaplan will drive me. I'm sure you don't mind."

Reina pulled up to the caboose and shut off the engine. She smelled of Juicy Fruit and lipstick.

"You're kidding me." she said.

"They hoisted one of their men from the front porch of A barracks before you had your morning coffee," he said. "And there's Fleischer standing next to the body all dressed up like he's ready for inspection."

"Are you okay?" she asked.

"You don't kill a man without it spoiling your day, even a man like Fleischer."

"What about Runt?"

"He's sporting a new necklace, but it didn't look serious to me. That little guy is pretty tough. I doubt anything's going to keep him away from his date with Amanda."

"Amanda is taken with him," she said. "That's obvious, though her father is less than happy about the situation. I don't know his history, but I suspect he's been hurt somewhere along the line. It's hard for him to let Amanda go."

"Runt may not be sophisticated, but he has the heart of a giant," he said.

"Word has probably leaked out about the atrocities that are being uncovered in Germany," she said. When she glanced over at Hook, her eyes welled. "It's too horrible, Hook, and some of those prisoners out there may well have participated in it. Things are going badly for them over there, and they seem to sense it in the camp. It's a dangerous time inside those fences."

"Foreman is convinced they've an active kangaroo court to take care of business," Hook said.

"We are so far away from the war out here that it's easy to lose sight of the struggles that might be going on in the camp," she said.

Hook opened the door to get out, then paused. "Reina, Foreman tells me that shakedowns are pretty much routine in these camps. Is that correct?"

"It's the only way to find contraband," she said, "or to detect escape tunnels, things like that. Prisoners expect them, plan around them, in fact."

"And discipline is strict?" he asked. "No one would take it upon themselves to execute a prisoner without the knowledge of the commander, right?"

"Right."

"Nor order a standoff on their own?"

"Not a chance," she said.

"Not even Fleischer?"

"Especially Fleischer," she said.

"And yet these are the very things that happened," he said. "Why?"

Reina rocked the steering wheel and stared out the windshield for several moments. She started the car and turned.

"It's almost like a diversion," she said.

"Exactly," he said, sliding out of the car.

# 28

THE SUN HAD nearly set by the time Frenchy's work train chugged down the track. Even at that, Hook had almost missed it, clambering up the grade just in time to get Frenchy flagged down. He swung up on the ladder, cleared a space to sit, and waited as Frenchy eased the throttle forward. The fireman snored from his chair, his hat cocked over his eyes, his arms folded over his chest.

Lighting the stub of his cigar, Frenchy looked over his shoulder.

"You just now getting up?"

Hook lit a cigarette, pointing his chin at the fireman.

"Can't sleep on the job like some I know."

Frenchy had it pretty much right. He'd slept late but awoke determined to get the caboose in order. As he cleaned books off the bed, one thing led to another, and first thing he knew he'd read a hundred pages of Ellery Queen's *The Murderer Is a Fox*. No matter. There should be plenty of time to clean the caboose before Reina came.

"Pot's just resting his eyes," Frenchy said, "or thinking. I can't tell which."

"Resting is better than thinking for all concerned," Hook said, leaning back against the cab.

Clouds boiled into the sky, their tops dark and ominous against the setting sun. The smell of rain drifted in, a sprinkle and settling of dust against the heat of the boiler.

"I hear tell you saved Runt's ass." Frenchy said.

"You're likely to hear lots of things around here."

"You got him reading those goddang books yet?"

Crossing his ankles, Hook studied the crease, deep as a mail slot, that ran horizontally across the back of Frenchy's neck.

"Some things can't be changed, like the Rockies, or the stink of that cigar of yours, or Runt's disinclination to read."

As he puffed on his cigar, Frenchy's shoulders shook. "That's good," he said. "Runt's on this earth for one reason, and I don't want no one messing with destiny. You clutter up his head with all those goddang books, he might forget his real calling. Life wouldn't be worth living if that happened."

As they rounded the bend into the yards, Hook said, "Let me off at the depot, will you?"

"Oh sure, sure," he said, setting the brake. "I'll just hold up the line from here to Chicago so's you won't have to walk back from the yards. It ain't no problem, no problem at all."

Swinging down, Hook gave him a wave, then stepped over the tracks to the depot. Joe leaned back in his chair, a magazine open in his lap.

"Hey, Joe," Hook said.

Jumping up, Joe said, "Goddang it, Hook, you got to slip up on a man like that?"

"I'll be up in the sleeping rooms. Send the callboy around about three o'clock, will you?"

Dog-earing the magazine, Joe tossed it on the desk.

"Them pickpockets ain't out at three o'clock in the morning. Besides that, them tramps took the packing out of a cattle car over at the Brace siding. She got a hotbox and burned up ten acres of Bill Epson's Bermuda. Eddie Preston's been chewing on my ass ever since, wanting to know where you're at."

"If he calls again, tell him I'm on my way to Brace to check it out, will you?"

"Why does everyone around here think I'm their caretaker? Well, I ain't. I'm the goddang operator."

"See you later, Joe," he said.

The callboy shined his flashlight in Hook's face and shook his shoulder.

"It's three o'clock, Mr. Runyon."

Hook rolled his legs over the side of the bunk and rubbed at his eyes.

"Is the Extra on time?" he asked.

"Yes, sir. I called out the crew already."

"Thanks," he said.

"It's raining cats out there, Mr. Runyon."

Hook looked at his feet, waiting for his brain to engage.

"I don't remember it ever raining here."

"No, sir, but it's raining now," he said, closing the door behind him.

Slipping on his britches, Hook walked down the dark hallway. The waiting room stank of cigar smoke and rancid coffee. Joe worked at his radio, a June bug clattering in the globe of his desk lamp.

When Hook opened the door of the depot, a cold rain swept into his face. Lightning ripped across the sky, and thunder rumbled away. He hadn't figured on rain.

"Damn," he said, closing the door.

"Ain't likely to melt a yard dog," Joe said, from the office.

"How far out's the Extra?"

"Ten minutes."

"You got a slicker?"

"Goddang it, Hook. It's behind the door. Who took care of you before I came along?"

Donning the slicker, Hook lowered his head and drove into the rain. The sky flickered with lightning. The rails, like silver threads under its glare, struck into the darkness. Thunder rumbled and growled about him, and by the time he'd gone a hundred yards, his pants were soaked to the knees.

Leaning into the gale, he worked his way toward the ice deck, its floodlights flickering through the sheets of rain. Cutting east, he crossed the tracks to the sand house, a building constructed on piling that were high enough so that sand could be fed by gravity into the engines. To prevent slippage when moving from a dead stop, the engineer could release sand under the drive wheels. Tonight Hook needed as clear a view of the ice deck as possible, and the sand house just might do the trick.

The storm deepened as he climbed the ladder. Hunching down on the metal catwalk, he pulled up the collar of the slicker and waited. Even from here, he could barely make out the ice deck through the sheets of rain.

Within minutes the whistle of the GFX Extra rose above the thunder, her light dim in the driving rain as she pulled her way through the labyrinth of tracks. A bolt of lightning split the sky, its smell of heat. The floodlights on the ice deck flickered, struggling against the white-hot force of the lightning.

He'd about decided that sitting on a metal catwalk might not be a good idea when another bolt crackled through the yards, leaping from track to track. "Damn," he said, shaking away the tingle that coursed through his body. The lights in the yard blinked once more and then went out, plunging the world into blackness.

About then headlights swung in from the road, the growl of a truck as it pulled alongside the GFX. The headlights were cut, and voices rose above the din of the storm, small and distant like children on a playground.

Hook drew down, waiting, the GFX idling at the ice deck, steam shooting from her sides like an ancient dragon. Her headlamp lit a distant cottonwood, its top sweeping in the wind.

The headlights of the truck came back on, and it turned about And then all went black once more. A flash of lightning froze the world, a split second as clear as day, but Hook couldn't make out anything except the pilothouse of the turntable and the small building that housed the steam jenny.

Water dripped from his collar and raced down his back as he descended the ladder, his hook clanging against the rungs. What splendid luck to get caught in the first rain since Noah floated his ark.

Sneaking his way along the GFX, he paused now and again to listen, to look for lights, to gauge the distance as best he could. The wind whipped down the right of way, spinning rain into his eyes. So far he knew no more than before, and he cursed his bad luck as he moved ever closer to the ice deck.

He could smell smoke and steam. He moved to the siding to take refuge behind the wheel carriage of a wheat car. The voices were gone now, only the chug of the Extra as she breathed and sighed in the storm. Lightning cracked, and the world lit. Directly across from him sat GFX, RD 114.

When the lightning settled, he dashed across the opening, taking cover behind the wheels of RD 114. He checked the bunker drain under the car with the tips of his fingers. Dry.

He searched for his sidearm under the slicker. With luck he could climb the ladder, check the contents of the bunker, and get back down without being spotted. But if the deck lights should happen to come on, there would be no place to hide, and at this point, he couldn't be sure what he was facing.

Pulling himself up the ladder, he slid onto the top of the reefer, lying flat on his stomach, worming his way along. With each flash of lightning, he froze, pushing himself against the top of the car. The only thing he could see was the cottonwood tree illuminated in the headlamp of the Extra.

As he approached the end of the car, he spotted the hatch of the ice bunker, which had been thrown open. Inching along, he stopped to listen. Someone might be standing guard below or across the way on the ice deck.

Atop the car he would be an easy target indeed. Crawling the last few feet, he waited for a flash of lightning in order to get a look into the bunker.

The blow came from behind, catching him across his ear and neck. Lights flashed, not from lightning this time, but from his brain sloshing inside his skull. Staggering, he dropped, twisting in pain. He had a weapon somewhere, if only he could remember, if only he could move.

The kick to follow tore away the cartilage in his nose and the soft flesh of his cheek. Hook lifted his head, blood spilling from his nose, washing down the side of RD 114. Lightning struck, outlining a man standing above him, his hands clenched at his side. Hook struggled to rise but unconsciousness swept him away.


Blackness surrounded him. The sound could have been that of a casket lowered into the earth, or a spade, shovelfuls of dirt cast into the grave. The air, stale and finite, stank of flowers and corruption, and a great sorrow filled him. He lifted his hand into the blackness, to touch the lace and silk and boundaries of eternity but could feel nothing. He thought to scream, but who would hear? Again the sounds, but they were sounds he'd known, sounds from before, from when he lived. He listened, trying to focus, *clickity clack, clickity clack, clickity clack,* the sound of a train. He remembered it now from his former life, the cadence of wheels against the spans of track. Then he remembered the open hatch, the ice bunker, and the man who stood above him. Touching his face, Hook found it dried with blood, deadened and stiff from the blows.

Rolling onto his side, he struggled not to panic, not to scream into the blackness or to gape at the remaining minutes of air like a fish tossed on the bank. Standing, he leaned against the side of the bunker, steadying himself against the lurch and pitch of the reefer car.

Somewhere overhead was the hatch, the only way out. Feeling along the wall, he found something, a box, or a crate made of wood. Pushing it against the wall, he climbed on top, his head spinning as the train banked in a turn. Reaching up, he felt for the hatch, and he pushed against it, tentatively at first, and then with all his strength. When it didn't move, panic seized him, and he fell to the floor, gulping for air, his heart pounding, blood coursing in his ears. This blackness would be his end and his grave, and the quiet swept over him once more.

When he came to for the second time, the clack of the wheels had slowed, and the whistle of the GFX Extra rose and fell like a dirge. Getting up, he searched for the crate once more. Bits of light flashed through his swollen brain as he climbed up on it.

Once again he tried the hatch. This time he could feel slack between the cover and the frame, but it would still not budge. Working the tips of his fingers in between, he discovered a wedge slid between the hatch and bracing, a piece of wood perhaps, a piece of the crate itself. If somehow he could work it free, he might have a chance, but not without tools, not with his air running out. Taking a deep breath, he tried to relax. There must be something he could do.

The idea emerged from somewhere, faint and jumbled from out of his battered brain. Taking off his shirt, he unbuckled the harness and removed the prosthesis. Steadying himself on the crate, he worked the hook under the hatch, inching the wedge forward a little at a time. Sweat ran into his eyes and dripped from his nose as he worked. When the hatch came free, he shoved it open, shouting, his voice reverberating in the confines of the bunker.

Overhead, the first rays of dawn shot through the retreating storm clouds. The air, washed and cleaned with rain, filled his lungs until they ached. Pulling himself out, he clung to the roof of the reefer, letting the wind blow in his face.

After slipping the prosthesis back on, he eased himself down the ladder. Ahead, he could see the gun towers of Camp Alva. The GFX Extra would be siding the reefer, and he had no desire to be seeing anyone just yet. Waiting until she'd slowed to a crawl, he jumped, striking down the track for the comfort of caboose and home.


Hook stood at the mirror, smoking a cigarette, checking the condition of his teeth and face. A plum-colored bruise ran from below his ear halfway down his neck, and the white of bone shone through his cheek. Blood matted his hair and clothes, and he smelled of rotting cabbage. While picking some of the debris off his clothes, he noticed that it was packing, old newspaper with foreign writing on it like he'd seen at Spark Dugan's shack. Seems he and Spark Dugan had been poking around in the same dangerous territory.

After cleaning up, he poured a shot of Runt's shine and downed a couple of aspirin. The muscles in his neck corded like cables, and his cheek throbbed with each beat of his heart.

Somehow he had to tie the ends together, to make sense out of the chaos. The one thing he'd learned as a special agent was that action and motivation were never isolated events, that risk rose from reward. Motivations might be different for different folks but were never absent.

And what did he have? purloined clothes, not worth more than a few dollars at best. He had reefers arriving from California with nothing but empty crates and packing material in the ice bunkers.

He had Favor Oil trucks leaving scheduled loads behind, and he had Ross Ague, the night foreman, who never saw anything, including Spark Dugan behind his train. He had a dozen POWs working the ice deck, two bums with the IQ of paste, and one Colonel Otto Hoffmann, Nazi extraordinaire.

But most of all what he had was one dead friend, Spark Dugan, and this morning, he had nearly joined him.

# 29

THE STORM HAD swept in like an angry giant, keeping Reina awake. As quickly as it came, it moved south in the direction of Waynoka, and the moon forged its way into the blackness of the sky. She lay in her bed listening to the last of the thunder and watching Hugh Favor's light wink through the row of elms.

But still she did not sleep because her life had changed forever. Evil had flown from the pages of her books and the theories of her classroom and gripped her soul in its icy hand.

She couldn't get the list of stolen Jewish paintings out of her head, the sadness of it, the disrespect. One painting in particular, Bellini's *Madonna and Child*, kept coming back to her like the refrain of a song. She had seen one in Hugh Favor's collection, but there were many artists who had done Madonna and child paintings. How ridiculous to think that Hugh Favor would own such a thing. This was America, the middle of America.

She climbed out of bed and pulled back the curtain. The light in

Favor's window had gone out. If only she could get a look at that painting, then she could be certain, could put the whole silly thing to rest. But how?

And then she remembered the key hanging at the back door of the cottage kitchen. Amanda's father kept the mansion's garage key there. Often on the weekends, Favor never even used the limo. But she might be spotted in the garden. It had happened once already, and a second infraction might not be so quickly forgiven. But then he *had* given her permission to enjoy the garden.

Putting on her clothes, she slipped around back, finding the kitchen door unlocked. On more than one occasion, she'd warned Amanda about such carelessness. Cracking the door, she retrieved the key from the nail and dropped it into her pocket.

The night wind smelled of rain as she crept through the garden. The last of the clouds drifted against the moonlight. At the swimming pool, she paused to catch her breath. The moon broke through the clouds, glinting and dancing on the water.

She checked Favor's window before cutting around the mansion to the side door leading into the garage. The bolt slid back, and she stepped in, easing the door closed behind her. Her heart beat in her ears, and she could smell oil and rubber in the darkness.

When her eyes had adjusted, she found the door leading into the kitchen and opened it. She stopped again, listening, considering what a foolish thing she had done. They called it breaking and entering, and she could be shot on sight. In this part of the country, burglars were considered fair game. When the grandfather clock in the foyer chimed, tingles zipped out the ends of her fingers.

The doors to Favor's collection were unlocked, and moonlight cast through the windows, lighting the paintings in its ivory glow. Reina looked at the engraved nameplate on the frame of the *Madonna and Child*.

"Oh, my God," she said.

When the light came on, she spun about, her heart pounding in her chest. Hugh Favor stood in the doorway, his eyes cold as glass.

"So," he said, "you've taken it upon yourself to visit my collection, have you?"

"This painting," she said. "Where did you get it?"

Favor came across the room, taking her by the arm. His fingers dug into her flesh, and his breath smelled of brandy. He hit her across the face with the back of his hand, and lights exploded in her head.

"I'll do the asking around here," he said.

Reina tried to stand, and Favor hit her again, spilling her onto the floor. She could taste blood, the tang of iron and salt. Scooting to the wall, she waited for his rage to calm.

"That painting is on the list of stolen Jewish art," she said. "Someone's paid with their life for it."

"How should I know where it came from?" he said. "This painting was necessary. Without it, my collection would not have been complete."

"And that is more important?" she asked.

Favor paused, his hands trembling. "Yes," he said. "It's more important." He looked up at the painting. "A collection such as mine will be the envy of the world. None can compare now that it is complete. The collection is whole, and in that compilation, I have created the ultimate masterpiece. It is I who have become the artist."

"These works were taken by the Germans from murdered Jews," she said. "To own one is to have their blood on your hands."

"Shut up," he said. "Someone would have bought it. Someone would have owned it."

"You have collaborated with the enemy," she said. "You are a traitor."

Favor stepped in, kicking her hard in the stomach. Bile rose in her throat, and her lungs emptied. The room tilted and then grew dark.

When she awoke, she had been moved away from the window. Her hands and feet were bound with tape, and her eye had swollen shut. Favor stood at his desk, talking on the phone. She couldn't make out what he said, but when he hung up, he came back, checking her bindings.

"You have been very foolish," he said. "And I cannot be responsible."

Reina didn't answer but lay still. Another blow might end her life, and no one would likely come this time of the night. Amanda's father would not miss the key until morning, if at all. By then, it could well be too late.

When she heard the voices at the front door, hope rose in their familiarity but quickly faded into despair. The chilling accent of Colonel Hoffmann was unmistakable, and she knew that her life now hung in the balance.

Favor closed the drapes over the windows and turned on the light. Colonel Hoffmann stood with his thumbs hooked in his belt. She recognized the two men behind him as Corporal Schubert from the kitchen and the slick-sleeved guard from the camp gate. The guard carried his army-issue rifle.

Hoffmann walked to where she lay. She could see the scuff of his jackboots, which had nearly worn through the toes.

"So," he said, "the Jewess has left her library. Perhaps you meddle for the last time."

"I caught her in the gallery," Favor said. "What are we going to do with her?"

Colonel Hoffmann looked up at the *Madonna and Child*.

"Disposing of the Jewess is not the problem, Herr Favor. The problem is this painting. We had agreed that the paintings were to be sold for redistribution. Yet you have taken it upon yourself to keep this one."

"But what difference could that make?" Favor asked, glancing about.

"The difference is that someone like her might recognize it and uncover our entire operation. This would be a problem, wouldn't you agree?"

Sweat glistened on Favor's forehead, and he wiped it away with the back of his hand.

"But she has been caught, hasn't she? So there is no problem," he said.

"Ah, yes, that would be true enough," Colonel Hoffmann said, "if she has not alerted anyone else. But there is no way of determining that now. You do see the problem?"

Favor moved toward the door, his face pale. The American guard shoved him back. Favor stumbled, grabbing hold of the fireplace mantle to steady his legs. The guard leveled his rifle, slipping off the safety. Reina's head spun.

"What are you doing?" Favor asked, his voice trembling. "I've made you a great deal of money. I can make you even more."

"I'm afraid it's much too late," Hoffmann said. "We'll have to move our operation elsewhere. Take him," he ordered.

Schubert and the guard grabbed Favor by the arms. Favor's legs collapsed under him as they dragged him across the room away from the window.

"Get that cord from the drapery," Hoffmann said to the guard. "It's far less disruptive."

Colonel Hoffmann took a cushion from the couch and covered Favor's face. Favor whimpered and begged for his life from under the cushion, but as the guard tightened the cord around his throat, his whimpers soon quieted. His legs twitched and then were still. And in that awful silence, Reina bit her tongue to keep from screaming out.

The guard stood, his breathing labored. "And the woman now?" he asked.

"No," Hoffmann said. "We might need her. Soon enough our absence from the camp will be noticed."

"What do we do?" the guard asked.

"Another delivery is scheduled later this evening," Hoffmann said. "It's far too valuable to not follow through. In any case, we cannot allow others to discover it. We'll stay here until it's time to make our move."

"And if someone should come?" the guard asked.

"Then we take care of that as the need arises," Hoffmann said. "In the meantime, fetch me a bottle of brandy from Favor's cabinet. His taste for fine spirits rivals his taste for fine art."

# 30

WHEN HOOK OPENED the door of the caboose, Runt stood there with a sack in his hand. Hook touched his swollen jaw.

"Hello," he said.

"You ain't going to blame that on my shine, are you?" Runt asked, handing him the sack.

"Come on in," Hook said. "Fix yourself some coffee while I get dressed."

Runt set the pot on the stove. "I've had bad nights before, eat up by ants and such, but I never came out of one looking like that."

Lighting a cigarette, Hook looked in the mirror. The cut on his cheek seeped blood.

"The GFX Extra came in at four this morning," he said. "I thought it might be a good time to check it out. Hadn't figured on rain."

"Rain ain't something you figure on in this country. Them fool hogs of mine near drowned looking up into the sky, wondering at the sight, and Essie, being the youngest, cried half the night. She hadn't never seen rain before." Runt poured the coffee and set the cups on the table. "You want a little Wallace sunshine in that coffee?"

"No more than to get my motor running," Hook said, pulling up to the table.

Pouring in a shot, Runt stirred it with a pencil.

"Shorty wouldn't cross the creek, being touchy about getting her feet wet, and Ma's chickens . . ."

"Will you stop?" Hook said, sipping on his coffee.

"Go on, then," Runt said.

"I climbed the sand house figuring to get a good view, but the rain fell in sheets, and the lightning turned fierce. And then the floodlights went out on the ice deck. What's a man to do but get in closer?

"One thing led to another, and I found myself inside an ice bunker with my head kicked in. It's a good job I had this hook, or I'd be arriving in Chicago about now."

"But why would someone do that?" Runt asked.

"Didn't want me snooping around that bunker, that's certain. That bunker had never been iced." The shine rounded the edge off the thump in his head, and he eased back. "I saw a truck there, too. Saw her lights. She pulled in and then shut off her lights."

Runt put tobacco in the Bugler machine and rolled himself a cigarette and watched the blackbirds gather along the tracks to pick wheat out of the rocks that had spilled from the cars.

"What did Major Foreman have to say?" he asked.

"He as much as admitted to being on the take, but it's petty stuff as far as I can tell. He claims Corporal Schubert came to see him but then wouldn't talk once he got there."

Runt lit his cigarette, then worked at the mud on his shoe.

"Corporal Schubert had something on his mind," he said. "Something's been eating at him, that much I can tell you."

"Major Foreman figured Corporal Schubert might put the squeeze on him for the blackmail stuff," Hook said, "but changed his mind."

"It don't make sense to me. Corporal Schubert has been pretty low, you know. Kept talking about dying in a strange land. He's in mighty deep, I think."

Reaching over, Hook lay some of the packing material on the table. "I found this stuck to my clothes. It came out of that ice bunker. It's the same stuff I found in Spark Dugan's cabin. Last I knew, they didn't put packing in ice bunkers. Something smells, and it isn't cabbage."

"Well," Runt said, "if you're going looking for trouble again, I hope you don't lead with your head. It's a mighty poor sight as it is."

"Thanks," Hook said, finishing off his coffee. "You sure know how to cheer a man up. Now suppose you drive me over to the Favor sheds? I need to check something out."

"Does that mean I'm still on expenses?"

"Until otherwise advised."

"In that case I'm ready to go."

Clearing a place to sit in the truck, Hook kicked his foot up on the dash and waited as Runt choked the engine against the dampness of last night's rain. When she fired, she coughed and sputtered, and blue smoke rolled by the window. Dropping her into low, Runt eased out on the clutch, and they lurched forward. Taking down an old toothpick that had been wedged between the header and the frame of the windshield, Runt parked it in his mouth.

Hook rubbed at the ache that crawled up his neck.

"I'd be better off in the ice bunker than this rattletrap," he said.

"She's a good truck," Runt said, patting the dash. "She'll run on drip as good as gas and backward good as forward. To top it off, the junkyard's stocked with parts, and they're all half-price."


They pulled up to the gate shack at the Favor sheds, and a man stepped out, holding up his clipboard.

Leaning down, he said, "Public ain't allowed beyond this point."

"Remember me?" Hook said, showing his badge. "We're here on official business."

Ducking his head to where he could get a good view of Hook, he said, "Well, then, make damn sure you sign out."

"Right," Hook said.

Most of the sheds were empty, and a "Gone to Lunch" sign hung in the window of the office. A truck had been parked in shed twelve, her wheel flaps clogged with mud, and a mongrel dog lay curled under the shade of the bed.

"Looks like that truck may have been out in the rain," Hook said.

Shutting off the engine, Runt looked at the dog. "It's a grand life for some, ain't it?"

"Come on," Hook said.

"Hell, what if someone's about?"

"They've all gone to lunch. Now, come on," Hook said.

"What if that dog bites?" Runt asked.

"He'd have to get up to do that, wouldn't he?"

"It's a point," he said, opening the door.

The smell of grease and gas hung like fog inside the shed, and it took a few moments for Hook's eyes to adjust to the dim light. One of the back tires of the truck was nearly flat, and a jack leaned against the bed.

"Give me a heft," Hook said.

"That's Favor property," Runt said. "You're going to wind me up in Sheriff Donley's jail, and it ain't all that pleasant, I can tell you."

"Will you hurry it up?" Hook said. "I'd like to get this done before the crews get back from lunch."

Bending over, Runt locked his fingers together, bracing his elbows against his knees. Hook put his foot in his hands and hopped up into the back of the trailer. Several moments passed as he searched the bed, probing into the corners.

"You find anything?" Runt called up. "I thought I heard something."

Hook said, "What about this?"

The dog peeked out from behind the tire to see if it might be edible.

"What is it?" Runt asked.

"Newspaper packing, the very same I found in Spark Dugan's shack and again in that ice bunker."

Dropping down, Hook let his knees absorb the shock. When he looked up, Roy Bench stood behind Runt. He had a crescent wrench in one hand and a Coca-Cola in the other.

Runt, seeing the look in Hook's eyes, made a slow about-face.

Roy set down his cola and bounced the wrench against the palm of his hand.

"Well, if it ain't the yard dog," he said, "poking around on private property again."

"You wouldn't happen to have met the GFX Extra last night, would you?" Hook asked.

"Maybe. Maybe not. Ain't your business one way or the other far as I know."

"Maybe we'll make it our business," Runt said.

"You might want to stay out of this, pygmy."

Hook moved to the side. With a little luck he could talk his way out of this, being disinclined to have his head banged up with a crescent wrench.

"It's railroad business," Hook said. "We think there's been some illegal trafficking. Just checking, that's all."

"What does that have to do with Favor Oil?"

"Thing is," Hook said, "your truck keeps showing up, like last night in the yards."

"This truck never left the shed last night."

"Then why she's covered with mud?" Runt asked. "It ain't rained for a year."

Roy lowered his crescent wrench to his side. "Shut the hell up, bug brain, if you want to live."

"Let me handle this," Hook said.

"Yeah," Roy said, "stay out of it before I pinch your fuckin' head off."

Hook didn't remember when the blow came, but it happened sometime just after the dog stuck his wet nose against his arm. Stunned, he dropped to his knees, in disbelief at having been slammed for the third time in twenty-four hours.

"Shit," he said, shaking away the fog.

When he looked up, Roy's hands were pinned behind his back, his face red as he struggled to free himself from Runt's grip.

"You want me to let him loose?" Runt asked. "So's you can whip him even up."

"Are you nuts?" Hook said, bringing his fist into Roy's belly. When Roy bent forward, Hook caught him on the chin with an upward thrust of his knee, waiting as he crumpled to the floor.

Wandering over, the dog sniffed Roy's face before returning to the shade of the truck bed.

"Jeez," Runt said. "You hit him before I could let go."

"Yeah, I forgot the rules for a minute. Now let's get out of here before the whole shop turns up."

As they approached the gate shack, Runt slowed.

"Keep it moving," Hook said.

"But they wanted us to sign out."

"I'll give them a sign," Hook said, rolling down the window.

Back at the caboose, Hook washed the blood off his face where Roy had caught him with the roundhouse swing.

Rolling himself a cigarette, Runt said, "You need to stop leading with your face. You ain't never going to be pretty at this rate."

Hook checked his face. "And you were going to let him loose."

When the knock came at the door, Hook took out his P.38, laying it on the table. He had no intentions of getting hit in the head again.

"You want to get it, Runt?"

Opening the door, Runt said, "Hello, Amanda. What you doing here? Come on in. Hook, this is Amanda Roswell."

"Hello," Hook said.

Holding her fingers over her mouth, she took a step back. "Oh."

"Sorry about the face," Hook said. "The world's been kicking it around of late, but you're every bit as pretty as Runt said."

Glancing over at Runt, she blushed. "I thought I better come," she said.

"Is there something wrong?" Hook asked.

"It's about Dr. Kaplan."

"Reina?"

"She rides to work with me in the staff car every morning, but this morning she didn't show. Finally, I went to her room. She wasn't there."

"Maybe she went in early."

Shrugging, she said, "That's just it. She didn't go to work."

"Well, not to worry," Hook said. "She probably had some shopping or an appointment."

"But there's something else, Mr. Runyon," she said, lowering her eyes.

"Oh?"

"Colonel Hoffmann is gone from the camp, so is Corporal Schubert and the second-shift gate guard, too. They've just disappeared."

Hook's hands grew damp, and he wiped them on his britches.

"Runt, you and Amanda contact Sheriff Donley. Tell him what you know. Have him call the highway patrol to block off the main roads."

"Major Foreman has already called the authorities," Amanda said.

"Then get hold of Joe, the operator at the depot. Make sure all outgoing trains are checked. I've got a bad feeling about this."

"But where are you going?" Runt asked.

"Camp Alva," he said, "to have a talk with Major Foreman."

Major Foreman dabbed at his nose and looked over the rim of his glasses at Hook.

"I don't know where Colonel Hoffmann is. I've contacted the authorities, and that's all I can do. I'd goddamn sure bring him in if I knew where he'd gone. Him, Schubert, and that guard just disappeared. He should never have been on duty, but what the hell you going to do? There are no able-bodied men left. You know that."

"And what about Reina Kaplan?"

"Look," he said, "I can't be responsible for everyone who doesn't show up to work."

Leaning onto Foreman's desk, Hook leveled his eyes at Foreman.

"Let me put it this way, Major. If anything happens to Reina, I'll personally see to it that you spend the rest of your career at Fort Leavenworth. Do we understand each other?"

Foreman's face flushed. "Yes," he said.

"Now, I'm going over to the library. I presume that's all right with you?"

"I'll alert the tower guards," he said.

The door to the library opened when Hook pushed on it. Unlike his caboose, the place was tidy, books shelved, trash can emptied. Even the curtains were arranged at half-mast. Checking the coffeepot, he found it washed and cold and the cups lined up on the windowsill.

"Where the hell are you, Reina?" he said under his breath.

Her desk, too, had been cleared for the night, with the exception of a small crystal clock that sat foursquare in the center. From the doorway, the whoops and hollers of the prisoners drifted in from the soccer field, and the smell of cooking cabbage hung in the air.

Sitting down at her desk, he opened the drawer, a half dozen sharpened pencils, index cards, scissors, a tube of lipstick. In the second drawer, he found the photos that she'd told him about, the vacant stares and swollen bellies, and under the photos he found the list of plundered art taken by the Nazis.

At first he didn't catch it, the pencil mark encircling Bellini's *Madonna and Child,* but when he held it to the light, his mouth went dry. Written in the margin in Reina's distinctive hand was the name Hugh Favor.

# 31

HOOK PICKED HIS way across the tracks. Ahead, he could see Favor Mansion. Dropping into a draw that ran from the tracks to Favor land, he skirted the mansion.

Swallows shot through the evening sky like fighter planes, and sunflowers bent against the southwesterly breeze, their smell still pungent from the day's heat. He couldn't be certain why Reina had circled the painting, or why she had penciled in Hugh Favor's name, but right now all clues led to this place.

At the stand of trees that encircled the grounds, he paused for a breather. He would come in from the back and work his way through the gardens. Once at the mansion, maybe he could get a look inside. It was not Hugh Favor who worried him, but Colonel Hoffmann, Schubert, and the guard were another matter indeed.

Taking a short run at the fence, he hooked his leg over, then dropped into a stand of bois d'arc that had been planted along the back wall. Darkness fell as he stole his way through the garden. The air swarmed with the rich smell of alyssum and spirea. Hugh Favor had built a paradise, created by dint of money and power, a garden of Eden in a vanquished land.

Hook dropped down at the bottom of the limestone steps that led up to the landing. From there he could see the back door ajar and a light on at the far end of the hallway. Earthen jars filled with papas grass were placed around the terrace, and in the center a cherub statue dashed and played in the water.

Slipping through the back, he crept down the hallway, stopping, listening, moving ahead. The door leading to the foyer was closed, and he put his ear against it. When satisfied that no one waited on the other side, he opened it: the chandelier, the painting of the little girl with her hands held out to the storm, the darkly paneled walls. For a moment he didn't see the body crumpled on the terrazzo floor beneath the painting.

Unholstering his P.38, Hook clicked off the safety and stepped into the foyer. Even as he turned over the body, he recognized him as Hugh Favor. Drops of blood trickled from the corners of his eyes like clown's tears. His glasses lay broken at his side, and his tongue distended from between his teeth. Fear was etched in his face. The digger had been right.

"Drop the weapon," a man said.

Raising his arms, Hook rose to face him. He wore the U.S. Army uniform, missing chevrons on the sleeves, and he had his rifle trained at Hook's head. Next to him stood Corporal Schubert.

"Well," Hook said, "if it isn't our missing guard and the corporal."

Schubert glanced away, but the guard leveled his eyes on Hook as he bent for the weapon, sticking it in his belt.

"No German souvenirs," he said, smiling. "It's the rule."

"This your handiwork?"

"Up the stairs," he said.

The doors at the top opened onto Hugh Favor's art collection.

With no room left on the walls, paintings were stacked on tables, and on the floor, and in the corners. There were opened wooden crates and newspaper packing with foreign print. Even Hook could see the scope and importance of the collection.

"Where are we going?" he asked. "What is this all about?"

"Keep it shut," the guard said.

When they entered the framing room, Colonel Hoffmann stood. Reina sat behind him, her hands bound. Red streaks extended across her cheek. When she saw Hook, she let out a small cry.

"Oh, Walter," she said. "Why did you come?"

"Ah, the railroad detective," Colonel Hoffmann said. "You've paid us a visit, I see."

"Caught him snooping around downstairs," the guard said. "Here's his weapon."

Taking the pistol, Colonel Hoffmann turned it in his hand.

"You and Corporal Schubert go back downstairs," he said. "I don't want anyone else wandering in here."

"A German officer's weapon," the colonel said to Hook. "I see you have the American's penchant for souvenirs." Sliding out the clip, he checked the bullets. "It feels good to have one of these back in my hands."

"What's going on, Reina?" Hook asked.

"Sit down, Mr. Runyon," the colonel said, pointing the weapon at him. "Over there, where I can keep an eye on you."

"He's killed Hugh Favor," she said

Moving to the cutting table, Hook sat down. "I saw. But why?"

Colonel Hoffmann moved aside one of the paintings to reveal a small wall safe. He spun the tumbler and took out a stack of money.

"Perhaps I can answer your question," he said. "It's quite simple actually. You see, this money is to be used to hasten the Führer's victory and the liberation of Camp Alva. Art has been shipped from

Switzerland to be sold to your fellow citizens, as you can see. Of course, it's degenerate art, worthless art taken from the Jews, but this makes little difference to the American collectors."

"The ice bunkers," Hook said, shaking his head. "It's coming in the ice bunkers."

"But of course," the colonel said. "We made arrangements with certain members of the Swiss Legation for the art to be brought through Gibraltar to Havana and on to Panama, and ultimately, of course, to Oceanside, California.

"A few dollars spread about with the likes of Ross Ague made for an easy icing schedule. Of course, Major Foreman, having been involved selling American supplies, failed to examine things as he should. An occasional upheaval at the camp kept him quite occupied as well. Your major has difficulty thinking about more than one thing at a time."

"They used Hugh Favor as their contact," Reina said, "He provided them markets for their scheme."

"Why would Hugh Favor do something like this for money?" Hook asked. "He hardly needed it."

The colonel smiled. "He sold the paintings or exchanged them for others to fill out his own collection, paintings less subject to scrutiny. At least that's what we thought until tonight.

"Mr. Favor had a masterful knowledge of the market, but the paintings, it appears, were too much of a temptation for a man driven by his passion.

"All had been quite civilized until Mr. Favor could not resist hanging one of them in his collection and then showing the collection to her. We underestimated his obsession, I'm afraid."

"The *Madonna and Child*?" Hook asked, glancing over at Reina.

"Yes, quite so," the colonel said, checking his watch. "And then, of course, she arrived on the scene with her suspicions. This put, as you Americans say, a crimp in our plans."

"When I saw the painting on the list," Reina said, "I remembered seeing it when I toured Favor's collection, but I couldn't be certain. I decided to find out. Favor caught me and contacted the colonel."

"A serious mistake on both their parts, I'm afraid," the colonel said.

"What about Spark Dugan?"

Sitting on the edge of the cutting table, Colonel Hoffmann lit a cigarette. He had a hole in the sole of his boot, and the cuffs of his pants were frayed.

"He showed up at the wrong time, an unfortunate circumstance, and saw more than he should from beneath the ice deck. It was a matter of placing Spark Dugan's body under the reefer car."

"And so you killed him?"

Drawing on his cigarette, he looked up through his glasses.

"Many more important have died for the Führer."

The guard stepped to the door. "Ague said he would have the reefer on the siding by ten."

Rising, Colonel Hoffmann put the money back into the safe.

"What do we do about them?" the guard asked.

"There would be a key to the wine cellar in the butler's pantry. Lock Mr. Runyon in the cellar. We'll take the girl with us. And then get Favor's limousine," he said. "Be careful of his driver. After we pick up the shipment, we'll come back for the money and finish our business here."

"Leave the girl," Hook said.

"I'll be all right," Reina said, glancing up at Hook, her smile crooked from her swollen lip.

"Indeed," Colonel Hoffmann said. "Quite safe."

"What about Favor?" the guard asked.

Colonel Hoffmann squared his hat, crossing his arms over his chest. His eyes creased at the edges, and his lip curled.

"Put him in the wine cellar with Mr. Runyon. They should have a great deal to discuss."

Reina's eyes were locked to Hook's and were the last thing he saw as the guard slammed shut the door of the wine cellar. In the blackness he listened to their footsteps fade as they climbed the stairs, the vanishing voices, the silence of the tomb.

Somewhere the body of Hugh Favor lay on the floor, corrupt in its stillness. The air was dank and suffocating and smelled of mold. Hook tried the door, just in case, but it wouldn't move, its massive oak planks, its wrought-iron hinges, its lock of brass and steel.

To be here when Colonel Hoffmann returned wouldn't do. What could be ahead but death? Of this he had little doubt, and for Reina, perhaps worse, a lot worse.

To complicate matters, the wine cellar lay far below in the bowels of the mansion. To call out would be pointless. Who would hear?

Dropping to his haunches, he leaned against the dampness of the wall. "Well," he said to himself, his voice huge in the confines of the cellar. "It's fancy company I keep at the least."

Hours passed, perhaps minutes, in the darkness, and with each moment the mounting certainty of doom. But somewhere in that time, the thought came again. Fancy company indeed. Who would have a key to the best wine cellar in the country? Who but Hugh Favor himself, the richest man in town?

God willing, it might be on him now. Getting on all fours, Hook searched for the corpse. He didn't fear death. He'd seen it often enough on the rails, touched it, smelled it, slept beside it, but always with deliberation. Now the thought caused his mouth to dry and his heart to pound. And when he did touch it, he jerked back his hand, catching his breath, the icy flesh, the beginnings of rigor mortis, the smell of cologne in the darkness.

Slipping his hand into Favor's pants pocket, he retrieved change, nail clippers, a money clip with folded bills. Reaching under, he gave him a half turn. Air escaped through Hugh Favor's vocal chords, and his voice purred in the blackness. Hook sat back and waited for his heart to settle, to gather up his courage to search again.

This time, it was there, a ring laden with the keys to Favor's riches. Scooting back to the door, he tried the first key, gathering it up, trying again, keeping each separate from the others as he tried the next and the next.

Sweat gathered on his brow, stinging his eyes, as he labored at the latch, and when the click at last came, he shoved so hard that he spilled headlong into the hallway.

As soon as he adjusted to the light, he checked his watch. Only an hour had passed, the longest hour of his life. From the hallway, he could see Hugh Favor's face in the column of light that struck through the door, his eyes open and unseeing.

"Thanks, ole man," he said. "It's about time you helped someone besides yourself."

# 32

THE GUARD SMILED and brought his rifle to his shoulder when Hook stepped into the foyer. Sitting on the floor were Runt, Amanda, and her father.

"What the hell?" Hook said.

"Thought I heard a rat," the guard said. "Why don't you join us?"

"Runt?" Hook said.

Runt shrugged. "Showed up to see my girl and found this guy in her house with everyone at gunpoint. Didn't mean to barge in, but he insisted I stay."

"Up against the wall, Runyon," the guard said, shoving him.

He checked Hook's pockets and found the cellar key.

"What's this?" he said.

"Oh, that? Hugh Favor loaned it to me."

"Guess it's mine now," he said.

"He came for the limo," Amanda said. "When Father opened the door, he just burst in. We didn't have a chance."

"Favor's dead," Hook said. "Hoffmann has taken Reina with him."

"That's enough," the guard said. "This isn't a family reunion."

Amanda's father clasped his arms about his knees, his face the color of paste.

"What are you going to do with us?" he asked.

"Well now," the guard said. "I hadn't thought it through just yet, but I figure that since I have the key, the wine cellar just might be the place for the lot of you. I'm sure Colonel Hoffmann will have a suggestion or two for your future when he gets back."

"I got one or two words myself," Runt said, "though I can't share them in polite company."

"How you figure on getting out of this?" Hook asked the guard. "Don't you know they shoot traitors?"

"Hoffmann's got connections," he said. "He's a big man back in Germany. I have a share coming, a big share if you need to know."

"If he comes back," Hook said.

"Enough talk," he said. "You people stand on your feet."

Hook glanced over at Runt. If they were shut in that cellar again, they would never get out alive.

The guard pointed his rifle at the door. "Down the stairs," he said. "Just remember this is an M-1 rifle, and she holds eight cartridges. That's plenty at this range even for a bad shot, and I've got an expert-marksmanship badge."

Hook went down first, followed by Amanda and her father, then Runt. Midway down the stairs, Runt whirled around and punched the guard straight in the crotch. The guard yelped like a shot dog and pitched off the side.

Runt grabbed Amanda and made for the door, her father and Hook following directly behind. They ran to the kitchen and out into the gardens. The moonlight winked on the waters of the swimming pool and lit the gardens in its soft light.

When one shot rang out behind them, marble sprayed from

the cherub statue, a shower of stone stinging their faces. They dove for cover, lying as flat as they could behind the statue. A chunk of marble the size of a man's hand had exploded from the cherub's leg.

"He's on the balcony," Hook said. "We're pinned down."

"He wasn't kidding about that marksman medal," Runt said.

Three shots thudded into the dirt an inch from Amanda's father. He covered his head with his hands.

"He's a madman," he said, his voice cracking. "We'll never get out of this alive."

Hook rolled to the side and peeked over the top of the flower bed. He could see the guard's silhouette against the moonlight.

"I've got to get to Reina before it's too late," he said.

Runt looked over the bed just as the guard popped off another round. Amanda screamed and grabbed hold of Runt.

Runt started to get up. "That son of a bitch," he said.

Hook yanked him down just as two more shots ripped into the cherub.

Hook rolled onto his back. "One shot," he said.

"Say what?" Runt whispered.

"He did say that M-1 held eight rounds, didn't he?"

"Hell, Hook, I can't remember. I've been busy cracking nuts."

"He keeps firing at the cherub, Runt. He thinks it's one of us. According to my count, he's one shot left before he has to reload. Do you think you could make it to the pool?"

Runt looked at the open space between him and the swimming pool.

"You don't count on your fingers do you, Hook?" he said. "'Cause you only got five."

"Next time he fires, wait a few seconds and then make a dash for it. He'll be too busy reloading to notice. Work your way to the deep end and wait."

"And what are you going to do while I'm playing target?" he asked.

"We're going to surrender," he said.

"Oh. Now, I hadn't thought of that," he said. "You know I don't swim so good, Hook."

"Better than a one-arm man, I figure. Anyway, I think this guy thinks that cherub is one of us. You come as close to a cherub as anyone I know, Runt."

"Now that's funny, isn't it?" Runt said.

"Stay close to the side. I don't think he can see you from there."

Runt prepared himself to run. Hook lifted his prosthesis above the flower bed. The shot from the guard's rifle slapped into it. Runt ran for the pool, slipping over the side.

"Okay," Hook said. "When I say, step up beside me. Keep as close to that statue as you can. This guy will be counting heads on his way down."

Hook waved his arm. "We surrender," he called out. "We give up."

"Stand up where I can see you," the guard yelled.

"Here we go," Hook said, standing up.

Amanda and her father followed suit, crowding in close to the statue. They stood as if frozen while the guard worked his way down. He kept his rifle on them as he came down the sidewalk next to the swimming pool.

"Step out here in the light," he said.

He'd no sooner spoken than Runt came over the side of the pool, snaring the guard's arm in his viselike grip. Like some monster from the deep, he commenced dragging the guard toward the pool. The guard struggled to maneuver his rifle around for a clear shot, but Runt's crushing grip caused him to lose concentration. He began howling and begging for mercy.

He kicked and screamed and plummeted Runt's shoulders but to no avail. Inch by inch Runt worked him closer and closer to the edge of the pool. Even as Hook ran to help, Runt dragged him down into the water, folding over his body, covering the guard's head and shoulders and forcing him under.

The guard thrashed beneath Runt, his arms flailing. Bubbles rose up in the moonlit water, and then all was still.

Hook pulled Runt up onto the side of the pool. Amanda wrapped her arms about him.

"Are you okay?" she asked.

Runt shivered and wiped the water from his face.

Amanda kissed him, and Runt glanced up at her father. "Don't mean to be disrespectful," he said.

Amanda's father took hold of Runt's hand and helped him up. "Nor I, ever again," he said.

Hook checked his watch. "I've got to get to the yards, Runt. Could you take me?"

"Sure," he said. "I reckon I could do that. Beats the hell out of being a target."

"Amanda, maybe you could call the authorities?" Hook said. "Come on, Runt, time's running short."


Hook shoved aside the tools and waited as Runt fired up the truck. She coughed and hissed and died. Runt spit in his hands and fired her up again. This time she leveled out, and Runt headed down the road, one headlight shining into the sky, the other into the grader ditch.

"Is this as fast as this ole crate will go?" Hook asked.

Runt looked over his shoulder. "We're headed downhill now. I've seen her hit fifty on a good day, what with a tailwind."

When she coughed and loped again, Runt glanced over at Hook. "What?" Hook asked.

"It's nothing," Runt said. "She's just catching her breath."

But as they made the corner, the truck slowed once again, stalling momentarily.

"Goddang it, Runt," Hook said.

"I forgot," Runt said, pumping the footfeed.

"Forgot?"

The truck wound to a stop and died. The lights faded to yellow, and the motor creaked as she cooled.

"We're out of gas," Runt said.

Hook looked at Runt through the darkness. His clothes were wet, and his hair lay in streaks across his forehead.

"We're out of gas? You're kidding me, right?" he asked.

"I'd intended to borrow a little drip on the way home, Hook. How was I to know you'd be wanting a country ride?"

"Damn it," Hook said. "How am I to get there now?"

Hook looked off into the darkness. Reina's life lay in the hands of a Nazi, a man bent on destroying America from the inside out.

He lit a cigarette and tried to think. Hoffmann had taken his weapon, and the guard's rifle now rested at the bottom of Favor's swimming pool.

Suddenly a light glowed on the distant horizon. "Runt," he said. "That's the southbound out of Chicago. How far are we from the crossing?"

"She's at the bottom of the hill, Hook. You could never make it."

"You said this ole heap could coast, didn't you?"

"Like a soapbox derby once she's rolling," he said.

"Come on, Runt. We don't have much time."

Runt slipped the truck into neutral, and they opened their doors, pushing as hard as they could. She groaned and gathered up speed. At the last second they both jumped in, slamming the doors shut. Runt strained to see the road ahead, whipping the wheel this way and that at the last second.

The southbound's light grew brighter in the distance. And then ahead, the red signal light on the crossing commenced sweeping to and fro. They gained speed, bumping and rattling down the road.

"I hope the brakes work on this thing," Hook said, leaning forward.

"I've been meaning to fix that emergency," Runt said, pushing the hair from his eyes.

Runt hit his brakes a hundred yards from the crossing, sending them sliding sideways in the road.

"Wish me luck, my friend," Hook said, bailing out just as the southbound roared through the crossing.

He ran through the open field. As he climbed the embankment, the southbound set her brakes for the Alva spur, sending a screech her length as steel on steel brought her down. Hook ran as fast as he dared, praying not to stumble and fall under the wheels.

When a grab bar came by, he latched on, swinging up. He struggled for breath. Even though he'd hopped many a car, it never came easily, and he was not getting any younger.

The smell of smoke and steam filled the night as the southbound picked up speed. In the distance, he could see the last of Runt's headlights fading in the darkness. Moving into the moonlight, he checked his watch. The southbound, made up mostly of deadheaded-grain cars, would be making time on her way to the yards. With a little luck, he just might make it.

# 33

LEAPING FROM THE southbound, Hook cut east to the roundhouse, its great archways like catacombs, steamers idling in the stalls, hissing and wheezing as if in slumber. And from the pits beneath the engines, the voices of workers rose as the men cursed and hammered at the iron. In the roundhouse there was always the heat from the boilers, the smell of oil and sweat and steam. High overhead, pigeons chortled, waddling back and forth across the steel rafters in a perpetual game of tag.

The floodlights were off on the ice deck, but from where he stood, Hook could see the switch engine and the chute that ran from the reefer car up to the ice plant. The chute had been pushed away from the bunker opening and rested atop the reefer's roof. A Favor Oil truck had been parked below. A man sat on top of the car, his cigarette a red point in the darkness.

Hook climbed his way over the turntable for a better look, taking cover behind the pilothouse. The driver and Corporal Schubert were on top of the reefer. The bunker lid had been tossed back.

Colonel Hoffmann and Reina waited on the far end of the ice deck. Her hands were tied behind her back. Just then, a match lit in the cab of the switch engine, and Ross Ague's face flared in the darkness.

Dropping down on his haunches, Hook deliberated on his next move. Ague had, no doubt, made certain that the regular crew would be out-of-pocket. Hook knew Hoffmann was armed. Corporal Schubert and the truck driver were probably not. In any case, there were too many of them for him to take on. He would never make it to Reina, and he didn't want to put her in more danger.

Darkness and surprise were his only advantages, and he'd have to use them with care. Colonel Hoffmann and his lackeys would have to be taken one at a time, and with a little luck, he wouldn't be detected. "Okay, Ague, you son of a bitch," he said to himself. "You're first on the list."

As he crawled up the ladder of the switch engine, the heat from the boiler wafted by in the cool of the evening, the stink of Ague's cigar on its crest. Steam shot from a pressure valve, and Hook pressed himself against the ladder.

As he reached the door of the cab, he could see the wink of flames from behind the boiler door, and Ague's arm and hand out the window of the cab. Hook braced his foot against the ladder and tapped Ague on the shoulder. When he turned, Hook caught him in the neck with a solid punch. Ague snorted and pitched forward, his cigar rolling onto the floor.

Climbing down, Hook stayed in the shadows along the track that ran parallel to the sided reefer. He doubted that he could be seen. He stopped to catch his breath and assess his situation, realizing that he was standing in the exact spot where Spark Dugan had spilled his bucket of coal not so long ago.

In the distance, the whistle of the northbound 5003 out of Clovis rose and fell as it approached the Cimarron crossing.

He moved under the reefer, waiting in the darkness. The truck driver sent Schubert into the bunker to bring up crates. Closer now, the 5003 chugged and hauled against the Belva grade, throbbing and thundering against the enormity of her load. Once she topped the grade, she'd pick up speed and roll into the yards with a hundred thousand tons at her back.

The Favor Oil driver stood, walking to the end of the car. When he took a drag off his cigarette, Hook recognized him as Roy Bench. Squashing out his cigarette, Bench unzipped and took a leak off the side of the car. He was big and mean, and Hook knew he'd have to make his move count.

He found the reefer ladder at the far end and climbed up. Peeking over the top, Hook could see Bench against the distant lights of the yard, sitting on a packing crate with his back to Hook.

"Come on, Schubert, goddamn it," he said. "We got to be out of here before the night crew gets back."

Schubert mumbled something from inside the bunker and pushed a crate through the opening. Hook slid along the top toward the driver. When his prosthesis clanked on the metal roof, a shock wave raced up his spine.

"Stop," Bench said, turning.

Hook looked around for cover, but there was none, and the only way out was over the edge. The drop from this height could be lethal. Just then Corporal Schubert climbed out of the bunker.

"Who is it?" he asked, his voice tight.

"It's that yard dog," Bench said. "He's got himself loose. You should have killed him back at Favor's."

Hook knew that there was a time to follow gut instinct and to worry about the consequences another day. Spinning about, he kicked high into the air in hopes of catching Bench off guard. But Bench anticipated his move, leaping back to maintain distance between himself and Hook. In the process, Bench shoved Schubert backward against the ice chute. Schubert teetered momentarily and then plunged off the side of the car.

Hook charged in, seizing Bench, but one hand against two had never been great odds. He shoved his leg between Bench's legs to neutralize his leverage, and then set the hook under Bench's rib cage. When he lifted, the air rushed from out of Bench's lung like a spent tire. With his good arm, Hook caught Bench under the chin, sending the man backward into the hold of the reefer.

Hook made for the ice deck. Colonel Hoffmann might have been alerted. He had little time to waste.

Corporal Schubert lay splayed in the bedding gravel under the car, his head leaking into the dirt. Hook climbed up the trestle to the ice deck. When he reached the top, he searched the shadows for movement. An opening at the end of the chute led into the ice plant, where the ice blocks were kept in frozen storage. Canvas tails hung over the opening to lessen the loss of cold air from the plant.

Hook heard a noise just as the moon broke through the clouds, and he spotted Hoffmann and Reina ducking through the chute opening. He took a deep breath and went in after them.

Crouching down, he waited for his eyes to adjust. A single bulb hung in the middle of the icehouse, illuminating the line of ice blocks waiting in the chute. A bar lay across the side boards to hold back the blocks until they were ready for receiving. Overhead, a fog drifted in the frigid stillness of the ice plant.

"Come out," Hoffmann said. "Remember that Dr. Kaplan is my guest."

Hook looked for the voice, locating Hoffmann behind the line of ice blocks. He could see the top of Reina's head next to him and their breaths rising in the cold. Just then the 5003 lay in on her whistle at the edge of town, her wail rising like a fire siren.

Hook stepped out.

"No," Reina said.

"You'll never get away with this, Hoffmann," Hook said.

Hoffmann stood and smiled. "Move under the light."

Hook circled around, stopping under the light.

"You're in the middle of America, Hoffmann. How do you ex-pect to escape?"

"Ah," he said, bringing up his weapon, "it is you who does not escape. We are here to stay."

In that second, Reina lunged against Hoffmann's back, pitching him forward between the blocks of ice. Hook dived, sliding across the frost-covered floor. He grabbed the chute bar, pulling it free.

The cracking sound raced up the line of blocks as they loos-ened under the pull of gravity. Hoffmann stood, uncertain as to the source.

Suddenly the ice lurched forward, crushing Hoffmann's legs between the blocks. The ice reddened about his knees, and his scream cut through the stillness like broken glass. Again the blocks lurched, inching forward, first a little and then more, gaining mo-mentum as they hauled Hoffmann down the chute.

He looked back at Hook, his eyes as cold and blue as the ice that propelled him to his doom. He thrashed his arms above his head as if waving good-bye, disappearing through the chute opening.

Hook retrieved his weapon and untied Reina. Her hand trem-bled in his as they made for the ice deck. Below them on the track, Hoffmann lay pinned under the blocks of ice.

As they turned for the stairs, the 5003 thundered from the darkness and into the yards, her whistle screaming, her brakes screeching, her bell frantic. Hook and Reina stopped, riveted by the inevitability of Hoffmann's fate. Reina buried her head against Hook's shoulder as the ice blocks exploded under the impact, a crystal spray that danced and shimmered in the light beam of the engine.

Hook and Reina sat in Favor's limo while the sheriff escorted Ross Ague and Roy Bench to the patrol car.

"That corporal's a goner. We found Bench in the ice bunker.

Every time he breathes, he whistles a tune out that hole in his side," the sheriff said. "We'll have to come back for what's left of Hoffmann. Hardly seems worth the trouble.

"The FBI will have to be called in on this thing, Hook, what with the crossing of state lines and all, and then there's all them stolen paintings."

"That's fine, Sheriff," Hook said. "I'll be happy to cooperate any way that I can."

"Good. Good," he said, taking out a chew. "And then there's a report to be wrote out. I figure you might do that, being it's on railroad property and all."

"I'll be down first thing," Hook said.

"Good. Good," he said. "You did a fine job, Doctor. Maybe you'd care to apply for a job on the force?"

"Thanks, but I need work with a little excitement," she said, smiling.

"Proud to have you in town."

"Thank you," Reina said, snuggling in against Hook. "I'm proud to be here."

"Give you folks a lift?" he asked.

"We'll be taking the limo back if you don't mind, Sheriff," Hook said, pulling Reina in close to him. "I believe it's a ride well earned."

# 34

WHEN HOOK HEARD Runt's truck pull in, he slipped out of bed and put on his shoes, covering Reina's shoulders against the morning cool. Going out onto the steps of the caboose, he waited for Runt to shut down his truck.

Rolling down the window, Runt said, "Morning."

"Morning. You want coffee? I'll wake up my special agent."

"Thanks, no," Runt said. "You might like to know that they've reassigned Major Foreman."

"Oh."

"Either Europe or Leavenworth. Guess he figured Europe might not be so bad."

"Be glad to put the coffee on."

"The library's being moved into the new barracks building. Thought maybe Dr. Kaplan would like the news."

"Thanks. I'll tell her."

"Oh," he said, reaching for a brown sack. "Brought you a little something."

"I still have some goods."

"It's my granddaddy's shine, forty years old and as fine as ever made. I wanted you to have some."

"I'm right honored. Where did you find it?"

"Where that old rooster died," he said. "My pa had it wrong all along. It wasn't in the bramble but in that stand of sumac, right there within spitting distance of the house the whole time. It's like he come back and showed me where to look. It's a fair price she'll bring, if a man sold her, I mean."

Hook turned up the collar of his robe. "Sure you won't come in? You're always welcome."

Reaching down, Runt cranked up his truck and waited for her to settle out.

"Much appreciated, but I'm stopping by the prison cemetery. Going to have myself a smoke with an ole friend." Slipping his truck into gear, he said, "You ever decide to hunt elevator rats again, call someone else, will you?"

As Hook turned to go in, he spotted Spark Dugan's coal box, empty beneath the steps. The dead often spoke from the grave, he supposed, Runt's granddaddy, Spark Dugan, too, in his way, reaching back for justice.

Crawling into bed, he pulled up the covers, then nuzzled into Reina's neck, her warmth, her smell of sleep, her breasts abundant against him.

"Today's Saturday," she said. "We'll miss the auction."

"Dr. Kaplan," he said, drawing her to him. "Some passions just can't be satisfied between the covers of a book."